You will all pay

That was the note he'd left all over town and now he planned to wreak his vengeance. How good it felt to be alive again! He'd chosen the perfect time—All Hallows' Eve. Maybe he wasn't hallowed, but he was evil—and this was his time.

For now, he could only move among the living for short periods during the day. But the darkness was a friend to a man who knew the town like the back of his hand.

Soon they would all feel the strength and vengeance of that hand. He was just toying with them all now; it pleased him to think of them confused and helpless. Tomorrow, their confusion would turn to fear.

The bottle in his hand demanded attention, so he tipped it to his lips and drank. Fire in liquid form poured down his throat—sweet, stolen liquor. They owed him food and drink and more. They owed him for the life they had stolen from him.

Tomorrow. She would pay. Lauren Kent would pay.

Dear Reader,

What better time to snuggle tightly with the one you love than on All Hallows' Eve—when things truly go bump in the night!

Harlequin Intrigue is ringing your doorbell this month with "Trick or Treat," our Halloween quartet—filled with ghastly ghouls and midnight trysts!

If Linda Stevens could have it her way, it would be Halloween year-round. In fact, Beardsville, Vermont, is her dream town, where Halloween is a real *event*. The holiday, she says, brings out the child in her and gives her the chance to display her wicked sense of humor.

Be sure not to miss any of the TRICK OR TREAT quartet this month.

Regards,

Debra Matteucci
Senior Editor & Editorial Coordinator

Fright Night

Linda Stevens

Harlequin Books

TORONTO • NEW YORK • LONDON
AMSTERDAM • PARIS • SYDNEY • HAMBURG
STOCKHOLM • ATHENS • TOKYO • MILAN
MADRID • WARSAW • BUDAPEST • AUCKLAND

ISBN 0-373-22252-1

FRIGHT NIGHT

This edition published by arrangement with Harlequin Enterprises B. V.

® and TM are trademarks of the publisher. Trademarks indicated with ® are registered in the United States Patent and Trademark Office, the Canadian Trade Marks Office and in other countries.

Printed in U.S.A.

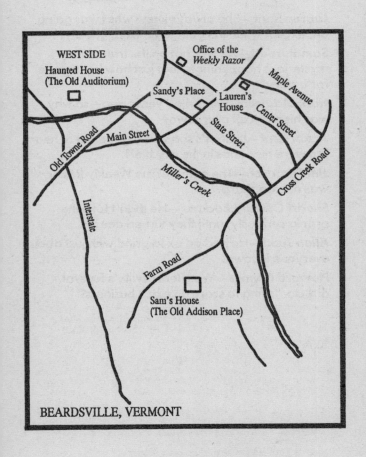

WEST SIDE

Haunted House
(The Old Auditorium)

Office of the
Weekly Razor

Maple Avenue

Sandy's Place

Lauren's
House

Center Street

Old Towne Road

Main Street

State Street

Miller's Creek

Cross Creek Road

Interstate

Farm Road

Sam's House
(The Old Addison Place)

BEARDSVILLE, VERMONT

CAST OF CHARACTERS

Lauren Kent—She always knew what was going on, except when the goings-on were ghostly.

Sam Burdett—He was hot on the trail of the mysterious happenings—but just how hot was he for a story?

Hank Addison—He'd died years ago—so why was his mark all over town?

Jason Kent—Lauren's son was a good kid at heart, but were his hands in the mischief?

Jim Ferguson—The editor of the *Weekly Razor* was not too sharp.

Sheriff Oswald Buckner—He didn't take the pranks seriously, until they turned deadly.

Allen Judd—He had an ax to grind with just about everyone in town.

Howard Conner—Was Beardsville's funeral director trying to scare up extra business?

Prologue

It was a cold, silent night in late October. Hidden deep in the shadows of a huge oak tree, a man with a haggard face and wild blue eyes stood looking out across the open meadow in front of him. By the dim light of a yellowish crescent moon, the rows and rows of cheap white grave markers seemed to him a sad, forbidding forest.

Potter's field. Last stop for the indigent. Although this place was like a final kick in the face by a cruel, unfair world, it had still been his home for a long time now, and in a strange way he was reluctant to leave.

But leave he must, for he was a man with a mission. The wind picked up as he left the shelter of the big oak, sending the fallen leaves swirling around his feet. With each stride he could feel the hot blood pumping through his veins. He ran deeper into the chill, black night, driven onward by the need within him.

This body was strong and hard, such a change from the pathetic hulk that lay buried in that poor plot of earth behind him. It would serve him well for the task ahead.

Someone must pay. They *all* must pay.

Chapter One

Lauren Kent parked her big four-wheel-drive truck in front of Sandy's Place at seven on the dot. As usual she was right on time, and as usual that meant she had beaten everyone else there. Clad in black wool slacks and a teal sweater that very nearly matched her eyes, she looked rather incongruous climbing out of such a rough-hewn working vehicle. But then, Lauren prided herself on being a contradiction.

She stood there for a moment breathing in the crisp early-morning air and enjoying that special kind of sunlight that can only be found in New England in the fall. As a lifelong resident of this small Vermont town, she would even go so far as to say that such light could only be found right there in Beardsville.

Smiling, she headed toward the café to see if Sandy had arrived to open up yet. Just as she reached the door, the woman in question came dashing out, her keys still in one hand and her purse in the other.

"Gangway!" Sandy propelled her considerable bulk straight past Lauren without a pause. "We'll see who does the paying around here! I'll get those rascals but good!"

Lauren spun on her heel and called after the other woman. "Which rascals?" she asked. "Pay for what?"

"See for yourself!" Sandy called back without breaking stride. "But don't touch anything! I want that lazy sheriff to come see it just like they left it!"

Chuckling and shaking her head, Lauren turned and stepped into the café. With only a week until Halloween, it was possible for almost anything to happen in Beardsville. This was a town that went collectively crazy the last week of every October. Little wonder.

It started with the penchant many New Englanders had for this time of year. Then came the incentives cooked up by the Beardsville Promotional Society, or BPS as it was locally known. Once this group of businesspeople started awarding prizes and cash for best decorations and costumes, the whole town got into the act. That meant the place became even more of a tourist attraction than it already was. With the arrival of all those tourist dollars, the floodgates opened wide.

These days, Beardsville became a spookfest in late October from one city-limit sign to the other. Every quaint, historic house on every tree-lined street was decorated in appropriately ghoulish style. Then came the now-famous haunted house, which was conducted in the old Beardsville auditorium all week long. Finally, on Halloween, there was a big parade, and later a wild and pricey charity cocktail party nicknamed the Weirdsville Bash.

All this naturally got everyone quite excited, and sometimes that excitement got out of hand. Of course, there were also those in the normally quiet town who did not much care for such a ruckus.

The BPS was considered the instigator of this Halloween pageant, and Sandy's Place was where they customarily met every Monday morning. It was only reasonable to expect some sort of token protest, which was why Lauren wasn't terribly alarmed by Sandy's outburst.

Until she saw the butcher knife.

It was embedded in the kitchen door, and covered with blood, or at least something red and sticky, as if it had been used for some grisly purpose. At the moment, it was being used as a period for a four-word sentence that had been scrawled on the door, also in sticky red. Whatever the author had used for ink, it had dripped down the door, making those four words look even more ominous.

You Will All Pay

Lauren shivered with unknown dread. Somehow this didn't seem to her like the usual harmless Halloween prank.

Suddenly a cold hand plopped down on her shoulder. She whirled around and darn near smacked the president of the Beardsville Promotional Society in the eye.

"Howard!" She leaned against a nearby booth, her heart thumping. "Don't sneak up on a person like that!"

"I didn't sneak," the man objected. "I'm simply quiet by nature. Force of habit in my line of work."

Howard Conner was in his early sixties, a tall, thin man with sad eyes and what Lauren considered an even sadder, albeit obviously necessary profession—he was Beardsville's funeral director.

"Then I suggest you clear your throat or something when approaching us live ones from behind," Lauren told him. "Or we'll be needing your services prematurely."

Howard simply smiled. Like most people in this town of less than four thousand, they knew each other well enough to trade jibes without fear of injured feelings.

"The only thing you're going to need prematurely is a hearing aid," Howard retorted. "From all that hammering and sawing you do."

Lauren cupped a hand to her ear. "Huh?"

Howard laughed. As the town's only building contractor, Lauren did do plenty of hammering and sawing. Since she was already a woman in a traditionally male trade, however, she was used to getting strange looks. She had no macho worries about wearing hearing protection on the job and Howard knew it.

He pointed to the kitchen door. "I take it that is what sent Sandy running down Main Street in such a tizzy?"

"Do you blame her?"

"Pranks are seldom funny," he said. "Except to the pranksters, of course."

"I don't know, Howard," Lauren said doubtfully. "This seems more serious to me."

Howard shrugged, then went over to take a closer look at the writing on the kitchen door. Lauren joined him. She made a face as he bent nearer the door and sniffed the red substance. Whatever it was, it had once been free flowing enough to write with, but had long since congealed.

"Well?" she prompted. "Is it what it looks like?"

He straightened and shrugged again. "In my professional opinion, you mean?" Lauren made another face and nodded. Howard smiled wryly. "Hard to tell. But, yes, it does have a rather reminiscent odor."

"All I want to know is who's going to scrub it off!"

Sandy was back with the sheriff, who did not look particularly pleased to have been dragged down the street from his office like this. He and Sandy were roughly the same size and shape, proof enough that married couples can come to resemble one another after many years.

Proof, too, that Sandy was a terrific cook and both were terrific eaters.

She was glaring at him. "Do something!" she demanded.

"And just what would you have me do, my love?" Sheriff Oswald Buckner returned with a long-suffering sigh.

"Your job!"

Another sigh. "I just got here. I suppose a cup of coffee is out of the question?"

"That does sound nice," Howard interjected, hoping to head off one of the Buckners' infamous rows.

Some other members of the BPS had arrived, and took this opportunity to voice their interest in coffee, as well. Sandy fixed them all with a disparaging gaze.

"You want some coffee, do you?" She pointed at the cryptic message written on her kitchen door. "Then go ask whoever did that, because they took it all with them. Took sugar for it, too, and a whole bunch of other stuff out of my kitchen. You just go look!"

With that, Sandy grabbed her purse and flounced out the door, presumably to go buy supplies. Sheriff Buckner stood there for a moment, then decided he'd better get busy or there would be hell to pay when she got back.

He looked around, then sent someone for his camera and took a few pictures. When he was satisfied, he carefully put the knife in a plastic bag, and the members of the BPS helped him straighten up. They were at their usual table answering questions when Sandy walked back into the café.

She must have been pleased, because there was hot coffee on the table in a trice, as well as a plate of jelly doughnuts. By then the sheriff had already determined that no one knew any more about this than he did. But he felt obliged to remain and partake of this sudden good fortune.

"I'll grant you it's strange," he said, waving a jelly doughnut for emphasis. "And I fully intend to take the knife to the forensics lab for further study. But in my opinion it's just a prank, plain and simple."

Lauren had known Sheriff Buckner all her life, and had found him to be a good man with his heart in the right place. She also had to admire the way he managed to look and sound so officious with a dab of strawberry jelly on his nose.

However, she did have to admit that he could be as slow to move as extra-fancy maple syrup in midwinter. "Since when is breaking and entering a prank?" she asked.

"They came in through the back window, Lauren," he replied, waving aside her comment. "There isn't even a lock on the darn thing."

Sandy came to refill their coffee. "And just whose fault is that, Oswald? You were the one who said you'd get around to putting one on and never did."

"I was going to call Lauren last week," he objected. "But then she got so busy with that fancy driveway the Booths are putting in that—"

"Last week!" Sandy interjected. "We've owned this place for over twenty years, Oswald! Don't you dare lay this on Lauren's doorstep."

"I did have plenty of time last week," Lauren felt obliged to add. "I don't do concrete—the whole town knows I've only been supervising subcontractors out there." She looked at Sandy. "I'll be glad to fix you up after the meeting. Drill one hole, put in a sixteen-penny nail and there you are, instant lock. Won't take me five minutes."

"Five minutes," Sandy repeated, gazing pointedly at her husband. Though she could see the jelly on his nose, such was her state of pique that she decided not to bring it to his attention. "And a nail. Not much to stop a burglary, is it?"

Sheriff Buckner thumped the table with his fist. "This was not a burglary! It was a prank, and done in part to get ammunition for other pranks."

"How do you figure?" Lauren asked.

"They took sugar for putting into gas tanks, eggs for throwing at cars and soap for smearing on windows," he replied, speaking to the group as a whole now lest anyone else decide to question his conclusions.

Lauren looked doubtful. "So what was the coffee for? To keep them awake while they do those things?"

"All I know is that there's been a regular rash of vandalism this year for some reason, from broken windows to firecrackers in mailboxes," he informed them, ignoring her sarcasm. "Somebody even stole a prize hog from Old Man Joseph's farm last night. I shudder to think where that'll turn up. But things will simmer down after Halloween like they always do, so I suggest you all concentrate on your business and let me get on with mine!"

With that the sheriff stood, grabbed another jelly doughnut and stalked out of the café. After a moment of stunned silence, Sandy apologized for his outburst.

"Don't mind his bluster. His cholesterol is up and Doc Randal is threatening to put him on a diet again," she confided. "Has him fit to be tied."

They all laughed, and finally Howard called the meeting to order. Whether it was the work of pranksters or not, there was naturally some debate over what the note could mean.

Was it a joke? A threat? Some form of veiled warning, perhaps? With Halloween and the days leading up to it being one of the town's most important and lucrative holidays, they all agreed that both it and the wave of pranks the sheriff described were complications they could easily live without.

However, since there was a small but vocal contingent of Beardsville residents who opposed both the BPS and its goals, specifically growth and progress for the town, the group also agreed that the note was most likely just sour grapes.

"Okay, let's get on with more important things," Howard said. "Lauren, how's the haunted house shaping up this year?"

Given her profession, it hadn't surprised Lauren or anyone else when she had been unanimously elected to oversee the construction and mechanical operation of the haunted house since its inception six years ago. Each year it had gotten bigger and better. This year promised to be no exception.

"My crew and I will be over there in full force this afternoon. We'll be ready for the grand opening tonight," Lauren assured them. Then she smiled. "Don't worry. It's going to be a real scream."

Chapter Two

The BPS meeting broke up shortly before nine, much to Lauren's relief. She liked being a part of the group, and usually approved of its goals, but it was much too nice a day to be stuck inside hashing over such mundane matters as whether there should be one or two pretzel vendors at the annual Halloween art fair and picnic on Sunday.

She had other things to think about, such as making a living. At this time of year, she mainly had the mechanical problems of the haunted house to deal with. But there was the Booths' driveway and patio, and Mr. Anderson had called last night about some loose shutters.

Although the sign painted on both sides of her truck said Lauren Kent, Building Contractor, Lauren wasn't very fond of that particular job description. It implied she just stood around drinking coffee and yelling at poor day laborers. In reality, she was almost always in motion on a job site, preferred diet cola as her source of caffeine and rarely yelled at anyone unless they deserved it. When they did deserve it, she could yell with the best, and the size of their bank account didn't matter to her a bit.

Actually, this driveway job and the subcontractors it entailed was a rarity for her. She usually worked alone, as a jack-of-all-trades from carpentry to plumbing. Since she didn't care to be called a handyperson, either, she had long since settled on "building contractor" as a sort of compromise. It also looked rather nice on a business card, and the sides of the truck, as well.

As her only vehicle, the truck was important to her in more ways than one. Most everyone in town was used to seeing her zip around in the big thing, in all manner of dress, though it did give the newcomers a start at first.

However, if anyone thought hers an improper profession for a woman, they certainly didn't say it out loud more than once. If they did, the next time their roof needed fixing or a fussy electrical outlet had to be re-wired, they might have to wait for some out-of-towner to make a service call.

Besides, Beardsville was a small town, and it wasn't long before any newcomer found out how she had come to be in the business. It had been her ex-husband's. The jerk.

They had married young, broke and pregnant. But Jack Kent had had a way with tools, and Beardsville, with its many older homes, a constant need for a repair-man. A repairwoman, too, on occasion. He taught Lauren all he could, and she was a quick study. Unfortunately, about five years into their marriage, Lauren caught him giving lessons of another kind.

It seemed his numerous trips to Montpelier had been to the lumberyard all right, but less for supplies than to bed a few of the cute little cashiers on the side. Lauren kicked him out, filed for divorce and then proceeded to raise their young son, Jason, alone.

It hadn't been so bad until the past year or so. Now she was thirty-two, and becoming very much aware of two growing problems. The first was her single status. The second was a thirteen-year-old son who was getting to be a real handful.

Which was probably why she found herself driving past the junior high school even though it wasn't necessarily on her way. Sure enough, there was Jason, hanging out in the school yard with the group of older boys he had recently taken up with rather than help decorate the building for Halloween like the other kids his own age.

With a sigh, Lauren drove on, unsure of what else to do. Having had a child at a young age meant she wasn't so far removed from her own teen years. Confronting him in front of his friends would definitely be uncool—though they probably had another word for it these days.

When he was younger he had been such a good boy. He wasn't really so bad now, as much as he'd started running with the wrong crowd, and Lauren knew that might mean bad wasn't too far off. Still, she couldn't put all the blame on Jason or his pals. She also knew that some of his troubles fell squarely on her own shoulders.

As a single parent she had to work twice as hard to keep afloat, which meant she wasn't there for him as much as she would like. There was also a smidgen of guilt thrown in, for no matter how good a mother she was, there was one thing she could never be. Male.

At this time in his life, Jason needed a positive male role model, someone he could talk to concerning things Lauren could only guess about, and ask questions a boy simply wouldn't ask of his mother, no matter how young minded or open she was.

His father more or less disappeared after the divorce, but was never much of a role model in any case. There were teachers, but again Lauren knew that teenagers tended to consider such relationships as an us-against-them proposition. Since Jason wasn't particularly inclined toward athletics, even that avenue wasn't promising—not that she considered the local potbellied, winning-obsessed football coach a fount of acceptable masculine knowledge, either.

But what could she do? Beardsville wasn't overflowing with unmarried men even near her age, nor was she too sure whether she *or* Jason were quite ready for that anyway.

It was certainly inevitable, though. For a long time after the divorce she had felt so betrayed that men in general hadn't interested her much. But eight years was a long time, and she was, after all, a relatively normal, most definitely healthy female.

Still, she was young, and with the way the town was growing someone was sure to come along. As for Jason, Lauren could only hope this was a phase and would pass, like spitting food and temper tantrums had in their own time. Best she steel her nerves, anyway, for the even more imposing dangers of driving cars and dating girls that approached.

With a shudder at the thought, Lauren put it all out of her mind as she nosed her truck into a parking space in front of an old stone building that housed Beardsville's local newspaper. It was a small, gossipy little publication unabashedly named the *Weekly Razor*.

Always on the lookout for another source of income no matter how small, Lauren worked occasionally as a sort of informal reporter for the *Razor*, mostly doing local color and progrowth pieces. To be honest, these days she did it more for her own personal satisfaction than the money. It was a small operation, with her old friend Jim Ferguson serving as publisher, editor, lead reporter and pressman.

This was Lauren's usual first stop after a meeting of the BPS. Jim, like all newspaper people, was a born snoop. As a business owner, he could be a member of the group himself if he wanted to, but always said he considered it a conflict of interest. The actions of the BPS were the very sort of news the *Razor* printed.

But since he didn't object to Lauren being a member, she thought he just didn't like to attend meetings. She had barely stepped into the office before he was asking questions.

"Heard Sandy dragged Oswald down Main Street by his ear this morning. What's the scoop?" he began. Then he scowled at her and added, "You got a picture, right?"

"Why, I'm just fine, Jim, thanks for asking," Lauren returned. "How are you today?"

Jim was a wiry man in his mid-fifties, with sharp, intelligent features and skin that looked as if it had been smoke cured. In a way it might have been, since he had spent most of his youth working all over the eastern seaboard for big-city newspapers back when the link between smoking and lung cancer was still considered a nasty rumor.

Though Jim had quit the habit himself a long time ago, he had somehow managed to hang on to the crabbiness of someone in the midst of a nicotine fit. At least, that's what Lauren told him. Jim told her he had been that way even before he'd taken his first puff.

In response to her sardonic jibe, he muttered something unintelligible—which was probably for the best. He then pushed off against his desk and rolled his office chair across the room to a battered old refrigerator. From it he pulled two cans of diet cola. One was for him, and the other he threw at Lauren as he rolled back across the room.

She caught it deftly. "Thanks." This was as much of an apology as she would ever get for his gruff welcome and she knew it. Lucky for her they shared a penchant for the fizzy stuff. "Sandy didn't exactly drag him by his ear. If she had, or ever does, you'll have that picture so fast the fixing solution will stain your shirt."

"I'd better." He popped open his cola can and had a big swallow. "Now then. What's all this about a bloody knife and some sort of warning to the BPS?"

Lauren came around the counter that divided the front of the newspaper office from the work area and had a seat at the other desk, facing Jim's.

"We don't know that the warning is to the BPS," she countered. "We don't even know it was blood on the knife."

"Then what *do* we know?"

Lauren filled him in quickly on the events of that morning, and of the meeting afterward. When she was through, her cola can was empty and she got up to get another from the noisy old refrigerator. She opened this one right away and took a gulp, then sighed with satisfaction.

"Still not indulging in our mutual soda obsession at the meetings, I take it?" Jim asked with the snide grin that normally passed for his smile.

"I consider it best not to."

"So you've said. But free diet cola! That's just not like you, Lauren. You've been sponging mine for as long as I can remember."

"I've earned every drop and you know it, Jim Ferguson," Lauren objected. "Some days it seems you only live to pester me." She gave him the evil eye. "Like today."

Jim shrugged. But Lauren knew better. It was a tactic he used to make others think he'd given up the attack, and all the while he would be sneaking up behind for an ambush.

"All I want to know is why you don't ask Sandy for a soda when she's serving the others coffee?"

"Too early," Lauren told him.

"Hah! Remember that blizzard? The one that caught us by surprise last Thanksgiving? I decided to stay put at your house until the plows arrived."

"So?"

"They got there at four in the morning! You popped one open then, and enjoyed it, too!"

Lauren blew out a deep breath. "All right! If you must know, I don't ask for one because it would make me look silly, okay? I'm already the youngest person at those stupid meetings. There would be all the big people drinking their coffee and me sitting there with my soda pop."

"I knew it!" Jim crowed. "That's all I wanted to hear. I just had to find out if you're really as brave as you make out or if there was something that scared you."

"Scared? Who said I was scared?" Lauren sat down on the edge of his desk and shook a finger at him. "Listen up, pal. I'll admit *you* frighten me a little. I also have a healthy respect for live electrical wires. And that case of hemorrhoids I got after my pregnancy." She shook her head and grimaced. "The thought of those coming back has caused me a sleepless night or two. But otherwise I'm virtually fearless, and don't you forget it."

On occasion Jim was actually capable of laughing, and he did so now. It was hard not to when this lively woman with the teal blue eyes and feathery blond hair put on a full-court tease.

Jim had known Lauren most of her life, having moved to Beardsville when she was just four. Even then she had been something of a tomboy, and had grown up as strong—and as strong willed—as any of the boys that teased her endlessly. Eventually she grew to her present five-eight and filled out in all the right places. That's when the teasing turned into hot pursuit. But he remembered her as being a fairly cautious young woman.

Obviously not cautious enough. It surprised the whole town when she turned up pregnant by Jack Kent, but none more so than her parents. They hadn't liked Jack, sentiments which turned out to be prophetic, and responded to Lauren's insistence on marrying him by moving out of state. They had expected her to cave in to their desires and go with them.

She married Jack in a little civil ceremony the very next day. The rift between Lauren and her parents eased a bit when Jason was born, and a bit more when she divorced Jack. But it was still there, and flared whenever they tried to badger her into moving away from Beardsville. It amazed Jim how much damage was done when parents forgot that everyone had a need for individuality, including their own children.

Then again, he was a bachelor with no kids of his own and supposed he wasn't in any position to preach. But he had kept an eye on Lauren over the years, helping her out when times got lean by giving her reporting assignments. Much to his surprise she proved good at the work, and now he was the one who often relied upon her.

However, she did have her moments. "All right, then, fearless one. I have an assignment for you. I'd like you to make it your personal and professional quest to get to the bottom of these pranks." He held up a sheaf of papers. "I'm hearing reports from all over town. Midnight, broad daylight, it doesn't seem to matter. Somebody out there is determined to have fun this Halloween even if it lands them in jail."

Lauren just laughed. "Oh, Jim. You make it sound like a crime wave or something."

"In a town the size of Beardsville this *is* a crime wave," he maintained, shaking the handful of telephone messages. "It's news, too. I'm serious, Lauren. You find the source of all these shenanigans, and I'll give you space on the front page to write all about it. And a per-word bonus to boot, the juicier the better."

"Stop the presses!"

Both Jim and Lauren spun around at the sound of the deep, masculine voice behind them. The man standing at the door grinned at them as he came the rest of the way in, closing the door behind him.

"Unless I'm hearing things, Jim Ferguson just offered to actually pay extra for something," the man continued. He looked at Lauren and pointed at the phone on Jim's desk. "Call the wire services! This man opening his wallet is worthy of a news bulletin!"

He laughed, and Lauren laughed with him. Jim glowered at them both for a moment, then finally grinned and rose from his chair to shake the other man's hand.

"Careful, Sam," he said to him. "Or I might never give you another real-estate tip again."

"That's a threat?"

"Your new digs not up to your expectations?" Jim asked.

Sam made a face. "Allow me to describe the color and texture of the water that came out of my pipes this morning."

"I told you it was rustic," Jim returned with a shrug.

"Rustic I was ready for. I did not, however, expect to be sharing my kitchen with a family of raccoons. Practically scared me to death."

"Come on. A big tough guy like you?"

"But a city boy, remember? I thought they were a new humongous breed of rat." Sam turned to Lauren again. "That your truck out there?"

"Lock, stock and grease spot," she confirmed.

"Then you must be Lauren Kent. Jim's told me a lot about you." He extended his hand. "Sam Burdett."

Lauren's eyes widened perceptibly. "Pleased to meet you, Sam. You do know that Jim is a habitual liar?"

"But everything he said about you was good."

"In that case, he's a wonderful man who's never so much as told a fib." She was still sitting on the edge of Jim's desk, regarding the man standing in front of her with open curiosity. "So you're the new owner of the Addison place?"

Sam nodded, a rather rueful expression on his face. "I notice you didn't say *proud* owner." He sighed, and his expression brightened again. "But I hope to change all that."

Lauren wished him luck, but managed not to say it out loud. Once a fine farm, the old Addison place had been driven to ruin by the last of that family's line, Hank Addison. If she remembered correctly, it had been taken over for back taxes around twelve years ago, and the land divided into parcels that had been sold to other nearby farmers over the years.

The last parcel to go was a fifteen-acre tract with a few outbuildings and the house itself, livable but in a state of disrepair. Since the place was a local curiosity, that made the person who bought it something of a curiosity, too, or rather even more of one than he was already. Sam

Burdett was still quite the mysterious stranger to Lauren and the other Beardsville residents.

They knew that he was a good friend of Jim's from New York who had been looking for a project house in the country, and that he had bought the old Addison place on his friend's recommendation, sight unseen. They also knew he had just moved in that weekend. To Lauren's knowledge, this was his first visit to town.

Other than those paltry facts, Jim had only told them that he was an intensely private man with something of a troubled past who would prefer to get to know people on his own terms. If that hadn't been enough to jump start Lauren's active imagination, Sam Burdett's occupation did the rest.

He was a true-crime writer who had done many pieces for television, and who specialized in the bizarre. In other words, Sam Burdett should fit right in around Beardsville, especially at this time of year.

One thing was for sure. Tall and darkly handsome, with chiseled features and piercing blue eyes, Sam Burdett was a good-looking man, and Lauren's imagination wasn't immune to that sort of speculation, either.

"So how do you like my chances?" Sam asked.

Lauren blinked. "Huh?"

"My chances for fixing up the place," he told her. "Or does that glazed look in your eyes tell the whole story?"

"Oh. Sorry. I was thinking of something else," Lauren managed to say, realizing she'd been staring at him. "I haven't actually seen the place in a while, so I really couldn't say."

Lauren slipped off Jim's desk and went to get another diet cola. Sam followed her with his eyes. Jim had told him about this sometime reporter who could also turn out to be his salvation in remodeling his new home. But Jim sure as heck hadn't told him she was so pretty.

Her hair, blond with sunshine highlights, was about shoulder length and feathered in a flattering, easy-to-manage style. She was trim, but not in that Fifth Avenue starvation-diet style that Sam had come to loathe. Where those so-called ideal women had angles, Lauren had curves, and lush ones at that, especially at the hips. Her legs, though concealed in black slacks, looked firm and strong.

It wasn't something he would ever say to a woman, lest she mistake his meaning, but to Sam she looked solid. As in healthy. Able to stand on her own two shapely legs and meet the world head on. Which by Jim's account she had. That meant she was mentally tough, as well. It was a trait Sam found very alluring, probably because he had spent so much of his life doing battle with the world himself.

Right now, Jim was chuckling and wearing a knowing smile. "I have an idea," he said. "Sam here has some newspaper experience behind him, Lauren. Why don't you two work together on this prankster story?"

"Prankster story?" Sam repeated. He pulled up a nearby chair and sat down, clearly interested. "Do tell."

Lauren returned to her seat at the desk, diet cola in hand. She was shaking her head. "Hold it. I'm not so sure there is a story, let alone enough of one to share."

"Well, I do, and I'm the editor," Jim said.

"Why don't we fill him in, then let Sam decide for himself?" Lauren suggested. Jim shrugged. She looked at Sam. "First of all, are you aware that Beardsville gets involved in Halloween in a big way?"

Sam nodded. "Jim told me. Most of the New England media run a special interest feature on it each year, too."

Lauren couldn't help but smile at that, since a lot of that publicity had been arranged by her and the BPS. "Well, this year it seems we're having some trouble with vandalism," she continued. "So Jim's gotten it into his head we're under siege."

"I never said that!" Jim objected. Then he grinned and scribbled something on the pad in front of him. "But I like the sound of it! Go on, tell him about the bloody note."

"For the last time, it might not be blood!" Lauren sighed, then told Sam about the events of earlier.

By the time she had finished, Sam had a grin on his face that mirrored Jim's. "Sounds like a story to me."

"Hah!" Jim exclaimed.

"Besides, someone broke into my toolshed sometime late last night or early this morning," Sam continued. "So even if this doesn't prove to be an organized assault on the town, I've got a personal stake in this, and I'd at least like to be in on the hunt."

Lauren still wasn't so sure. "Well, I don't know..."

"You can keep all of this tightwad's money, and if there is something worth writing about, you can have the byline, too," Sam told her. He smiled thoughtfully. "I might have bigger fish to fry."

"Oh?"

"This might make a good piece for *True Behavior*."

"The television show?" Lauren asked, eyebrows arched.

Sam nodded and cleared his throat. "I'm in a little hot water with the producers right now. They think I'm in a slump, and they could be right. But something like this could get me out of it. I'd be happy to let you share credit on the piece—if it turns out to be a piece, that is. It'll have to be more than a couple of kids acting up."

"Deal," Lauren said, without much thought. "It's not as if I get a chance to work with a professional writer every day."

Jim straightened in his chair. "I resent that remark!"

"Oh. Sorry," Lauren told him, smiling mischievously. "But you know what I mean."

"I suppose, and consider yourself lucky that I'm such an understanding soul," Jim said. He looked at Sam. "As for you, I suspect an ulterior motive."

"What?" Sam had been admiring Lauren's teal sweater, and the curves it couldn't conceal, so Jim's accusation gave him a start. But he was quick to recover. "Well, of course I have an ulterior motive."

Lauren gazed at him curiously. "Oh?"

"I've just moved into a dilapidated old house, and you're the local fix-it person." He smiled at her. "It would behoove me to stay on your good side, right?"

"You'd better believe it," Lauren agreed.

She liked his smile. In fact, so far she liked Sam Burdett in every way. That probably meant some major fault lay just beneath the surface, waiting to crush her fantasies.

"Speaking of which, would you mind telling me why you're moving out here to the country, Sam?" she inquired.

He frowned. "It's a long story. Let's just say I've been too long in the city and need some space to sort out a few things."

"I see." But she didn't. Was he a burnout or a serial killer? "I guess we all feel pursued at one time or another. Is anyone in particular chasing you, or just the world in general?"

"Oh, for heaven's sake, Lauren!" Jim said. "Give the poor guy a break."

Jim was laughing again, the second time in one day. Lauren was starting to worry he might be ill. "Whatever do you mean, Jim?" she inquired innocently.

"I mean stop looking for the crack."

Sam was confused. "Crack?" he asked.

"In your armor," Jim told him. He still didn't seem to understand. "Never mind. Suffice it to say Lauren likes to look before she leaps. I told you her history. Can you blame her?"

"Jim!" Lauren exclaimed. "Get a little personal, why don't you!"

"Oh, come on, Lauren. This is Beardsville, remember? I haven't told him anything he wouldn't find out with one question and five minutes in Sandy's Place."

She slumped in her chair. "Too true."

"What's this all about?" Sam asked.

"She wants to know if you're the devil in disguise."

"And am I?" Sam wondered.

"Maybe. Do you have that article I asked you to write?"

While Lauren looked on warily, Sam went to retrieve some papers from the briefcase he had left by the door. He handed them to Jim, who scanned them quickly. His eyebrows arched and he nodded.

"Yes, I do believe you're about to sprout some horns, Sam," he informed his friend. "In Lauren's eyes, at least."

Jim gave the article to Lauren, who scanned it, her eyebrows arching just as Jim's had done. She then read it more carefully, and by the time she finished, she had indeed found the major flaw beneath Sam Burdett's intriguing image.

His article was on Beardsville from the viewpoint of a newcomer. It was very well done, and full of surprising humor. But it was very much antigrowth. Sam had moved there to get away from the constant push for progress and economic expansion.

Lauren got to her feet, and threw the sheaf of papers down on the desk. "How dare you!" she exclaimed.

"How dare I what?" Sam asked, totally baffled.

"Don't you think it's just a tiny bit hypocritical of you to move someplace and then try to stop others from doing the same?"

"I certainly do not," Sam returned calmly. This woman had a quick and fiery temper, something he would have to remember. It did nothing to make him dislike her, though. In fact, he rather enjoyed the fire flashing in her eyes. "Someone has to take a stand, and it might as well be me."

"The only place a newcomer should stand is in line, behind all the people who've spent their lives here, working for a better tomorrow."

Jim stepped between them. "Perhaps I'd better explain something before you two go at it," he said. "Sam, Lauren is a very active member of the Beardsville Promotional Society. In other words, she has spent a great deal of her time over the past few years pushing this town in the exact opposite direction you propose in your article."

"And you didn't think that was something I should know before I met her?" Sam asked, staring at him incredulously.

"I thought about it," Jim said. Then he smiled. "And I decided it would be more fun this way." With that he stepped out of their way. "Let the games begin!"

Chapter Three

Lauren didn't have much patience with the antigrowth contingent in town, and wasn't very happy to see such a well-spoken addition to their ranks.

She folded her arms and met his calm gaze with one of defiance. "Tell me something, Mr. Burdett."

"I much preferred Sam," he said.

Lauren ignored his attempt to mollify her. "You're like all the others moving out of the city looking for a safe haven, aren't you?"

"Could you be more specific?"

"The ones who have already made their fortunes by crushing the masses underfoot, or have an outside income that isn't dependent upon the local economy. What do you care if we're barely scraping by, as long as you can park your BMW in front of a mansion in the pines."

"Crushing the masses underfoot?" Sam repeated. He looked at Jim. "What have you gotten me into?"

Jim just chuckled, clearly enjoying himself. "Leave me out of this, you capitalist pig."

Sam sighed and faced Lauren again. "For your information, writers are usually among those getting crushed. I know my bank account has taken a beating lately. But I can't argue the point about my income and the local economy, except to say that I'm sure there are people who've lived here all their lives who are in the same boat," he told her. "Former state employees on pension, for instance. Or retirees on Social Security. Right?"

"Yes," Lauren conceded. "But that's part of it, too. Our seniors are a great asset, but a town needs younger people to remain vital. In a lot of small towns, the only jobs they can get are service positions. If they want a career, they have to leave. A town this size can only support a handful of professionals."

Sam nodded. "I understand that. But in a way it's also my whole point. You can't have it all. Everyone has to make his or her own choice about what they want out of life, and if what they want isn't near home, they have to leave."

"Or they can encourage their home to *grow,*" Lauren maintained. "In my case, the more the town grows, the more jobs there are for me to do, and the more secure the future for me and my son."

"I'll buy that up to a point," Sam said. "But how about the people who live here *because* it's small, or who move here for the same reason? We have the right to speak out, as well. I'm sure I'm not your only opponent in this."

Lauren chuckled ruefully. "No. That bloody knife and note this morning might be the work of some of them."

Jim clapped his hands and hooted. "Now wouldn't that make a sensational headline!"

"If it is, maybe they have reason," Sam said.

"What!" Lauren exclaimed, eyebrows arched high.

"Don't get me wrong. I'm not advocating that sort of thing," he assured her. "But won't there come a time in this growth scenario of yours when you and the other members of the BPS become the ones who are crushing the proverbial masses underfoot for your *own* goals?''

"Of course not!" she exclaimed, taking a step back from him. "We want sensible growth, not urban sprawl."

Sam leaned against the counter and gazed at Lauren, smiling. "I'm sure you do. What about the rest of your group? Are you certain they all feel the same way?"

Lauren scowled. There were a lot of people in the BPS who didn't care how big Beardsville got, as long as they were making money on the deal. There were always people like that around, and Sam knew it.

This was a dangerous man. She had stepped right into his trap, and it didn't help that she was the one who'd given him the rope to make a snare.

"Point taken," she replied at last. "So save me the clichés about power and greed."

"Actually, I was going to use the one about how hard it is to get the genie back into the bottle."

"Whatever." Lauren no longer had her arms folded over her chest, but the defiant light was still in her eyes. "All that means, though, is that it's necessary to set guidelines and keep an eye on those in charge. The basic need for growth to secure our future remains. It's vital!"

"Is it? I wonder."

Sam was still smiling. He was enjoying himself. It had been a long time since he'd met a woman who had more on her mind than her next close-up. But that was his own fault for dating models and television actresses. Lauren was an entirely different sort, maybe even a different species.

"Surely business can't be as bad as all that?" he asked her. "Otherwise you would have already been forced to leave."

"The summers are usually good. In fact, I have trouble keeping up," Lauren admitted warily, smelling another trap. "But there are also slow times, like right now. If I didn't have the haunted house, I'd be out hustling for work."

"But you *do* have the haunted house."

"Thanks to the BPS," Lauren pointed out quickly.

"And more power to you all on that score. The print ads I've seen are marvelous. That sort of growth is good."

Even Jim was surprised at that one. "You like it?"

"Sure. It's the perfect kind of growth, because it's internal. The town doesn't get bigger, it just becomes a bigger attraction, and just once a year at that."

Finally, something they could agree on. "That's right," Lauren said. "People come, spend lots of money and then leave. I'm just saying that if they did stay, my business would be better, that's all."

Sam was shaking his head. "Only for a while, Lauren. Right now you have the market pretty much to yourself. You said if you didn't have the haunted house, you'd be out hustling up jobs. Would you find them?"

"Well, there's always something," she replied.

"But what about if the town grows much more? Wouldn't a need for another business like yours appear? You said yourself you could barely keep up this summer."

Lauren sincerely wished he would stop using her own words against her. "Maybe," she said.

"Sure it would," Sam told her. "Supply and demand. But the slow times would come again, as they do to every business no matter what size the market, and only the best funded or strongest of you would survive."

"I suppose." Lauren was regarding him through narrowed eyes now. She could tell where this was leading, and didn't like his logic one bit—mostly because it made perfect sense. "But I'm a survivor."

Sam didn't doubt that for a minute. "Then you would either have to gobble up the other contractor—which usually means assuming their debts and liabilities, as well—or let yourself get gobbled up and lose the control that makes self-employment so attractive. That sure as heck doesn't sound very secure to me. But if that's the life-style you want, you'd be better off just moving to a bigger city."

Jim snickered. "By the way, Lauren, I think I forgot to mention where Sam got his journalism experience."

"Don't tell me," Lauren said with a sigh. "The *Wall Street Journal*, right?"

"Only as a stringer for a couple of months," Sam told her. "But it was a real education. I decided I'd much rather write about your normal everyday ax murderer than some of the ghouls in the financial trades."

"I can imagine. And as much as I'd love to stay here and get beaten over the head with my own rhetoric some more, I have things to do." Lauren grabbed her purse from Jim's desk, giving him a sidelong glance at the same time. "I suppose you're still serious about us being partners on the prankster story?" she asked, indicating Sam with a wave of her hand.

"More than ever! It should give the story a real edge, don't you think? That's why I had Sam stop by this morning." He grinned. "Other than for the sheer entertainment value of introducing the two of you, naturally."

"You better watch it, pal," she warned him. "Or you'll be the one getting bloody messages, and I'll start with that big nose of yours!'' With that she turned to Sam, tipped an imaginary hat to him in way of salute and stalked out the front door.

"Quite a woman," Sam said, watching as she hopped into her truck and sped away. "But I think we may have gotten off on the wrong foot." It was his turn to glower at Jim. "Thanks a bunch, old friend."

He was still grinning. "My pleasure! Really!"

"I noticed. Did it occur to you that Lauren and I might actually hit it off?"

"Of course! What do you think just happened?"

Sam frowned. "Not to beat my own drum, but I think I just won a debate. Unfortunately it was against the most fascinating woman I've met in a decade, with whom I would have much preferred to make friends first."

"What you won was a minor skirmish," Jim informed him. "Since you expect to live here, and talk out against growth, you and Lauren were bound to lock horns. All I did was make sure the first encounter took place in the presence of an impartial referee."

"Referee? Hah! You acted more like a spectator at a boxing match."

"Okay, so I enjoy a good fight. Sue me. The fact remains that I'm partial to both Lauren and you, which is why I'm going to give you some advice, Sam. First of all, Lauren Kent is fascinating to you because she isn't like any other woman you've ever known."

Sam thought of her strong physique, and of the fire in her eyes as she defended her position. He smiled. "Certainly among the top five."

"I'm serious," Jim said. "She's tough, Sam, mentally and physically. All you would have gotten by avoiding a confrontation with her is scorn. There's only one way to make friends with Lauren, and that's to earn her respect first. You did that by going head-to-head with her."

"If you say so. But where do I go from here?" Sam wanted to know.

Jim looked at him with exasperation. "What do you think, for heaven's sake? She's a woman and you're a man!"

"In other words you haven't the slightest idea."

"Nary a clue," Jim admitted. "I will tell you one thing, though."

"What's that?"

"In light of what this particular woman does for a living, I'd tread lightly on the growth issue for a while. At least until you get your plumbing fixed."

LAUREN'S HOUSE was on Maple Avenue, just off Main at the northern edge of what constituted Beardsville's downtown area. It wasn't the largest house on the block, but it stood out anyway, mainly because it was always in tip-top shape.

A Victorian-style two-story, it was freshly painted in shades of slate blue and bone white, with turquoise and rose flourishes where appropriate on the gingerbread trim. There was a waist-high cast-iron fence surrounding the property, with red brick pillars at each corner and an ornate gate in front. Lauren had put in a cobblestone walk up to the porch, and planted an herbaceous border along its edges that filled the air with a lovely scent, even this late in the fall.

Still in a snit over her encounter with Sam Burdett, she pulled her truck up in front of the house and gleefully ran over the remains of a jack-o'-lantern that some prankster had thrown into the gutter. Maybe Jim was right; maybe this was an epidemic.

Unfortunately, as she got out of her truck, she stepped smack in the middle of the orange goo. This she blamed on Sam, for having rattled her to the point where she hadn't been looking where she was going.

She went inside to change from her slacks and sweater into her normal working attire of blue jeans and sweatshirt. The sweatshirt was green today, since that was the color Mr. Anderson wanted his shutters painted after she fixed the broken hinges. Lauren then went into her small upstairs office and checked her answering machine.

The only message was from Mrs. Booth. Evidently the concrete subcontractor had arrived at the job site and had backed into and subsequently squashed their bird feeder. Rather than call to apologize, Lauren decided to do it in person, after stopping by the feed store for a replacement.

The Booths were most appreciative, and gave her a big piece of homemade pumpkin cheesecake for her trouble. This she took and ate in front of the subcontractor while telling him about the deduction she was making from his pay. It wasn't a very nice thing to do. She blamed it on the bad mood Sam Burdett had put her in.

Then she was off to see to Mr. Anderson's shutters. When she arrived, she saw that most of them were creaking in the light breeze that had blown up. It was an appropriate sound for Halloween, and went well with his decorations, which included a group of scarecrows storming his porch with pitchforks.

"That's why I want them fixed," the elderly gentleman told her when she asked. "The noise is giving me the creeps."

Lauren went to have a look, and found that almost every hinge on all twelve shutters needed to be replaced, an easy but time-consuming task. She got out her cordless screwdriver and got down to business.

As she worked, Lauren finally started to calm down enough to ponder both Sam and the things he had said. He was definitely the most interesting man to hit Beardsville in a long time. Much to her chagrin, he had also scored some major points in their debate.

She realized now that she had been working toward the goal of promoting growth without really thinking about why she wanted to attain that goal. More specifically, she hadn't given much thought to what she had lost along the way. When she was first married, back before her ex-husband's affairs, she had been perfectly happy with Beardsville and the amount of work to be done.

Now she couldn't fill her days enough to suit her, and that often meant working until she was exhausted. In fact, she was starting to like being exhausted, because then she didn't have time to think. It wasn't good for her, nor for her son, Jason. Why had she been pushing herself so hard?

An answer had presented itself that morning, in the form of Sam Burdett, with his confident masculine air and haunting blue eyes. Was she sublimating? Had she traded love, sexual satisfaction and her happiness for her work?

She did like to work, and found great satisfaction there, but there was more to life and she knew it. Indeed, she had once had those things. Lauren felt certain she could have them again. But not if she was up to her elbows in concrete and green paint when the next opportunity came along. One thing was certain. Sam had given her much food for thought—and stirred up more than her temper.

When the last shutter was fixed and painted, Mr. Anderson insisted that Lauren share his lunch of homemade macaroni and cheese and a fresh cucumber salad. At this rate, she wouldn't need any supper.

Finally Lauren arrived at what she considered the most important chore of the day, indeed of the whole week. The Beardsville haunted house.

The haunted house took place in the old Beardsville auditorium, a spooky, dilapidated structure that was scary even without the gruesome special effects so painstakingly constructed there each year. It was little wonder the place had become famous—or rather, infamous.

For a fee, stouthearted thrill seekers were given a guided tour guaranteed to elevate their adrenaline levels. Late Halloween evening, however, the tours were reserved for those well-heeled enough to pay for a tour *and* a ticket to the Weirdsville Bash. This combination costume ball and cocktail party featured live music, dancing and a lavish buffet. It also served as a fund-raiser to help retire the debt for the new civic center, as well as for other local projects.

Each year the series of scary tableaux that made up the haunted house got more technical and complex, which was both good and bad for Lauren. She enjoyed the challenge. In the case of certain electronic devices, she had even become computer literate. On the down side, complex machinery tended to break more often and take longer to fix. Since the BPS paid her by the hour to keep on top of it all, however, Lauren supposed she should count her blessings.

She stopped to check in with Nancy Cooper, the person in charge of running the business end of this year's house. As usual, the crew who would be the various ghosts, goblins and vampires guiding guests and operating the effects had hit some snags during their Sunday practice session. Lauren took the list of their complaints and went to work.

An hour later, she had pared the list down to a balky mechanism on the guillotine. She was balanced atop a ladder, probing at the blade release with a screwdriver, while Nancy helped her from below.

"Try it now," Lauren told her.

Nancy tugged on the lever. The blade remained where it was. "Zip." She brushed her long black hair out of her eyes. "Hurry up, would you? This guy gives me chills."

"Which guy?"

Nancy glanced at the fake head resting in the basket below the guillotine. "Shifty Eyes down here. Sometimes I wish you weren't so darned clever." She shivered again, watching the creepy pair of weird green eyes move back and forth, as if the severed head were watching a tennis match. "How'd you get his eyes to do that, anyway?"

"Just a simple little mechanism inside," Lauren replied. "This scary stuff is big business. You'd be surprised how much they have available."

"Who? Ghouls 'R' Us?"

Lauren laughed. "Something like that."

"Well, I still say this guy's looking up my skirt."

"Could be. After all, as the script for this tableau says, the poor guy already lost his head over a woman."

"Right. Shall I pull the lever again?" Nancy asked.

"Go ahead."

This time there was a click, and the wicked-looking blade zoomed down its guides, hitting home with a loud thunk. Something red oozed down the front of the blade, splattering the upturned face of the dummy head.

"How's that?" Lauren asked from atop the ladder.

"Gross!" Nancy exclaimed.

"That's good!" Lauren climbed down and stood beside her, admiring the effect. "Nice blood. New recipe?"

She nodded. "Leon came up with it. We're using it in the mad scientist's lab, too."

Lauren grabbed a rope at the side of the guillotine and raised the blade back into position, then wiped off the dummy head and reattached it to its body. "There you go, Shifty. All ready for opening night." She looked at the rag she had used to wipe off the fake blood. "Is Leon keeping track of this stuff?" she asked thoughtfully.

Nancy shrugged. "Who knows? He mixes it up by the bucketful out back. Why?"

At the close of the BPS meeting, they had all agreed to make as little of the bloody note on Sandy's wall as possible. She hadn't been about to try that with Jim, of course, and Sam was in on it now, as well. But she felt obliged to draw the line somewhere—not that any secret lasted long in Beardsville.

Lauren shrugged, too. "I just thought it would make a nice statistic," she replied, inventing a cover-up for what she'd been thinking. "You know. Twenty gallons of blood were spilled in the making of this year's haunted house."

"That's disgusting!" Nancy exclaimed. "I think you've been doing this for too many years."

Lauren laughed wickedly "No, *you* just haven't been doing it long enough. It's the first-year jitters."

"First and maybe last," Nancy replied, again looking askance at the moving eyes of the soon-to-be headless man.

"Hey, this is just the warm-up! Wait'll Fright Night."

"Fright Night?" Nancy asked uneasily.

"Halloween after dark," Lauren said. There were some other workers around, painting, practicing and otherwise getting ready for the grand opening that evening. She waved a hand to indicate this unusual crew in general. "When our special guests pay top dollar to come through. If you think *I'm* bad, wait until you see some of these guys then."

Nancy turned a bit pale. "Is it too late to back out?"

"Much too late. You're one of us now." Lauren laughed, and then tugged at Nancy's sleeve. "Come on. I'll buy you a cup of coffee to steady your nerves."

As they walked toward the exit together, Lauren did have to admit the place gave her the creeps sometimes, too. With its unearthly beasts and horrible monsters, well-timed strange noises and carefully planned shadows, their haunted house was frightening even in broad daylight with the houselights up. She knew the place like the back of her hand, and would still bump into something unexpected around a corner every now and then.

Tonight, with the lights down low and a full crew waiting to do their worst, the Beardsville haunted house would again earn its well-deserved reputation.

The haunted house itself took up only about half of the old auditorium. Once past the exit barrier, macabre decorations gave way to those of a lighter tone, one of jack-o'-lanterns and Halloween fun. Here, in the remainder of the building, the Weirdsville Bash would take place on Halloween night. There were simple refreshments available there now, coffee, punch and, of course, a supply of diet cola for Lauren.

On Fright Night this part of the main auditorium would be filled with the delicious smells of a fantastic buffet, and the potables would include more adult fare.

There would also be music, dancing and games with prize giveaways.

Nancy got her cup of coffee, but was called to the phone before she could sit down. Lauren decided to take her soda outside and breathe some fresh air. By design, the atmosphere in the haunted house was pretty claustrophobic.

She strolled out to her truck, enjoying the sun. It was a little after two in the afternoon. Normally by this time of day, Lauren would be thinking about getting home if she could, since Jason got out of school at a quarter to three. Today, however, he had an after-school function to attend and wouldn't get out until around three-thirty or four. So she relaxed against her truck and drank her soda.

That's when she spotted it. It was just a flash of color, a sort of burnt orange flurry at the very edge of her vision moving around the back side of the auditorium. But when she turned her head to look, it was gone.

From such a tiny glimpse she wasn't even certain if what she'd seen was human or animal. She decided, however, that she'd better have a look. There was a door around back that led to an off-limits section of the auditorium, so if it had been anyone other than a member of the haunted house crew, Lauren wanted to know where they were going and why.

Feeling rather foolish, she nevertheless tried to walk as quietly as possible as she approached the edge of the old building. Last year, the sheriff had caught two high school kids necking in one of the scrub-oak thickets back here. If they were at it again, she could scare them off and save them the embarrassment.

"Then why am I creeping up on them?" Lauren muttered under her breath. "Oh, heck. It's been so long, maybe I can pick up some pointers."

When she got to the corner, she carefully poked her head around for a peek. Nothing. She walked on, more boldly now, to the door in the middle of the building. It was unlocked.

"That shouldn't be," she said aloud, taking some small comfort from the sound of her own voice. Then she blew out a deep breath, exasperated with herself. "Nancy was right. I've been doing this too long." Next thing she knew she'd be jumping at shadows.

Lauren opened the door and stepped inside. This part of the old auditorium was behind the backstage area and had always been used for storage. It therefore had stuff stacked around its cavernous interior spanning its entire existence.

There were old sets from the various plays and pageants that had been staged there over the years, as well as some things from past haunted houses, and just general junk. Lauren knew this place, too, knew the entire auditorium intimately, in fact, from the fire-sprinkler plumbing she'd installed a few years ago in the rafters to the wiring she'd tapped into in the subbasement.

But that familiarity didn't make it any less spooky. The lighting here was dim at best, provided by a few dirty bulbs and some equally filthy skylights. Directly across from here were the large double doors that led to the stage and auditorium proper. They were closed, but not soundproof, and the voices of the other people in the building filtered through. Still, they didn't ease her fears. The cavernous open spaces beneath these high-vaulted ceilings caused sounds to echo all around. She pulled a flashlight out of her back pocket and switched it on, but even that didn't help. The beam only made shadows dart and whirl among the leftovers of long-ago Halloweens.

As she moved farther toward the center of the huge space, gingerly stepping among the various props, boards and building supplies, Lauren had the uneasy feeling someone was watching her. Was that sound the muffled voices of other workers talking? Or was it someone breathing, in the shadows to her left?

Lauren gasped as one of those shadows took on the shape of a man. She spun and pointed her flashlight directly at it, but it was only the remnant of a suit of armor.

Then she heard a footstep behind her. She whirled again, crouching low to make herself a smaller target. But if it was a footstep she had heard, her ears must be overreacting, because all the beam of her flashlight discovered was a mouse, cleaning its whiskers and watching her curiously.

"Oh, what are you looking at?" she asked it.

It just squeaked and ran away. Which was exactly what Lauren felt like doing at that moment. She made her way toward the doors on the far side of the room that would take her backstage, then onto the stage itself and in sight of everybody. For some reason, that was where every nerve ending in her body was telling her she should be.

These doors were locked tight. Naturally. Just when she needed them open. She fumbled with the ring of keys she carried on her belt when working the haunted house.

Since the ring held every key for every lock in the place, it would take a while to find the right one. As she tried them one by one, she began to get that feeling again, as if she was being watched. She could almost feel the cold, hard gaze of some maniac as he crept toward her, butcher knife raised. The hair on the back of her neck prickled and her hands started to shake, making the task of finding the right key even harder.

Finally one of them went into the lock and turned. Lauren paused, however, her hand on the doorknob.

This was silly. There was nothing behind her. To run without looking would be to give in to her fear, admit that she was scared. That was for the rubes, the guests who paid money to file through a haunted house she had helped create for the past six years. There might well be ghosts, but Lauren didn't think they haunted the living, and there were scarier things on the evening news than in the imagination of even the most twisted horror writer.

Lauren took a breath and slowly turned around....

Just in time to see one of the fake walls of an old set slowly tip over toward her. She jumped aside, and the wall came crashing down on the floor at her feet in a spray of dust, ancient flaking paint and splintered two-by-fours.

Bravery would have to wait. She jumped back over the wreckage and yanked the double doors open, propelling herself out into the backstage area without so much as a backward glance. But this time the trouble was ahead of her.

It was pitch-black. She dashed onstage, but found it even darker there, if possible. Then, as she wrestled with the heavy velvet curtains, someone grabbed her from behind.

"Help!" she screamed. "Someone please help me!"

Chapter Four

"I thought that's what I was doing," Sam Burdett told her as he unwrapped the curtain from around her. "You were about to topple off the stage." At last he got a look at her face. "Lauren!"

He still had his arms around her, preventing her from falling into the orchestra pit. She leaned against him. "I don't know what you're doing here," she said. "But thanks."

"Anytime," Sam told her. "I just got here when I heard the crash and came running. Actually, I came to see you. But nobody told me you were part of the entertainment!"

Lauren noticed that several of her co-workers had come to find out what all the noise was about. They were looking curiously at her, and at the way Sam had his arms wrapped around her. She straightened and gently disentangled herself.

"Thanks," she told him again, making a show of looking off the edge of the stage. "I would have had a heck of a time explaining how I broke my leg running from a ghost."

"Is that what you were running from?" Nancy asked with a wry grin. She looked pointedly at Sam. "Things that go bump in the night?"

"More like things that go crash in the storeroom," Lauren said smoothly. One couldn't be too careful in a town this size. Rumors got started on far less evidence than the position she and Sam had been caught in. "Has anyone been in there recently?" she asked, as much to direct attention away from herself as anything.

They all shook their heads. "How could we?" someone asked. "You're the only person the BPS trusts with all the keys. Nancy just has one for the front doors."

Someone else had gone to check backstage, and came back with that coveted set of keys, handing them to Lauren. It was Leon Wells, who was Beardsville's blacksmith, welder and horseshoer when he wasn't whipping up a bucket of blood or serving as propmaster for the haunted house.

"Didn't see anything unusual," Leon told her.

Lauren waved it off. "I found the back door open and was checking things out. It could have been unlocked since last year, for all I know. As for the crash, I probably just nudged a board or something as I walked by and one of the old sets fell down behind me."

She didn't bother telling them that it almost flattened her. Nor did she see any reason to talk about the way she had felt right before it happened. It was just her imagination.

Nancy cleared her throat. She was still looking at Sam, as were the rest. Lauren quickly made amends.

"Sorry, everybody. This is Sam Burdett. He's the new owner of the Addison place."

This brought about several moments of introductions, and more than a few questions concerning Sam, his

intentions for the old Addison farm and especially his
profession. It wasn't long before everyone in the building took a break and came to see what was going on.
More than one of them had either read Sam's work or
seen the pieces he'd done for TV.

Sam, Lauren noticed, was one of those men who had
a way with people. Not slick or pandering, but honest
and in tune with the way normal, everyday people
thought and talked. It was undoubtedly what made him
a popular writer in a medium that sought to entertain
millions at a time. Whatever, she had been right in her
assessment—Sam Burdett was going to fit in just fine
around there.

"Would you like a tour?" Lauren asked, indicating the
wall that divided the auditorium in half. "All hell breaks
loose on the other side."

The others laughed and cajoled, urging Sam to go in
from the front to get the proper effect. Lauren thought
it a good idea, too. It would serve as a dry run for this
evening's performance. Sam agreed, which sent them all
scrambling for their positions. Lauren led him out the
side door and around the front of the building.

"Of course, we don't have a full crew on yet," she told
him. "These are just the folks who managed to get time
off from their regular jobs today. But you'll get the idea."

"I'll try to act properly terrified," Sam assured her.

She smiled. "Tough guy, huh?"

"Not tough so much as jaded, I suppose," Sam replied.

"Oh?"

"I once interviewed a man who had killed his boss,
then cooked and ate most of him," Sam told her. "After being in the same room with someone like that, you

tend not to jump very high when somebody in a monster mask yells boo."

Lauren shivered. "I see your point." She ushered him through the front door and into a darkened hall that served as the entrance. "But then again, this is not your average haunted house. I guess someone with a true-crime background could think of it as a walk down memory lane."

As Sam pondered what Lauren meant by that, he noticed that the darkened corridor began to narrow. He reasoned this was to make the guests proceed in orderly single file. He also noticed that he was now almost in total darkness.

Suddenly he felt a blast of fresh air and was bathed in a bright, disorienting light. As his eyes adjusted to the searchlights, he saw that he had emerged into the first tableau. Or had he? Sam looked down to see that he was standing on what looked like asphalt, with a double yellow line running right between his legs. Then he looked up again and his eyes widened in disbelief. The lights shining in his eyes weren't searchlights, but *headlights*.

The sound of an eighteen-wheeler roared in his ears, bearing down on him. An air horn blared and the lights were headed right for him now, the shiny grillwork between them grinning at him like some evil demon as the behemoth truck came closer and closer. In an instant it was right on top of him and he could hear its engine clatter, feel the rush of air that signaled approaching doom.

As suddenly as it had begun, the ordeal was over. Everything went dark and all was deathly quiet again. Or almost everything. Just ahead of him, Lauren chuckled.

"You should have seen your eyes!" she exclaimed.

Sam cleared his throat. "I was just startled, that's all," he said.

Lauren took his hand and led him onward. "Come on, tough guy. We're bound to find something you like."

"No, really. That was great," Sam assured her. He wiped a bead of perspiration off his brow with the back of his other hand—carefully, so she wouldn't see. The lights were coming back up again. "Very realistic."

"It should be. A special process was used in filming that truck, allowing us to project it on a wraparound screen. The sound was done professionally, too, and plays through a barrage of speakers arranged around the room. If you listen carefully, you can hear crickets in the background." She laughed. "Just before you get squashed like a bug."

As the path twisted and turned through the modern-day house of horrors, Sam found a great deal that was realistic. That, Lauren assured him, was the whole idea. Today's thrill seeker demanded a lot of bang for his or her buck, and Beardsville had earned a reputation for giving the best scare money could buy. Much of the haunted house was given over to modern-day terrors right out of current headlines.

There was also more ordinary fare, but artfully done for maximum effect. Some, like the mad scientist's lab, went for the simple gross-out with buckets of blood. Others played on the basic human fear of death, such as a very eerie tableau of a giant grim reaper swinging his scythe over a freshly dug grave. As each guest stepped up to look in, a hidden camera placed his or her image in the coffin.

Overall, Sam was very impressed. With a full crew, Lauren had a perfect right to expect even the most jaded souls to walk away with an elevated heartbeat.

One particular tableau, however, came more into his bailiwick than the others. It was a reenactment of an execution in a gas chamber, and he felt obliged to make a suggestion.

"It isn't your acting," he assured Missy Jenkins, the woman who was to play the doomed mass murderer. "Your face was perfectly grotesque after the gas pellets fell."

"Gee, thanks!" Missy said.

"It's just that I once had the dubious honor of actually seeing one of these chambers in use," Sam told the workers who had assembled to hear his comments. "Believe me, not even an Oscar winner could duplicate the effect. And quite frankly, I think it's in poor taste for anyone to try."

Lauren could tell by the slight tremor in his voice that Sam wasn't kidding. In fact, all those present were silenced by the haunted look in his eyes.

"I've never been too wild about this tableau myself," Lauren announced. "But it's a bit late to come up with something to take its place."

"I have an idea, if that's okay," Sam told her.

She shrugged. "Why not?"

"This is the last tableau," Sam said. "And the ones leading up to it are harrowing, to say the least." He made a show of letting his shoulders sag as he blew out a sigh of relief. The crew chuckled. "So what do you say we give them a bit of a break. Do this one campy."

"Campy?" Lauren asked, frowning.

"Well, sort of." Sam approached Missy Jenkins. "You're supposed to be a vamp who lured men up to her apartment and then hacked them to bits, right?" She nodded, leering at him with an evil smile. "That's the ticket!'' Sam exclaimed approvingly. ''And dress the part, too. Something revealing.''

''Not too revealing, Missy,'' Nancy interjected. ''I'll not have Sheriff Buckner shutting the place down for indecent exposure while I'm in charge!''

Lauren leaned closer to Sam and whispered, ''Missy was an exotic dancer in New Orleans before she married and moved here a year ago.''

Sam raised his eyebrows and nodded his understanding. ''Yes, well, you get the idea, I'm sure. Play it for fun, not for real. And, Lauren? Do you think you could cook up a gadget that would temporarily fill the gas chamber with some kind of smoke or fog?''

''Atmosphere is Leon's department,'' she replied. ''Leon?''

He was nodding. ''We've got an extra fog machine left over from a gag we pulled last year. I can rig it to fill the chamber fast, but it'll dissipate rapidly.''

''Perfect. The way I see it, Missy sits there, looking fetching but evil, leering at the guests the way she pretended to leer at me a second ago.''

''Who was pretending?'' Missy said with a sly smile.

Sam cleared his throat. ''Anyway, the executioner throws the switch, the room fills with fog, and when it clears, she's gone.''

''Gone where?'' Nancy asked suspiciously.

''Out the back and around,'' Sam told her, tiptoeing around the mock-up chamber to show them what he meant. ''When she gets to here, she'll jump out, weapon of choice in hand, and start moving toward the guests.'' He advanced upon the crew, waving an imaginary ax. ''Maybe she can even grab the guide, who will then tell them to run for their lives.''

Sam wrapped an arm around Lauren's waist. She tried to look properly horrified and pointed toward the exit. "Get out or she'll kill you all!" she cried.

"Very nice," Sam told her. "They do so, running right out the exit with an adrenaline rush they'll remember but also a good laugh and a sense of relief. Bingo, you're ready for the next batch."

The crew applauded Sam's little scenario, including Lauren. It was a perfect solution to a sticky problem and they were all impressed. So much so that Lauren had another idea.

"Why don't you join us, Sam?" she asked.

"You mean take part in all this? As a guide or demon or something?" he asked incredulously.

"Yes!" Leon exclaimed. "There are still lots of costumes available. We never have enough help."

Missy grinned at him. "He can help me practice leering."

"He can help *me* collect tickets," Nancy objected.

"Hey! I'm a newcomer," Sam told them. "Why don't I just float around wherever I'm needed until I find a niche?"

Though Lauren had been the one who asked him, she was actually surprised he'd accepted. "You'll do it?"

"Wouldn't miss it," Sam replied.

"Great," she said.

Was it really? First she would be around him during the day, looking into the prankster story. Then they would be together at night there at the haunted house. She had calmed down since their debate earlier, but she hadn't forgotten it. They could make a volatile pair.

But so what? What was she afraid of? If they avoided talking about the growth issue, they'd get along just fine. If not, it was something they would have to come to terms with sooner or later. Lauren couldn't deny that she was attracted to Sam, and that attraction was growing as she got to know him better. It was therefore only natural for them to spend time together. How else would she find out where that attraction might lead?

Nancy got called to the phone again, and the others went back to their duties. Lauren took the opportunity to ask Sam the question that had been on her mind since he'd prevented her from falling off the stage.

"Don't get me wrong, Sam," she began. "You probably did save me from an embarrassing broken bone. Your timing was marvelous. But what brought you here in the first place?"

"I wanted to see if you were willing to come out to my place sometime soon," Sam replied. "Maybe you could help me estimate what needs to be done and how much it'll cost. I'd like to do as much of it as I can, but I'll need help."

He certainly would. But again Lauren kept her snide comments to herself. She nodded. "I'd be glad to," she told him. Then she couldn't resist one little dig. "I'm sure there's enough work for the both of us."

"I'm sure," Sam muttered. He looked at her. "As for my timing, I guess that was just fate. Maybe I was meant to save your bacon so you can save mine."

She laughed. "Maybe. But it'll have to be tomorrow. I need to get home and see my son," she said. "Once the haunted house starts, about the only time we have together is just before school and later when we cook dinner."

"Cook?" Sam asked. "That's that thing people who have stoves do, isn't it?"

"You don't have a stove?"

"I have one," he told her. "It doesn't work."

"Why not?"

Lauren was already walking toward the exit. Sam was following. She was pretty sure he was only fishing for an invitation, and she needed a moment to decide how she felt.

"If I knew why it didn't work," Sam replied, "I wouldn't have been forced to make coffee in the fireplace this morning, now would I?"

"Touchy." But she had to laugh. "I'll be glad to look at that tomorrow, as well," she informed him. For better or worse, she had made her decision. It was a big one, because asking a man home meant a great deal when there was a curious thirteen-year-old waiting there to complicate matters. "In the meantime, why don't you come have dinner with Jason and me?"

"Why, thank you, Lauren! I'd love to."

She was still chuckling. "As if I took you totally by surprise."

"Actually, you did," Sam told her. "I was expecting you to recommend a good restaurant."

"You may come to wish I had. It's Jason's night to do the cooking, and he's awfully fond of beans and wienies."

Rather than disgusted, Sam seemed pleased. "A boy after my own heart."

"Oh, no," Lauren groaned. "Not you, too?"

They had arrived at Lauren's truck. Sam walked to the vehicle parked in the spot in front of her. She had been too angry that morning to pay any attention to what he drove. It certainly wasn't a BMW.

"You're kidding, right?" she asked, looking it over.

"What?"

"It's a cab!"

Sam looked incensed. "It's a Checker!" He cleared his throat. "Well, okay, so it used to be a cab. But I have all the maintenance records and it's as solid as a brick." He patted the boxy vehicle on the fender.

"Right. A big yellow brick!" Lauren was laughing so hard she had to hold her sides. "I don't know why I'm surprised. What could be more natural than a New Yorker in a cab? Did it come with the meter?"

"No, it didn't come with the meter," Sam returned, scowling at her. Then he grinned and opened the driver's side door. "But they did throw in this nifty beaded seat cushion!"

That made Lauren howl even louder. "Oh, my!"

"And a can of mace, which I'll use on you if you don't stop laughing at my transportation. They say there's a psychological connection between the car a man drives and his manhood, you know."

Lauren was leaning against the bed of her truck now, struggling for breath. "I'm almost afraid to ask, but just what does this particular connection between man and machine indicate?" She gasped.

Sam folded his arms over his chest and pretended to look thoughtful. "I'm not sure. But I have noticed that whenever someone whistles, we both get excited."

This set Lauren off again. She hadn't laughed this much in a very long time, and it felt good. Finally, however, she managed to get into her truck and start the engine. Much to her surprise, Sam's ex-cab fired right up and purred like a kitten.

He pulled up beside her and rolled down his window. "I'll just follow you, okay?"

"Okay. But not too close," she instructed, on the verge of breaking up again. "Someone might whistle and, after all, we only just met this morning."

Chapter Five

Lauren's son, Jason, was tall and gangly for his age, all elbows and knees. His eyes were almost teal blue, like his mother's, and his hair a thick, sandy brown as his father's had been. He would be a handsome young man someday, but at the moment his face didn't quite fit him, particularly his strong, prominent jaw.

Naturally he was intensely aware that he was a mishmash of components waiting to come together, and thus self-conscious. When Lauren introduced him to Sam, he held out his hand uncertainly, still at odds with this masculine ritual.

Realizing his predicament, Sam took the opportunity to let Jason know how he wanted the relationship to begin. He grabbed the boy's hand with a firm, no-nonsense grip and gave it a couple of quick shakes, then let go.

"Strange custom, shaking hands. Do you know why we do it?" Sam asked him.

Jason frowned. "Something about not being able to hold a weapon at the same time, right?"

"That's what they say." Sam looked at his own hand. "But when you think about it, we've just exchanged about twenty different viruses. It's another form of

competition, really. May the best immune system win."
He looked up at Jason. "I much prefer video games."

Jason glanced at his mother, then back at Sam, unsure of how to react. He settled on a noncommittal shrug tempered by a half smile. "Me, too," he replied, waving Sam into the family room. "I got the latest version of Batsbane for my birthday. You want to play?"

"Only if I can be Pekoe, the demented monk." With a quick grin at Lauren, Sam turned and followed closely on Jason's heels. "What level are you on?"

"Third."

"In that case, let me take the first couple of runs at that door. It's only fair. I'm on the fifth."

"Cool! How'd you get past the wolf fairy?"

There followed a rapid exchange of clues and methods. As far as Lauren was concerned, the pair were speaking a different language. Video games were not her forte, to say the least. She had barely managed to last two minutes at the helm of a jet fighter in an air-combat game that Jason had mastered in half an hour and now considered lame.

Sam already had a game controller in his hand and was busy zapping his way through some multicolored fantasyland. This wasn't just his way of trying to find a means of relating to Jason. Teens, Lauren knew, had built-in manure detectors. Sam was actually enjoying himself, a fact Jason realized and was responding to in kind. In less than ten minutes they had found common ground and were exploring it together, laughing all the way. They were male bonding right before Lauren's startled eyes.

To be honest, she had to admit that that had been on a sort of hidden agenda when she had invited Sam home with her. Strangely, though, it was now making her realize that she should be careful what she wished for.

Whether it was territorial, maternal or something else, she was actually envious of the rapport Sam had so quickly formed with Jason. It was great to see them having fun, but she wanted to be part of it.

"Can I play?" she asked.

Sam smiled and offered her his controller. But Jason moaned. "Oh, Mom, not now! Sam was just showing me the key to the fourth level!"

She held up her hands in surrender. "Okay! I'll go change and check the answering machine."

Clearly Jason had staked his claim on Sam's attention for the moment and was quite protective of that claim. As she changed into a pair of heavy gray denim slacks and a jade green chamois cloth shirt, Lauren tried to pretend that it didn't bother her, but it did. A lot. On this point, however, the reasons weren't so clear.

Was it possible she was also envious of *Jason,* for all the attention Sam was showing *him?*

That thought rattled her so much that she was almost relieved to find a message on her machine that instantly put her mind on another track. Some of her neighbors had suffered from pranks that day. The way Sam and Jason were going, Lauren would have plenty of time to interview them.

"I'm going next door to talk to Mrs. Perkins," she announced. "Don't drive Sam crazy, okay, Jason?"

He looked at her as if she were now speaking a foreign language. "Huh?"

"I'll be fine," Sam assured her.

"I can see that." Lauren sighed, then left.

Sam and Jason were both adept enough that they could talk and play the game at the same time. As he had expected, Sam found himself to be the main topic of discussion.

"What's it like, writing for television?" Jason asked.

"It's a lot of fun most of the time. But sometimes the people in charge can be a drag," Sam replied. "All they care about are ratings and selling commercial time. Which is fine. It is a business, and there's a lot of money in it."

"Yeah?"

Sam chuckled. "Yeah. When you're working, that is."

"But you're not working now, are you?" Jason wanted to know. He was regarding Sam curiously.

"Watch that pothole," Sam told him, pointing at the television screen. Once Jason had quickly averted disaster, Sam answered him. "No, I'm not. I got into a fight with one of the people in charge. A producer. She felt I was spending too much time, uh, playing and not enough time working."

"Were you?"

Sam grinned. The directness of youth. "Yes. I just wasn't happy doing the sort of stories they wanted me to do anymore, so rather than do them, I goofed off."

"I'm that way with school sometimes," Jason said, nodding in understanding. "Mom jumps on my case."

"A lot?"

Jason shrugged. "I guess. More now than she used to." He glanced at Sam. "I guess I've been goofing off more than usual. School's boring."

"Boring how?" Sam wanted to know. "Not challenging enough? Or just not interesting?"

Another shrug. It was, Sam had noticed, a gesture most teens had honed into a separate form of expression. This one seemed to mean Jason hadn't really thought about it.

"I don't know," he said at last. "It's plenty hard, especially math." He made a face. "But mostly there's other stuff I'd rather do. Like video games."

"Tough to make a living playing video games," Sam said.

"That's what Mom says."

"Now designing the games," Sam pointed out, "that's different. I do know a guy who makes his living that way. It's still tough, real competitive, but he does okay at it."

Jason seemed truly interested. "Yeah?"

"Takes a lot of math, though."

The boy's face clouded a little at that, but he quickly recovered. "Math's not so bad."

"If you say so," Sam returned. "I'm not very good at it myself. English is more in my line. I'll bet your mother has to know math pretty well, doesn't she?"

"Yeah. She's always figuring something out. My math teacher says Mom knows more about how to use trigonometry and geometry for real-life stuff than he does. That's why he rides me on it. Says I should be doing better because she's around to help me."

There was undeniable pride in Jason's voice, but something else, as well. Having just met Lauren and her son, Sam was reluctant to get involved.

But he had touched a nerve in his debate with her that morning when he'd mentioned the effects of increased business. In the interest of keeping harmony between them, he decided he'd best find out a little more about why that nerve was raw.

"Does your Mom help you?" Sam asked.

"Sometimes. She's been pretty busy."

Sam nodded. "The world can be a tough place sometimes. Like it or not, you have to earn a living. It's why I never got married or had kids. Just too busy. I regret it.

I'm sure your Mom regrets not having enough time for you, too.''

Jason concentrated on the video game for a few moments. But there was something else going on in his head as he did so. Sam could tell, and was almost positive what his next question would be. It was one Sam knew he'd best answer very, very carefully.

"Do you like my Mom?" Jason asked at last.

Bingo. It was Sam's turn to shrug, with what he hoped was the right amount of nonchalance. "We just met this morning. But, yes, I like her. She's nice."

"So you're going to be hanging around for a while?"

That was one Sam hadn't expected, but probably should have, given what had happened with Jason's father. This, too, would have to be answered carefully.

"Well, your Mom and I have a mutual friend, Jim Ferguson, and he wants us to work on a piece for the *Weekly Razor* together. And then there's that old house I moved into. It needs a lot of work, and I hope to hire your Mom to do some of it," Sam informed him. "So, yes, I'll be around for a while. I like Beardsville."

Jason seemed satisfied. "Cool." He pointed at the video screen. "You just got eaten by the wolf fairy."

"You tricked me!" Sam bellowed in mock rage just as Lauren came back from interviewing the neighbors. She seemed pleased to find he wasn't invulnerable.

"Poor baby. Did the coyote get you?"

"It was a wolf," Sam objected haughtily. "With big snarly fangs and an invisible shield. But, yes, he got me. What did you get?"

"I'll tell you later. Right now I want my supper." She looked pointedly at Jason. "It's your night to cook, Jason. Will we be having the usual?"

He shook his head. "We're out of wienies, remember?"

Lauren closed her eyes and groaned. "I was supposed to pick some up on my way home, but Sam came along and I—"

"In that case it's my fault," Sam interrupted. "So I propose I take us all out for dinner. To celebrate my first real night in town with my first real Beardsville friends."

"Aren't you forgetting Jim?" Lauren pointed out.

"You mean the man who talked me into buying the Addison place? That's not what I call a friend," Sam joked.

Jason grinned slyly. "But he introduced you to Mom."

"True," Sam agreed. "Perhaps we can invite him the next time you cook your specialty, Jason."

"He hates wienies."

"All the better," Sam said.

Lauren was glad to accept Sam's invitation, what with the grand opening of the haunted house that night to worry about. Of course, by the way Jason dashed to turn off the television and get his coat, she doubted he would have let her turn Sam down anyway.

No doubt about it, Jason's relationship with Sam was growing much faster than her own. Lauren didn't know how she felt about that. She didn't really know how she felt about Sam, either. Inviting him home had been a nice, neighborly thing to do, but she was well aware there was more going on in her mind than that. It had been a very long time since she'd been around a man who interested her, so there were things going on elsewhere within her, too.

Whatever the outcome, all she could do now was hang on for the ride and do her best to steer things in the right direction, because it was much too late to turn back now.

"That's your car?" Jason asked as they stepped outside.

Sam gave him a look. "You have a problem with that?"

"No! I think it's cool!"

"Why am I not surprised?" Lauren asked with a sigh.

Like most places in New England, the hills within a few miles of Beardsville boasted a number of country inns that featured fine restaurants. Sam inquired as to their favorite, and Jason promptly provided the name of one that made Lauren groan. Her parents always took her and Jason there when they were in town.

She insisted they try somewhere else. The one she suggested, however, brought gagging sounds from the back seat, where Jason had insisted on riding like a fare.

"Their burgers suck."

"That's because they specialize in seafood. And in the future, please use another verb when describing something you don't like, young man."

"All right. They stink."

Lauren shook her head and sighed. "Not much better. Besides, a little fish wouldn't hurt you, you know."

"I only like fish sticks," Jason announced, sticking his head over the back seat. "With lots of ketchup."

"Sit back down and put on your seat belt!" Lauren exclaimed. "Honestly! I can't take you anywhere!"

"Is that why you never do?" Jason groused.

Lauren looked over at Sam. "Isn't this fun?"

He laughed. "I'm having a good time."

"Masochist."

Once ensconced at a table in the cozy nearby inn, however, Jason settled down and Lauren started having a good time, as well. There were already quite a few out-of-town visitors coming in for the Halloween festivities, which meant the inn was busy. This pleased Lauren, and especially pleased the owner of the inn, but didn't much thrill Sam.

"This is what it's like all the time in the city."

"It's not so bad," Lauren objected. "And look at it this way. At least you know the place will be in business the next time you want to eat here."

"True, but then again, you also know it won't always be like this. You know there will be slow times when you could come here for a quiet, romantic evening," Sam pointed out. "Bring your population up much more and that might not be so easy anymore. Think about that."

Lauren did. Especially the romantic evening part. It had been so long since she'd had one of those that she could scarcely remember what one was like. But she did miss them. In her case it was lack of opportunity, not overcrowded restaurants. Still, she realized that meant Sam was right. There were a lot of sides to this growth issue that she had failed to think through from the perspective of a couple because she was no longer part of a couple.

To Sam, however, all she would admit to was a small degree of doubt. "I'm thinking," she assured him.

He nodded. "That's all I ask."

After dinner it was time to go help with the haunted house. Since it was still early, Lauren agreed to let Jason tag along, much to his delight.

They had barely arrived when Nancy took charge and immediately pressed them all into service. "Hurry, Lauren! We turned on that fog machine and blew a circuit breaker!" She pointed in that direction and then turned her attention to Sam. "Leon's waiting for you in wardrobe, Sam. That's to the left of the stage where you saved Lauren earlier."

"You saved Mom?" Jason asked. "From what?"

"Just a fall," Sam reassured him. "She got confused in the dark and—"

"Small talk later!" Nancy interrupted. "Go!"

Sam gave her a crisp salute. "Yes, ma'am!" he exclaimed, and marched off through the haunted house.

Nancy then turned her attention to Jason. "How would you like to help me take tickets tonight?"

"Do I get to wear a costume?"

She nodded. "Sure. I think I saw a pirate mask around here somewhere."

Jason made a face. "Oh. Don't you have anything with the eyeballs hanging out?"

"Hmm. Well, I'll see what I can do," Nancy told him, turning a bit pale at the thought.

"And can you make the eyeballs squirm around a little or something?" he asked hopefully. "Or maybe drip some blood?"

Nancy groaned. "I'd say your mother was raising a monster, but she'd probably just consider it a compliment."

Meanwhile, Lauren was on her way to the circuit breakers when a chilling scream rang out, stopping her in her tracks.

Chapter Six

Horrible yells were an integral part of the haunted house, of course, but this one had sounded for real. As Lauren turned in the direction of the noise, someone hollered again. "Help! The slime machine's gone crazy!"

She breathed a sigh of relief. "Just unplug it!" she yelled back. "I'll be there in a minute."

Her reaction to the scream surprised her. Evidently, the incident in the storeroom earlier still had her jumpy. But she'd best get hold of herself, because it looked as if it was going to be one of those nights.

When the haunted house was in full swing, the old auditorium resounded with unearthly groans, shrieks and the occasional terrified scream of a satisfied customer. These Lauren took in stride as she roved about, watching for any mechanical difficulties. Occasionally a yell of a different sort would crackle softly over the little pager clipped to her belt, and she would be off to the rescue.

"Lauren! The grim reaper's head just fell off!"

"On my way!"

In order to blend in with the rest of the crew as she went about her duties, Lauren was clad in a dark brown monk's robe. The hood served to hide her face, since she could hardly do her job while wearing a mask, and the deep folds concealed the tool belt she wore around her waist. She still jingled as she walked, but that actually lent an eerie quality to her movements around the haunted house and drew uneasy glances from the already disconcerted guests.

She popped the grim reaper's head back on and quickly disappeared into the shadows again. Moments later, she was scampering to the other end of the horror trail.

"Lauren! The guillotine just started spewing blood!"

"So what?"

"That last lady in the white jeans was not amused!"

"Oh. On my way!"

There had been a few other opening-night glitches, but all had been easily fixed, including the problem with the fog machine in the execution tableau. Much to the delight of Sam and everyone else, his brainchild was rapidly becoming a big hit with the crowd.

In fact, Sam was quite a hit himself. Hanging around all those television people must have rubbed off on him, because he was turning out to be a great actor. The niche he had settled into was that of a guide, which he performed with just the right blend of menace and deadpan humor.

His costume was perfect. At the start of a tour, he simply looked like a well-dressed Victorian gentleman. As he guided his little group deeper into the haunted house, however, he started to surreptitiously change his demeanor and appearance. Finally, on the darkest part of the horror trail, he would insert a very real-looking set of bloody fangs and show himself as the vampire he had been all along.

As the evening wore on and her problems eased, Lauren finally got time to make a phone call. Then she went up front to make sure Jason didn't give the person she'd called any trouble. It was Teri Simms, a neighbor who kept an eye on Jason when Lauren wasn't around. She arrived a bit later to take him home and make sure he went to bed on time.

Running the haunted house was fun, and all for a good cause, but it was plenty of work. By closing time the crew was elated and exhausted at the same time. Another banner year was off to a good start. As the only full-time member of the crew, Lauren usually stayed late to shut everything down and lock the doors. Sam felt obliged to volunteer for this, as well, especially since they had come in his car.

They made sure the doors in back were all locked, including the one to the storeroom, then made their way through the haunted house. It was after midnight, and the place was even scarier than before.

"When I was a kid, I saw this movie about an evil wax museum," Sam told her as they made their way back along the horror trail. "Scared me silly. For months afterward I had this recurring nightmare about being locked up in a place like that."

"Sounds awful," Lauren said.

"It was. Not that I can really remember much of it." He looked around at the shadowy monstrosities surrounding them. "But something tells me it was a lot like this."

Lauren shivered involuntarily. "Would you shut up?"

"I thought you'd be immune after all the time you've spent here."

"So did I. In fact, I thought I was." She frowned. "I don't know, Sam. This sounds silly, but there's something different this year. Something . . . sinister."

Sam chuckled. "Hey, that's pretty good. Can I use that in my spiel tomorrow night?"

"I'm serious!"

He looked at her face as they stepped around the open grave and its guardian, the grim reaper. "You are, aren't you? Can you put a finger on it?"

"No. It's just a feeling." Lauren shrugged. "I don't know what's causing it. That note on Sandy's wall seemed to set the mood, and then this afternoon, in the storeroom, I thought I felt someone watching me."

"Felt?" Sam asked dubiously.

"Don't tell me you've never had the feeling you were being watched."

Sam bent to pick up a gum wrapper somebody had tossed into the head basket beneath the guillotine. "Hey, where I came from there are so many people around you that you usually *are* being watched. I guess it's a feeling I've gotten accustomed to and probably don't notice anymore. I believe the proper term for it is paranoia."

"I'm not paranoid!"

"Too bad," Sam told her. "It's actually a pretty fair defense mechanism. Always being prepared for an attack is far better than thinking it could never happen to you."

"If you say so." Lauren paused, sniffing the air with disdain. "Do you smell something?"

Sam took a whiff and made a face. "Is Leon experimenting with something new for the mad scientist's lab?"

"Not that I know of."

"Well, I didn't smell it earlier."

"The vent fans were on earlier," Lauren informed him. "I just shut them down. Come on, we'd better see if a rat crawled in here to die or something."

They moved onward, into the tableau that was usually voted top gross-out by the haunted house visitors every year. It was made to look like a cross between a laboratory and an abattoir. What with Leon so elated with his new recipe for fake blood, it was gorier than usual.

"Oh, geez!" Lauren exclaimed. "What a stench! I think I'm going to throw up!"

"I believe the in word these days is *hurl*," Sam told her. "But whatever the term, we'll both be doing it if you don't turn those fans back on."

Lauren was more than happy to oblige, since it took her out of the immediate vicinity for a moment. When she returned, the air was already starting to clear, since there was a duct right over this particular tableau. But what had caused the stench? It couldn't be Leon's artificial blood; they were using it all over the haunted house without any problems elsewhere.

She found Sam investigating what was supposed to be a mock-up of a corpse undergoing dissection. He was holding a white handkerchief over his mouth and nose with one hand. In the other he held a pen, which he was using to poke at the thing on the marble slab.

"What is it?" Lauren asked, swallowing thickly. "Or do I want to know?"

"Entrails," Sam replied.

"That's the fake stuff Leon put together."

Sam shook his head. "No, they're real, all right, and starting to get mighty ripe."

Her eyes went wide. "Real! That can't be! What—"

"Give me a second!" Sam interrupted. "I'm a crime writer, not a surgeon. One liver looks pretty much like another to me." He grimaced. "Hang on. I think I found part of a head in here."

"Oh, yuck!"

Sam probed around some more, obviously not enjoying the process one little bit. Finally he stepped away from the table, gladly leaving his pen behind.

"Well?" Lauren asked.

"First of all, I think I've just decided to become a vegetarian," he announced. "But somewhere, somebody else is going to be dining on pork for a long time. It's a hog, or rather what's left of one after a pretty expert butchering job."

"Old Man Joseph!" Lauren exclaimed.

Sam raised his eyebrows. "Were you a friend of the deceased?"

"No, that's who owned it. One of old Henry Joseph's prize hogs was stolen last night," she informed him. "Come on. We have to go call the sheriff."

They hurried up front to the box office and Lauren made the call. It took Sheriff Buckner quite a while to answer, and when he finally did he was none too pleased.

"Land sakes, Lauren!" he bellowed over the phone. "Do you know what time it is?"

"Didn't you hear me?" she asked. "We just found the remnants of that stolen hog strewn around the haunted house!"

"Well, maybe somebody decided you needed a touch of realism or something," the sheriff said. He yawned. "I don't know what you expect me to do about it."

"I expect you to come look at it!"

"Why on earth would I crawl out of a nice warm bed to come look at a pile of hog innards?" he asked.

Lauren was starting to get mad. "Because it's your job, that's why! Has it occurred to you that the knife Sandy found stuck in her wall might have been the one that was used to slaughter this hog?"

Sheriff Buckner yawned again, but when he spoke there was an edge to his voice. "Now you listen to me, young lady. I'm an elected official of this town, the people's choice. And I've been doing my job since you were in diapers! As it happens, I already knew that the substance on that knife was pig blood."

"You did?"

"I did. The lab report came back late this afternoon."

"Why didn't you tell me?" Lauren asked.

"Now just when did they go and put you on my staff, Lauren?" he returned. "Do you honestly expect me to come report every little thing I do to you?"

She sighed. "I simply meant that you should have told the BPS, Sheriff. We do have an interest in this, you know."

"Well, of course I do! That's why I told Howard. He is your president, after all. And you can hardly blame me if he didn't think to tell you about it, now can you?"

No, she couldn't. It made Lauren even madder to know that Howard Conner hadn't bothered to contact her with this information. But she knew it wouldn't do her any good to yell at Sheriff Buckner, or Howard, either. They were both aware she was a pipeline to Jim Ferguson and the *Weekly Razor,* and therefore a possible weak link where information control was concerned. Since neither of them wanted to make a big thing out of the note on Sandy's wall, any information she got she would have to dig for. Well, so be it.

"All right," Lauren continued, regaining her composure. "So you know the knife was probably used to butcher this hog, and that whoever did it was therefore probably the one who wrote the note on Sandy's wall. Doesn't *that* concern you in the slightest?"

"Not particularly," he replied. "Why should it?"

"Because it could be a threat of some kind," she said between clenched teeth.

"Is that the story you and Sam Burdett are cooking up?"

"Excuse me?"

"Come on, Lauren. It's all over town that Jim hired you and that crime writer of yours to put some kind of sensational story together about all these pranks."

Lauren squeezed her eyes shut and muttered a curse under her breath. Leave it to the people of Beardsville to know about a story she and Sam were going to work on before they had even started to investigate. The part that really bothered her, though, was the way the sheriff had put it. That crime writer of *hers*.

She opened her eyes. "Sheriff Buckner," Lauren said in measured tones. "It's my understanding that the theft of livestock is a crime, not a Halloween prank."

"It's a more serious prank, to be sure, but under the current circumstances, and until something or someone comes along to change my mind, it is still a prank. If you and Mr. Burdett want to pretend there's something terrible going on in Beardsville, I guess I can't stop you. Freedom of the press and all. But I don't have to buy in to it myself."

"So you're not going to investigate further?"

He yawned long and loud. "What's to investigate? I have no leads. There were no fingerprints on the knife. And Old Man Joseph was insured for the loss of his hog. Take my advice, Lauren," he told her sleepily. "Dump those entrails and go home to bed. Good night."

With that he hung up the phone. Lauren did the same, though much more forcefully. "As usual, he's not going to do anything," she told Sam. "All he said was to clean up the mess and go home."

"On that score I must agree with him," Sam said. "It's late and I'm beat. Let's get it over with."

They did so, then closed up the auditorium and piled into Sam's car. As he drove her home, Lauren told him about what had happened to her neighbors. Sheriff Buckner's opinion notwithstanding, neither of them was in much of a mood to call theft or especially the dumping of entrails a prank.

"My next-door neighbor is missing some homemade canned goods. And a man down the street had a navy blue pea coat and some blankets stolen right off the clothesline," she informed him. "In broad daylight yet."

"You said Sandy's place was raided of basic staples?"

"Coffee, sugar, stuff like that," Lauren replied. She looked at him curiously. "Your shed was broken into, right? Was anything taken?"

He nodded. "As a matter of fact, they made off with an old kerosene camp lantern I'd found lying around. And now we find this hog carcass minus most of the usable meat."

"It's as if someone is using Beardsville as one big shopping mall!"

"Exactly," Sam agreed. "And normally I'd say it was the work of some light-fingered transient. Except—"

"Except for the note," Lauren interjected, on the same wavelength. "'You will all pay.' Do you suppose that's what the note means? Is somebody planning to rip us off until they're either satisfied we've paid enough or they get caught?"

Sam pulled up in front of Lauren's house. He turned to look at her, his face serious. "If so, I say we make it the latter. Tomorrow we dig into this thing in earnest— after you look at my house, that is. How about it, partner?"

"You got it." She held out her hand, and Sam shook it. "And we'll do it with or without the help of the authorities."

He laughed. "From the look of things around here, I'd say we don't have much choice."

"Still like small-town life?" she asked, teasing.

"I'm afraid a hog murder wouldn't carry much weight in the city, either, Lauren," Sam pointed out. "And there you have to wait fifteen minutes to even talk to a cop, let alone get one to listen."

Lauren nodded thoughtfully. "You're a dangerous man, Sam Burdett."

"In what way?" he asked curiously.

"Lots of ways, I suspect," she replied. "But at the moment I mean as an opponent. Darned if you haven't got me questioning my stand on this growth thing, and I haven't even known you a full day yet."

He leaned closer to her. "I'm just warming up."

"That's what I'm afraid of." She slid across the seat and opened the door. "Thanks, Sam. See you tomorrow."

Lauren noticed that Sam waited until she was inside before he drove off. Nice guy. But dangerous. Luckily, the day had been too long and she was too sleepy to dwell on all that had happened. She checked on Jason, who was fast asleep. It wasn't long before she was, too.

As BEARDSVILLE SLEPT, a thin, wispy fog began to form, first in the low-lying areas around Miller's Creek, then spreading outward. It hugged the ground and dewy streets like a blanket, whirling at the slightest puff of wind.

The old auditorium was silent now. At long last all the fools had gone home to their snug little beds. It was time for the ghosts and shadows to come out and play, writhing beneath the thin, dirty moonlight that filtered in through the skylights high above. One of the shadows smiled, showing hard, white teeth.

How good it was to be alive again! For now, he could only move among the living for short periods of time during the day. But that wasn't a problem. For now, he had what he needed. And the darkness was a friend to a man who knew this town like the back of his own hand.

Soon they would all feel the strength and vengeance in that hand. They would all pay. He was just toying with them now, because it pleased him to think of them confused and helpless. Tomorrow, or maybe the next day, their confusion would turn to fear.

The bottle in his hand demanded attention, so he tipped it to his lips and drank. Fire in liquid form poured down his throat, sweet stolen liquor. It went well with stolen bread and meat.

But no! Not stolen! They owed him food and drink and more. They owed him the life they had stolen from him. A tear trickled down his beard-stubbled cheek, part sorrow, part alcohol sting.

"They'll all pay." He spoke to the darkness around him, his voice raspy, an unfamiliar surprise to his ears. "Because a friend in need is a friend indeed."

Like a wraith, he moved through the building on silent feet, wearing the boots of a hunter. His clothes were warm and quiet. He could pull knowledge from lives gone by, a butcher, baker, casket maker. This town, these people, the very building in which he crept, were all in his memory, too.

There was a place he knew nearby where pain and death lay waiting, humming softly and beating its wings. To this place he went, quietly, so as not to wake it.

Tomorrow. Someone would pay.

Chapter Seven

"Oh, man! I miss all the good stuff!" Jason exclaimed.

Lauren had decided to tell him about last night, so he wouldn't think she was keeping things from him in case word got out—which it undoubtedly would.

"I wish *I* had missed it," Lauren said. "It was gross."

"Cool! I'll bet Sam wasn't grossed out."

She chuckled at the memory. "Let's just say he won't be wanting any wienies with his beans for a while."

Lauren handed Jason his lunch money. Until his last birthday he had allowed a kiss on the forehead as part of the school-morning ritual. Now she had to settle for patting him on the back. He was growing so fast.

"Have a good day," she said. "You're coming right home after school today, aren't you?"

"Yes, Mother."

"Good. I have to go out to make Sam an estimate on his house this morning, and then we're going to interview people for that prankster story I told you about. I'm not sure how late I'll be. You'll be okay, right?"

Jason looked skyward. "Yes, Mother."

He jumped on his bike and was gone down the street in an instant. Lauren went to the refrigerator and got herself a diet cola, then went up to her office.

There was only one item on her agenda today besides going to Sam's place, and she decided to get it over with before she headed out there. Not that she thought it would do any good. She dialed the phone, sipping at her cola.

A man answered in a kind, quiet voice. "Conner Mortuary. How may I be of service to you?"

"Hold the sorrow, Howard," she told him. "It's only me."

"Hello, Lauren. I understand you had an unexpected mess at the haunted house last night?"

"So you've already heard. Imagine my surprise."

"Oswald and I had coffee together this morning. I'm sorry you were stuck with the cleanup."

Lauren took a big gulp of her soda to wash down the memory. "Goes with the territory, I suppose. May I assume you and the sheriff are in agreement on this?"

"Meaning?"

"You still think the note on Sandy's wall was a prank."

Howard cleared his throat. "As a matter of fact, I do," he replied. "Naturally I'm appalled by all that's happened. Someone poured soap flakes into the fountain out in front of the funeral home, for heaven's sake! It was a terrible mess. Suds all over the place. But I'm confident that Sheriff Buckner is doing his best to find the perpetrators." He cleared his throat again. "Speaking of which, I think it best for you to stand aside and let him do just that."

"I don't plan on getting in the sheriff's way, if that's what you're asking," Lauren returned. "But I'm sure you also know that I'm working on a story for Jim. Like it or not, Howard, this is news."

"Granted. But you can be careful about the way you go about digging into it, can't you? For instance, I would prefer it if this incident with the hog didn't get around too much. We wouldn't want to scare away the tourists.''

Lauren just laughed. "Oh, come on, Howard! If you'll forgive the implication, the kind of tourist we want to attract would eat stuff like that right up."

"Maybe," he said. "Just go easy, will you?"

"Don't worry, Howard. I don't really have that much to talk about anyway," she assured him. "See you later."

With that she hung up the phone. It was true, she didn't have much yet. But she would figure it out, and when she did, she'd make up for lost time—in writing.

Since Lauren didn't figure to be doing any dirty work today, she had forsaken her usual jeans for a pair of tan cotton twill slacks, which she topped with a comfortable navy blue V-neck sweater.

She wanted to look nice when asking around town about the prankster. Of course, looking nice for Sam had entered her mind, too. And if fixing his stove proved difficult, she had coveralls in her truck. On the way out the door she grabbed another diet cola for the road.

Lauren was curious about visiting Sam's house, and a bit uneasy, as well. After all, she really didn't know him at all, now, did she?

It wasn't that she thought she might find someone sleeping in a coffin, waiting for the dark of night—though around Beardsville at this time of year anything was possible. However, she had certainly seen the sort of stories he did for television, and couldn't help thinking that if a person wrote about the twisted things other people did for long enough, it was bound to twist him a bit, too.

The old Addison place was about five miles outside of town down a heavily treed country lane. Lauren drove along in her truck, with its ugly but functional utility bed and massive toolboxes. All she cared about was that it got her around in any weather, and had a good heater, which in these parts was vital in the wintertime.

But it was another pleasant day, so she had the window open, enjoying the crisp breeze and the smell of fall. The rolling hills were still a riot of color, though the lane itself was covered with dry, brittle leaves that scuttled and crunched as she drove along.

As she approached the farm, Lauren started a mental list of the needed repairs she could see. A gate across the gravel driveway was off its hinges. The driveway itself was deeply rutted and full of potholes. All the trees needed to have dead branches removed, and the sugar maples, a valuable asset to any piece of Vermont property, were in special need of attention.

The amount of work to be done on the farmhouse proper was daunting even for Lauren, and that was just the outside. It was a once-proud, Victorian-style two-story not unlike her own home, with a rather Gothic-looking turret structure on one end. But there the similarity ended. Its slate gray clapboard siding was faded and peeling. The broad front porch sagged. The overall dilapidated condition of the house gave it a forlorn, melancholy appearance. Little wonder some of the townfolk thought it haunted.

As she pulled up in front of it, she was starting to think of the place as a potential gold mine. But then she cautioned herself that she could only guess at Sam's finances and plans for the place. For all she knew he might even be a capable do-it-yourselfer. Then, too, she was beginning to consider him a friend.

Still, this was how she made her living. From the looks of things, business was about to pick up. "Good morning," she said as Sam came out on the porch to greet her. "Sleep well?"

"As well as can be expected with strips of wallpaper falling on me," he replied. But he was smiling. "Actually, I slept fine. You?"

"Like a log. Ready to give me the grand tour?"

He shrugged and ushered her inside. "I can stand it if you can."

It wasn't as bad as he was making it out to be, but there was much to be done inside. The wood flooring was sound, but would have to be either carpeted or refinished. There was a great deal of ornate woodwork, including a lovely staircase, which was also in need of new finish. As for the structure, there was nothing a foundation shim or two wouldn't cure. Most everything else was simply a matter of reversing the damage that years of dirt and neglect had caused.

"I can tell you one thing," Sam said as he led the way upstairs. "If I ever meet the guy who let this place fall apart like this, I'll punch him in the nose."

Lauren was using her penknife to probe at a suspicious-looking piece of wood at the top of the staircase. "I'm pretty sure you're too late," she said absently.

Sam looked startled. "To save the stairs?"

"No," she said, laughing. "That's just a bit of dry rot. No big deal. I meant it's too late to punch Hank Addison in the nose. He died a while back."

"Really?"

She nodded. "Jim undoubtedly knows the particulars, if you're interested. Not a nice story to hear, though. He was destitute and eaten up by alcoholism."

"Oh. Well, then, I guess I shouldn't speak ill of the dead. Still, this must have been a nice home once."

"It can be again," Lauren assured him.

Sam looked doubtful. "In my lifetime?"

"That would depend on what you want to accomplish and how much of it you really want to do yourself," she told him.

He had made a start on some things, such as stripping old wallpaper and preparing several rooms for paint. Much to Lauren's relief, he did have some ability, and more important, didn't seem afraid of hard work.

"What would you like to do with the place?" she asked.

As they continued to stroll around the house, Sam described the things he liked about it and hoped to restore, as well as those he would just as soon tear down. Lauren listened with an experienced ear, and then went over her own list, including those things she had noticed on the way up the driveway. From the questions he asked, she could tell he would most definitely need her help.

They ended up outside, taking in the house as a whole. Lauren was nodding. "I think you have some reasonable expectations," she said. "Of the house, that is. As for what you expect of yourself, I'm not so sure. You seem pretty handy with a paintbrush and a putty knife. How are you with power tools?"

"I'm a fast learner," he assured her.

She looked at him thoughtfully. "That would imply someone would be teaching. I thought you were looking to hire a worker."

"I am, but I'm not made of money, either. Besides, I really do want to learn how. Would it be possible to work together on some of this?"

That certainly answered her question about finances. He was not filthy rich. In a way, that made her feel better about all this; he would have a personal stake in the place, not just a financial interest. Lauren liked that. She took pride in her work and expected others to, as well. It also meant he planned to stick around for a while.

But she could foresee problems. When a man and a woman got together on physical projects, the man usually wanted to take over. Lauren wouldn't allow that.

"I don't know, Sam. I usually work alone. You could probably save a few bucks on materials. Like windows, for instance. The kind you want are really expensive, and you'll need a bunch of them."

"I didn't say I was broke, Lauren. I knew what I was getting into." He grinned. "Well, for the most part, anyway. But I did arrange for rehab money as part of the mortgage deal. And that type of window will save me money in the long haul. What can I say? I have expensive taste."

Lauren was still gazing at him thoughtfully. She liked that he wasn't willing to scrimp on quality. It meant he wanted the place to last. It also seemed he could afford to keep her busy for a while without going bankrupt.

"All right," she said at last. "I'll take this on, and you can lower the labor cost by the sweat of your own brow. But there's one condition, and it's a biggie."

"Shoot."

"I'm the boss. Period. What I say goes and it goes without discussion, unless I ask for your opinion as the homeowner," she told him seriously.

Sam didn't blink an eye. "Of course. I'm hiring you to do the work and helping you so I can save money and maybe learn a thing or two. Naturally you're the boss."

"Then we'll try it." She held out her hand and they shook on the bargain. "One more thing. As far as this helper business goes, don't get carried away. When I ask for your help I'll want it, but when I don't, I'll want you out of my way. I'm stronger than I look."

Sam didn't doubt it for an instant. She was also a very self-assured woman. All those attributes in one beautiful package. He had to admit that when he'd first arrived in Beardsville, he'd wondered if country life was really for him. Now he was becoming enamored with everything country, especially Lauren.

"Like I said, you're the boss," he assured her. "I'm really looking forward to working with you."

She chuckled. "We'll see how you feel after we start stripping those hardwood floors."

They continued to stroll around, looking at the property and enjoying the lovely weather. Lauren had been tense when she'd first arrived, but now she was starting to relax. She noticed Sam was, too. That was good, because there was a lot she wanted to know.

"If I hit a nerve, tell me to back off," she began. "But it seems to me you're running away from something by moving out here."

Sam's expression clouded. "And you perceive that as bad, right?"

"Not really," Lauren returned. "I think it depends on what you're running from. I ran from my parents when I eloped with Jason's father. It later turned out they were right about him being a jerk, but I don't regret running, because in a lot of ways that's the day I became an adult. Sometimes you have to run to grow."

Now Sam smiled at her. It was a rather sad smile, she noticed. "Or to survive. That's what I'm doing, Lauren. Running for my life."

"Sounds ominous," she noted, frowning.

"Don't worry. The only person I ever tried to hurt was myself. You see, I spent a great deal of my life in dark little city grottoes doing what a good many writers of my ilk do."

"And that is?" she asked.

"Starve, sulk and swill booze until we either break or get a break. Mine came several years ago."

"With all the interest in true-crime stories and shows?"

He nodded. "They were right up my alley. I could write about crime with a realistic voice because I had witnessed plenty of it right in my own neighborhood. But let me tell you, it'll take its toll on you, writing about other people's misery. I made a lot of money at it, too, and that added guilt to the mix. The people I chose as my friends diagnosed it as stress, and prescribed heavy doses of partying as a cure. It wasn't long before my work started to suffer."

"So you ran?"

"Right into Beardsville. So here I am, thirty-six, with most of my sanity and brain cells miraculously intact. Within reason, I can afford to live where I want, write what I want and do what I want. For the time being, anyway." His expression cleared and he looked around at the property around him. "At the moment that includes fixing up this old house with my own two hands. The way I see it, it's a form of therapy, and probably cheaper than a shrink."

They had stopped at a fence made of wooden rails that had seen better days. Lauren leaned against it gingerly, regarding Sam in a new light. "Sounds like a good plan to me, Sam. And you took the right first step by hiring me."

"Oh?"

"While you work through your therapy, I'll do what I can to make sure you don't cut your own two hands off with a power saw in the process. I shudder to think what would happen to you without me around. A psychiatrist might be cheap in comparison."

"I'm perfectly capable of taking care of myself, thank you very much," Sam told her.

"Uh-huh. Do you want me to look at your stove now?" she asked pointedly.

Sam tilted his chin up proudly. "I already fixed it. Now, shall we go to town and see what we can dig up on this mysterious pork-loving fiend?"

With that he turned and started back toward the house. Lauren followed. Was there a problem with his stove in the first place? Or had it been a ploy to get her to invite him home with her?

"I'm impressed," she said. "What was wrong with it?" He muttered something, but Lauren was too far away to hear. She hurried to catch up. "Excuse me?"

"I said it was a technical problem."

"The wiring?"

"In a way."

Lauren was frowning. "In what way?"

"That's right. Not enough watts."

"I see." And she did, too. Finally. "In other words, it wasn't plugged in, right?"

Sam glanced at her sheepishly. "Right. How was I supposed to know you had to plug it in before it would work? It's a gas stove, for crying out loud! I tried a match!"

"Electronic ignition," she told him sagely. "And with the newer ones, the gas won't flow unless the igniters have juice. Safety feature."

"Well, it sure made me feel dumb."

She patted him on the back. "That's okay, Sam. It happens to all of us."

"You make stupid mistakes?"

"Of course not! I'm a professional," she informed him haughtily. "I only make highly educated mistakes. When I screw something up, it stays screwed up!"

He laughed. "In that case, maybe I'm glad you didn't look at my stove."

"Oh, those I make certain I fix properly. Making a mistake with gas appliances is a good way to blow yourself up. Of course, it would also be a good way to blow somebody else up, too."

"I'll make sure I stay on your good side, then."

Lauren grinned. "You do that."

Chapter Eight

Lauren was well-known and liked, so it was easy for her to go where she needed to, and to ask anyone in town just about anything. Since Sam was in her company, he, too, received a kind reception. It was a good way for him to meet and get to know the people of Beardsville.

Of course, a few already felt they knew him, having heard every bit of gossip about him that was going around. Sam handled these characters with admirable grace. Not that he had much choice. Beardsville was full of characters. Most had their opinions concerning what was going on in town.

"If you ask me, that old coot did it himself."

Sam leaned against the porch railing and smiled patiently at the wizened woman who sat before him in her rocking chair. Lauren was standing beside him.

"Which old coot is that, Marge?" she asked the woman.

"Henry Joseph, of course."

Sam raised his eyebrows. So far he had heard theories blaming Beardsville's Halloween prank wave on everybody from alien beings to someone within the BPS itself. The latter was a widely enough held belief that Sam was seriously considering looking into it. There were some deep-seated rivalries to be found, especially between and toward the business owners. It seemed possible that at least some of what was going on could be grudge-related.

But Marge's accusation was a first. "You think Mr. Joseph reported his own pig stolen, butchered it and used its blood to paint that note at Sandy's Place?" Sam asked.

"Of course!"

Lauren didn't bother concealing her amusement. The only reason she had stopped to talk to Marge Tandy in the first place was in the hope she had seen something firsthand. On the elderly woman's lap sat a pair of very high-powered binoculars, which she used to keep track of the whole town, or at least as much of it as she could see from her windows and front porch. Her neighbors had long since learned to keep their curtains drawn when doing anything they didn't want Marge to see—and subsequently tell everyone else.

"Marge, you're a hoot," Lauren told her, laughing. "For starters, Henry Joseph is ten years older than you are. Hauling a hog carcass around in the middle of the night isn't something he could do."

"Oh, you'd be surprised what he could do," Marge told them sagely. "Cornered me in the produce aisle at the store the other day. Tried to pinch me in the melons."

At that, Sam totally lost his composure. He laughed so hard he started to choke, and had to bend over to catch his breath. Marge didn't seem to mind his outburst. She simply rocked forward and peered at him.

"You all right, boy?"

"Yes . . . yes, ma'am," Sam managed to croak.

"It's that city air you been breathing. Clogs up your lungs. But you'll be right as rain in a couple of months."

Sam straightened and tried to look serious. "I'm sure I will, Miss Tandy."

"Now as I was saying," she continued, "Henry Joseph is your man. Poor perverted soul. Who else would've done that terrible thing where all right-thinking citizens could see?"

Lauren frowned, lost. "What thing?"

"Why, that thing with the scarecrows over at Tom Anderson's place, of course!" She pinned Lauren with a critical gaze. "Child, you're going to have to stay better informed if you expect to make it as a reporter."

Marge thrust the binoculars at her. Lauren took them and lifted them to her eyes, adjusting the focus as she slowly scanned the neighborhood. The Anderson place came into view and she stopped, trying to figure out what Marge was talking about. She was glad to see that his shutters were still up and looking nice. Then she realized what had changed since she'd been there yesterday.

The scarecrows were no longer storming Mr. Anderson's porch. In fact, they had apparently disappeared. "All I see is a big pile of leaves covered with sheets," she said, handing the binoculars back.

"Those aren't leaves, child. They're his scarecrows. And they're covered with sheets because I called him up at six this morning and made him do it."

"Why?" Sam asked.

"Because Beardsville isn't a peep show, boy!"

"I think we'd better go over and have a look for ourselves, Sam," Lauren said, just as puzzled as he was. "Thanks, Marge. You have a nice day."

She shook her finger at them as they left. "It'll turn out to be Henry Joseph, you mark my words! Horny old goat!"

Lauren stepped up to the large sheet-covered lump on the Andersons' front lawn, wondering what could have set Marge off like that. As she bent to peek beneath one of the sheets, Tom Anderson came out, a wry grin on his face.

"I thought you two might come around," he said, joining the pair. He introduced himself to Sam and they shook hands. Then the older man waved a hand at the pile. "That's why I left them the way I found them this morning. Make an interesting anecdote for that story you're working on."

"May I?" Lauren asked, grabbing an edge of the sheet.

He nodded. "Hope you're not easily embarrassed."

She pulled off the sheet. For a moment, she didn't comprehend what she was seeing. It was the scarecrows, all right, arranged in various poses. Gradually Lauren realized what she was looking at. Her eyes widened and she blushed.

The scarecrows were having an orgy.

Sam was laughing. "Well, at least it's more creative than blowing up mailboxes." He turned his head sideways. "That's an interesting position," he said, pointing to a pair that were particularly contorted.

"There's more," Tom said, pulling off the rest of the sheets. "You should have heard Marge Tandy howl at me over the phone this morning when she saw them. Must have fogged up her binoculars."

Lauren didn't doubt it. She hadn't quite recovered herself. Still, she couldn't help but look. The human-size, straw-stuffed figures looked ludicrous and erotic at the same time, posed as they were in intimate encounters with arms and legs akimbo, yet with their silly painted-on faces and ragged clothes.

"Marge thinks it was Henry Joseph," Sam told Tom.

He laughed. "I doubt old Henry is this educated in such matters, if you know what I mean."

"Neither am I!" Lauren managed to say at last. She walked around the pile of intertwined scarecrows, shaking her head. "Talk about some exotic positions!"

Sam gazed at her, a slight smile lifting the corners of his mouth. "Oh, I don't know. Unusual, perhaps, but hardly all that exotic."

She looked up at him. "To you, maybe!"

"Anything you'd like me to explain?" he asked.

Lauren's blush deepened. She did in fact have questions. Her ex-husband had been okay in bed but hardly inventive. The only diversity he sought had been other women to do the same old things with.

Apparently Sam was more well versed in such sexual matters. However, as much as he had aroused her curiosity, now was hardly the time or place.

"Maybe later," she replied, then looked at Mr. Anderson. "Thanks for keeping them for us, Tom. I think. Do you need any help putting them back where they were?"

"No, thanks. Untangling them could prove to be the best time I've had in years. But we'd better cover them up again, for Marge's sake. I'll get to it after lunch."

Lauren started to do so, and Sam came to help. He was grinning widely now. "Maybe later, huh?" he asked quietly, so Tom wouldn't hear. "That sounds promising."

"In your dreams," she returned.

He sighed. "Yes, I imagine I will be a bit restless tonight after this."

She gave him a sidelong glance, then waved to Tom and walked away. Sam caught up with her, still chuckling under his breath. Together they headed down the street toward where Sam had parked his car.

"I'm hungry," Lauren announced.

"Me, too. What do you say we pick up Jim and force him to buy us lunch?"

"Good idea. We can hash over what we've learned while we eat. Maybe he'll have some helpful input."

Sam opened the car door for her, then got in himself and headed for the *Razor*. "I certainly hope so, because the only thing I'm working on is a half-baked conspiracy theory."

Lauren looked at him, nodding. "You mean one where some person or group is trying to make the whole town so angry they'll turn on the BPS?"

"That's the one. Like I said, half-baked." He glanced at her. "And the only motivation I've come up with so far is an antigrowth sentiment," he added apologetically.

"Maybe." She frowned. "And maybe not. I was amazed at some of the resentment we encountered this morning from some of the *business* people. Obviously the BPS isn't doing such a great job of representing all their interests."

"It was pretty clear some people feel they're being forced to participate in all the festivities without getting much monetary return from it," Sam agreed.

"Well, I guess I wouldn't get much money out of it, either, if I weren't involved in the haunted house."

"It's something to keep in mind, anyway."

"We'll run it past Jim, too," Lauren said. "See what he thinks."

They couldn't get Jim out of the office with dynamite, but did manage to con him into ordering out for pizza. As they ate, they described their day so far. He roared at Sam's description of the scarecrows. As for their conspiracy theory, however, he didn't think much of it at all.

"Bull squat!" he exclaimed loudly.

He hurled a diet cola at Lauren, who caught it without batting an eye. Sam waved him off, preferring to go get his own. Jim rolled his chair back across the room to his desk and glowered at Lauren.

"It's pretty clear to me that there're two different kinds of things going on here," he continued. "But neither of them is the work of normal adults."

With a little cola to get her going, Lauren thought she saw what he meant. "You know, Jim, you may have just put your finger on something there."

"Of course I did!" Then he frowned. "What?"

She laughed. "There *is* a pattern of sorts to this madness. Without a doubt we have a prankster problem. As you well know, quite a few people have had their mailboxes blown to smithereens. Plenty have had windows broken and even I had a pumpkin splattered in my driveway."

"Every street in town has at least one house on it that's suffered some kind of damage," Jim agreed, waving his notepad for emphasis. "What are you getting at?"

"Just that even the scarecrow incident has something in common with the rest," Lauren replied thoughtfully.

"A creative lack of good taste?" Sam offered.

She shot him a look. "The key word here is juvenile. You're right, Jim—none of this seems like the work of normal adults. However, as I've been telling the sheriff all along, there's a difference between soaping a window, or even breaking it, and the theft of a coat or a hog. Neither are socially acceptable. But there's nothing juvenile about stealing things, even if the person doing it is one."

Jim was staring at her, his eyebrows arched high. "So you think kids are doing the petty stuff, while *someone else* is responsible for the hog guts and the rest?"

"I do," she replied. "We may still find out that there's some connection, of course. For instance, an adult may be directing the kids. But for the time being I say we concentrate on the real criminal activity and let Sheriff Buckner chase the punks."

Sam agreed. "I like it. It fits." His blue eyes fairly gleamed. "It could also turn out to be a heck of a lot more interesting than a bunch of juvenile delinquents with an attitude."

"I smell a story, people," Jim growled. "A real one for a change. And I want you to go out and get it for me." When they didn't move right away, he thumped his fist on his desk. "I meant right now!"

They each grabbed another piece of pizza and bolted out the door. Neither of them was sure where to go, but both agreed the first priority was getting anywhere out of Jim's sight. Once in the car and cruising down Main Street away from the *Razor,* they finished their lunch and decided to talk with the people who had been robbed of something.

"Whoever it was, they're mighty fond of peaches," Lauren's neighbor, Mrs. Perkins, informed them.

Lauren had talked to her briefly yesterday, but hadn't concentrated on the particulars. Besides, the woman was a saint who played down her own problems while fretting over her neighbors'. Seventy and going strong, she had long been widely known as the best home canner in Beardsville.

"The thing is, I would have gladly given some away, or sold them if they didn't want charity. I used to do that when I was younger," Mrs. Perkins said. "Sell my goods, that is. It kept me in pin money, don't you know."

"Could you show us where you keep your canned goods?" Sam asked. "Maybe whoever stole them left a clue."

She nodded and led them toward the rear of the house. From there, Sam could see the extensive garden Mrs. Perkins maintained in her backyard. Most of it was fallow now, in preparation for the approaching winter. But she still looked to have some squash and a few other late crops to harvest soon. He marveled at her energy.

"They're down there," she told them, opening the door to her cellar. "It's warm enough they don't freeze, but cold enough to keep 'em happy."

She turned on a light and Sam peered down the stairs, where he could see several shelves full of mason jars containing various fruits and vegetables.

"They broke into your house?" he asked.

"Heavens, no! There's an entrance from the outside. Used to be a coal chute. My dear departed husband put a padlock on it back in '52 and I don't think it's been off since—until yesterday, naturally. What's left of it is still out there on the ground by the door."

Lauren and Sam went to take a look. The padlock had been a good one, though undoubtedly weakened by its years of weathering outside. Even so, it had to have taken a pretty good blow to pop it open.

Sam looked around and found the tool that was used, an ordinary hunk of stone. Hard enough to have broken the lock without shattering but not particularly heavy.

"It looks as though you were right, Lauren," he said, hefting the rock in his hand. "I don't think a kid did this."

They looked around some more, but found nothing else of interest. After thanking Mrs. Perkins for her time, they went down the street to visit the man who had lost his navy blue pea coat and some blankets.

He was a fairly large man, which seemed to fit in with their theory. But otherwise he couldn't tell them much and they found no other clues, so they climbed back into the car and headed for Sandy's Place.

Lauren showed Sam the double-hung window at the rear of the building through which the thief had gained access. Though it was now secured by her makeshift lock, once she removed the sixteen-penny nail it opened freely. It was a fairly large window.

"Just about anybody would fit through there," Sam noted. "That doesn't mean it was an adult, of course, but at least it didn't *have* to be a kid."

"True," Lauren agreed. "So far, so good, but nothing very definite, either."

Since Sandy had already cleaned up the kitchen, it was doubtful there would be any clues left. So they headed out to Henry Joseph's farm. It had once been a long way out of town, but Beardsville had caught up to the place. That could have presented a problem, but by then he'd reached an age where he no longer raised hogs on a serious basis. Now he only kept a few as a sort of hobby.

Whatever he may have gotten up to with Marge Tandy in the past, that afternoon Henry Joseph was acting every one of his eighty-nine years. He simply pointed to the pen where the hog had been kept and sat down in a chair on the front porch to keep an eye on them.

"No melon pinching today," Sam observed.

Lauren smiled. "Maybe Marge just brings out the beast in him. But you see what I mean—a suspect he's not."

They looked around the hog pen, though neither of them was even sure what they were looking for. Then Sam spotted what he thought might be a clue.

"Does the old boy smoke cigars?"

Lauren shook her head. "Doesn't smoke at all as far as I know. How do you think he's lived this long?"

Sam pulled a toothpick out of his shirt pocket and bent down, poking at the cigar butt he'd found on the ground. It was soft and fresh. When he'd skewered it, he straightened and held it up for her to see.

"Sort of funny looking," she observed.

"Special kind," Sam informed her. "I used to indulge on occasion. Just at poker games. Made the cheap liquor taste better." He sniffed the twisted cigar remnant and nodded. "Sweet. They marinate the tobacco or something."

"Expensive?"

He made a face. "On the contrary, dirt cheap. More of a novelty than a cigar, really. You can get them at any convenience store."

While Sam went to ask Henry Joseph if he or anyone else had been smoking out by the pen lately, Lauren continued to scout around.

"Well?" she asked when he returned.

"We're the first visitors he's had in days," Sam told her. "Apparently even Sheriff Buckner just took his statement over the phone."

"Figures," Lauren muttered. But that information made her question something she had just seen on the far side of the pigpen. She motioned Sam to follow. "No visitors at all?" she asked.

"None. Except for the thief, of course. Why?"

She pointed at the ground near the pen gate. There, perfectly outlined in the thick mud, was the recent print of a boot. A big boot.

Sam put his own foot up beside the print. "Wow! Must be at least a size thirteen."

Lauren frowned. "Even in boots Henry Joseph's feet are smaller than this. Something odd about the pattern, too."

"Looks like those rubber-soled jobs for mud and snow. You know, the ones with the leather uppers people order from that woodsy catalog company."

"You're right," Lauren agreed, leaning over to study the pattern more closely. "And that adds an interesting dimension to this mystery."

"Oh?"

She straightened and looked at him. "Those kind of boots are currently in vogue with the BMW-driving yuppies I told you about. The ones buying places in the country and then spouting antigrowth."

"Oh, yes. So that's what they wear when crushing the masses underfoot," Sam recalled, grinning. He pointed to his own feet. "See? Well-used high tops. It's the urban look. Not very good for crushing."

Lauren chuckled, but she was serious about the implications. "You know what I mean. In fact, you said it earlier. An antigrowth sentiment could be the motivating factor here."

"Maybe. I should point out a few things, though," he said. "First, this sort of boot has been a bestseller for a long, long time. Secondly, I can't envision a yuppie loading a five-hundred-pound hog into the back seat of a Beemer, or anything else, for that matter. Last but not least, I don't think hog butchering is taught as part of an MBA in most ivy-league schools anymore, now, is it?"

She sighed. "I suppose you're right. But that reminds me of a question I wanted to ask Henry Joseph."

They went back to the house, where the elderly man was still sitting on the porch, watching them. He looked a bit livelier now, and Lauren noticed that sitting there resting had put a certain gleam back in his eyes. She also noticed that those eyes spent a great deal of time focused on the bit of cleavage that showed at the V-neck of her sweater.

In that regard, Lauren had always been direct. "Marge was right," she said. "You are a dirty old man."

"Looking's about all I can do anymore, girl," he said mildly. "You begrudge me that?"

She frowned at him and cleared her throat, but decided it wasn't an issue worth pressing. "Anyway, I wanted to ask you, is it hard to butcher a hog?"

"Always was for me," he replied.

"I meant, does it take a lot of experience to do well?"

He leaned forward and rested his forearms on a pair of bony knees. "Sure, there's an art to it. I never really did much of it myself, though. The slaughterhouse takes care of all that, you see. A farmer just sells them. And when you need one for your own table it's easier to hire somebody who knows what he's doing."

"A butcher?"

"Or just a fella who does it a lot," Henry Joseph told her with a shrug. He leaned back in his chair, reminiscing. "Around these parts we used to call Hank. He was a mighty fine hog butcher. About all he was good for, in fact, especially toward the end when he really started drinking. He'd do it for a share of the meat. But I think he kind of liked doing it, too. Hank was one mean drunk."

Sam raised his eyebrows. "Hank Addison, you mean?"

"Sure." Henry Joseph nodded. "Did you say you bought his house?"

"That's right."

"Darn shame what he did to it. The Addisons were real nice folks, but that Hank..." He trailed off, shaking his head. "Not much of a surprise when he lost the place. Except to him, I suppose. But he's out of his misery now. Poor soul. I hear tell he ended up a ward of the state and died without a cent. Didn't even get a proper burial."

"How awful," Lauren said.

He nodded solemnly. "It'd be nice to see someone fix up the old Addison place like it used to be."

"That's what I intend to do," Sam assured him.

"Good." He stretched and got slowly to his feet. "If there's nothing else I can do for you, I'd best be getting dinner for me and my hogs."

"Thank you for your time, Mr. Joseph," Lauren told him.

He grinned. "Thank you for letting me look, ma'am."

She didn't want to encourage him but couldn't help chuckling. Neither could Sam. They both turned to leave.

"Say, I just thought of something," Henry Joseph said.

They turned back again. "What's that?" Sam asked.

"That cigar you showed me. Maybe it's just because we were talking about him, but I seem to recall Hank smoking cigars like that. Smelled sweet. Funny, you finding that butt near the hog pen."

"Real funny," Lauren said, frowning.

But Sam just laughed. "Do you suppose it was Hank Addison's ghost that stole your hog?" he asked.

"I've been around a long time, son," Henry Joseph said. "And if there's one thing I've learned, it's that just when us human beings think we know everything, something comes along and shows us how ignorant we really are."

Chapter Nine

As Sam drove them back to her house, Lauren went over what they had learned that day. Of course, Henry Joseph's parting words still rang in her mind. Maybe they didn't really know anything at all.

"So what do you think?" she asked Sam. "Are we looking for a large, cigar-smoking woman with big feet?"

He laughed. "Maybe, but I doubt it. I'd say our thief is male. Although the coat he took was larger, he could still be almost any size, since big feet don't always add up to a big man," Sam explained. "Whatever size man we're dealing with, he's strong enough to crack open a fairly decent padlock."

"And wrestle a five-hundred-pound hog around without making much noise," Lauren reminded him. "It's probably safe to say this is not a small man."

Sam continued. "To sum it up, we're after a fairly large male who smokes cheap cigars and knows his way around farm animals, to include the efficient butchering thereof."

"Gee, that must narrow it down to, what?" Lauren asked sarcastically. "About half the population of rural Vermont?"

"Indeed," Sam replied with a sigh. "I need a break from thinking about it, that's for sure. If I were to invite you and Jason out to dinner again, would you think I was trying to buy your companionship?"

"No, I'd think you were trying to buy your way out of eating wienies, since my invitation to dinner still stands," she told him, laughing. "I can't speak for Jason, but I'd love to eat out again. It's something of a luxury for us, you know."

Needless to say, Jason was ecstatic, to the extent he graciously consented to go anywhere his mother chose. She opted for the seafood restaurant, and off they went.

Lauren had to admit she could get used to this. As they were eating, she and Sam exchanged glances across the table, and she could tell the feeling was mutual. When one of the increasing number of strangers in town mistook them for a family, Sam sounded almost sad when he corrected the man. Clearly he had been lonely much of his life and was looking to change that status.

Still, there was resistance on Lauren's part to think beyond the moment. She knew it was silly to resent the way Sam had with Jason, but she did. On the plus side, there was little doubt the growth issue was starting to resolve itself between them. Indeed, Lauren could no longer say for certain why she had wanted Beardsville to change in the first place. Maybe so she could meet a man like Sam?

After dinner, it was back to Lauren's. Since Jason had homework, there would be no haunted house for him that evening. Lauren called Teri Simms again, who would look in on him every now and then to make sure he did his studies before anything else. Then it was off to work, though neither she nor Sam really saw their duties at the haunted house that way.

"Bigger crowd tonight," Sam observed as the crew got ready to open the doors.

"Running true to form," Lauren said. "There'll be more tomorrow night, and even more the next. Halloween is wild."

Everyone kept a sharp eye out for anything gross or suspicious, or at least anything that wasn't supposed to be that way. But things went smoothly, especially for Lauren. As closing time drew near, she was even starting to get a bit bored. So she decided to go find a dark corner and catch Missy Jenkins's performance in the public-execution tableau.

The buxom young woman was turning into quite a crowd pleaser. As the guests gathered around, a crew member posing as Missy's guard strapped her into the seat at the center of the fake gas chamber. All the while, she leered at the men and writhed in abandon, giving them quite a show.

Then the houselights went down, leaving her beneath a dramatic spot. She made the most of it, rocking her head and heaving her bosom in fear. There was a noise, which was supposed to be the sound of the gas capsules dropping. The fog machine kicked in, and the chamber quickly filled with a dense vapor, bringing a gasp from the crowd.

Lauren waited for Missy to appear from around the back of the chamber, waving her ax. When seconds passed and she didn't show, Lauren realized something was wrong. Perhaps the hidden quick release on the straps was struck.

Then Missy Jenkins started screaming.

The crowd wasn't sure whether this was part of the act or not, and therefore didn't move. Lauren had to push them aside as she made her way quickly to the front of the chamber. By the time she got there, the fog was starting to clear.

And that's when Lauren saw them. Wasps. Hundreds of them. They filled the gas chamber like a cloud, swirling around poor Missy, who was pulling on the chamber door to no avail. The sheer, low-cut gown she wore offered her no protection against their sting, and they covered every inch of her exposed skin. She fell to the floor, still screaming at the top of her lungs.

"Oh, my God!" someone cried out. "It's for real!"

"They'll kill her! Somebody help!"

There were a lot of people yelling now, and the scene quickly gave way to total chaos. One woman fainted. Several men surged forward and started beating on the window at the front of the fake gas chamber, trying to break in. But it was made of thick, tough plastic and wouldn't give. Instead, the noise seemed to anger the wasps even more, and their hum took on the vicious sound of a buzz saw. Above it all, Missy's terrified screams of pain went on and on.

Lauren ran to the back of the chamber, where she found Leon, Sam and a few others trying to batter down the door.

"That's useless!" she exclaimed, pushing them out of the way. "I ought to know, I built the thing."

She pulled a claw hammer out of its loop on her tool belt and hit the doorknob a solid blow right where it met the surface of the door. The knob popped off and rolled across the floor. Lauren then stuck a screwdriver into the hole where the knob had been and pried out the lock. It, too, hit the floor, and the door swung open. Missy lay on the floor in a heap, covered with the furious stinging insects. Her screams were now shrill and hysterical.

Wrapping the hood of her monk's robe around her face for protection, Lauren bent down and grabbed one of Missy's arms. Leon grabbed the other and together they pulled her out of the room.

Meanwhile, Sam had gotten a carbon dioxide fire extinguisher and was spraying all three of them and the air around them in an attempt to knock the wasps off and freeze them at the same time. It worked. The ones that fell to the ground he quickly stomped into oblivion.

Once Missy was safe, Lauren slammed the chamber door shut again and wedged her screwdriver between it and the jamb to keep it shut. "Somebody call an ambulance!"

"It's on the way!" Nancy had arrived and took charge of the situation, barking orders like a drill sergeant. "Leon, get those gawkers out of here! Lauren, you and Sam help me get Missy to the exit! Somebody go see if there's a doctor or nurse standing in line out front. And for heaven's sake, would someone please go find some bug spray!"

THE FLASHING LIGHTS atop Sheriff Buckner's patrol car washed over the small group gathered near the front of the auditorium, bathing their concerned faces in alternating hues of red and amber. It was mainly the haunted-house crew, the sheriff having politely dispersed everyone else.

Sam and Lauren were among those remaining. He had his arm around her for comfort, and Lauren needed it. She was worried sick and furious at the same time.

At last, the sheriff got out of the cruiser and ambled over to them. He was smiling, and there was a collective sigh of relief before he even spoke.

"I just heard from the hospital. Missy'll be fine," he announced. "But sore as all heck for a while. They say she took enough stings to kill her if that doctor hadn't been here to head off an allergic reaction."

"In other words she almost died, right?" Lauren asked.

The sheriff looked around uneasily, to see if there were any tourists lingering nearby. "Now, Lauren, you're not going to make a big deal out of this, are you?"

"You don't think attempted murder is a big deal?"

"Attempted murder!" he exclaimed. Then he looked around again. "Let's talk this over inside, shall we?" he asked quietly, motioning for her to follow him back into the auditorium, away from prying eyes and ears.

"I'd better come along and protect you," Sam said.

Sheriff Buckner looked annoyed. "For Pete's sake! I'm just going to talk to her!"

"I know. You're the one I'm coming along to protect."

Lauren chuckled and shot him an appreciative glance. It was good to see her smiling again, no matter how brief. When they were inside, she confronted the sheriff.

"I'm getting tired of asking this question," she said heatedly. "But I may as well give it one last shot. What do you intend to do about this?"

He leaned against the box-office counter with a sigh of resignation. It was midnight and he was tired. "Well, Lauren, I thought I'd go out and round up a few suspects. Shouldn't be too hard. They're usually in their nests at this hour."

"How can you make fun? A woman almost died tonight!"

"I know that! What I don't know is what you expect out of me! Did you check out that fake gas chamber?"

She nodded. "I did. And, no, I cannot conclusively prove that the nest was put in there deliberately. But I've spent enough time working outdoors to know wasps, and they do not build in places like that. They're reclusive."

He looked unconvinced. "What about the door?"

"Again it's hard to tell. I had to pretty much trash the lock to get it open. We were in something of a hurry."

Sheriff Buckner rubbed his tired eyes and yawned, then looked balefully at her. "I'm just a small-town sheriff with limited resources and manpower, Lauren. I couldn't go door-to-door interrogating people even if I had probable cause, which I don't really think I do," he informed her. "Now I happen to know that you and Sam have been trying to do just that in pursuit of this story of yours and to be honest with you, I sincerely wish you luck."

"You do?" Sam asked, surprised. He'd been expecting the sheriff to tell them to butt out.

"Yup. I can't be everywhere at once. If by snooping around the two of you stop even one prank, that's one I won't have to attend to. I'm about flagged out."

Lauren could see that was true, and had started to calm down. "I'm sorry I keep climbing all over you, Sheriff. It's just that this is so frustrating."

"Tell me about it. I watch one side of town, the darn pranksters hit the other. I increase my patrols at midnight, they strike at noon."

"They?" Sam asked.

"I'm beginning to think there's a whole army of them."

"Sam, Jim and I think the pranks are separate from the more criminal activity," Lauren informed him. "And if this incident was deliberate, it wasn't a Halloween prank. Like I said, it's attempted murder."

"Well, I still wouldn't go that far," Oswald objected. "And if I did, Howard would likely have my guts for garters without more proof. But you may be right about there being two separate problems, and only a fool would try and pretend both of them aren't getting more serious by the day. As for the haunted house, I think I'd better put a man on duty here."

Lauren was pleased—and utterly shocked. "Really?"

Oswald had to laugh. "What did you think I was going to do? Sit around like one of those lawmen in the old horror movies, telling folks everything's just fine, while in the meantime the thing from outer space eats his hat?"

Sam was laughing now, too. Lauren broke down and joined them. After a moment, Sheriff Buckner pushed himself away from the counter and headed slowly for the door.

"I'll arrange for that guard," he told them. "Do you have a spare key to the front doors, Lauren?"

"Sure." She accompanied him outside, handing the key to him. "Everything's shut down for the night except the lights. Do you want me to stick around and help?"

He shook his head. "You two go on home. No reason for all of us to lose sleep."

They bade him good-night and took off in Sam's car. He stopped in front of her house. The heater was on against the chill night air. For some reason, Lauren was reluctant to leave him just yet.

"You handle yourself well in an emergency," she said. "I never would have thought to hose those wasps down with a fire extinguisher."

He shrugged. "Seemed like a good idea at the time. I'm just glad it worked. Speaking of which, you can really wield a hammer. You hit that knob in just the right spot without so much as a practice swing, and with a heck of a lot of force, too.''

"That's not so big a deal. A nail head is a much smaller target. And I've driven a heck of a lot of nails in my life, believe me.''

"It shows.'' He put his hand on hers. "You really are stronger than you look.''

The sleeves of her sweater were pushed up, and Sam's fingertips slowly traced their way up her bare forearm, following the curvature of her muscles. Lauren felt her skin tingle beneath his touch. It had been so long since a man had touched her like this.

How much she missed all the simple things! Dinner out, a touch, a soft word, a kiss. She put her hand on Sam's shoulder and turned toward him, tilting her head, knowing it was a bold gesture. But she didn't care.

Sam did seem surprised at first, but he wasn't about to let the moment pass. He dipped his head and touched his lips to hers. Her scent surrounded him, warm and spicy, like cinnamon. When he pulled back slightly, she sighed, her breath warm on his cheek, and he immediately kissed her again, his lips parting hers, seeking her tongue.

The kiss deepened and Lauren felt his arms wrap around her, strong and gently demanding. Her hand slipped inside his jacket and along his rib cage, thrilling at the warmth of his body as their tongues dueled in her mouth.

At last she pulled away with a moan of indecision. Lauren looked at him, and found his blue eyes full of desire. She had no doubt it was mirrored in her own.

"I...I don't know what got into me!'' she exclaimed softly. "It's just been such a trying night and—''

"Was it so bad?'' Sam asked, his voice husky.

"Bad? No! It was . . . I just . . ." She trailed off, unaccustomed to the feeling of shyness after all these years. "The last relationship I was in was long-term, Sam," Lauren said after a moment. "One tends to forget how to be subtle when you've been together that many years. I just needed to be close to someone."

"You needed a kiss. And you asked for it." Sam pulled her close again. "Like I'm asking now."

Again he pressed his lips to hers, felt the smooth, quick heat of her tongue against his. Lauren moaned again, softly, every fiber of her being longing for his touch, all the while telling herself they were being foolishly impetuous. But what was wrong with that? In fact, it made the moment all that much more exciting.

Still, there was something vaguely reminiscent about it, as well. Her son had been conceived in a situation much like this one, although it had been the back seat of her ex-husband's flashy red Chevy, not the front seat of Sam's funky old cab.

Honestly, though, she preferred the cab. And she much preferred Sam. He was gentle, almost tentative, and yet skillful. Lauren leaned into his touch as his hand slipped beneath her sweater and ran along her back. She half expected him to unhook her bra, but quickly discovered that was not his intention. He simply wanted to touch more of her soft skin, feel more of her warmth.

They drew apart once more. Lauren kissed him again lightly, a quick, sweet touch. She wanted more. She could tell by the look in Sam's eyes and his accelerated breathing that he did, too. But Lauren was no longer a teenager, and knew there were other things to consider in her life. Besides, this was not the time, and certainly not the place.

As if to punctuate that fact, something suddenly hit the windshield with a sharp crack. They faced forward, disentangling themselves, just in time to hear another crack and see a second egg splatter against the glass.

"Hey!" Sam exclaimed in outrage. "Who the—"

He was interrupted as another egg hit the car, this time on the driver's side window. Suddenly they were under full-scale attack. Eggs pelted them from all sides, covering the windows with a mixture of shattered shells and slimy yellow goo that totally obscured their vision.

Then, as quickly as it began, the onslaught ceased. They heard rapid footsteps and hoots of triumphant laughter disappearing down the street. And then all was quiet.

They got out of the car, carefully avoiding the drips and glops of raw scrambled egg that dripped off the doors.

"What a mess!" Sam cried. He looked both ways, up and down the street, yelling and shaking his fists. "Real funny! You'll get yours, punks!"

Lauren was laughing. She couldn't help it. "That was perfect! There I was feeling like a teenager necking in my boyfriend's car and then we get egged!" Pointing at the slimy cab, she laughed even harder. "And look! The color almost matches!"

Sam couldn't bring himself to laugh, but he did manage a wry grin. He came around the car and gave her a hug. "I felt like a kid myself. Still do. I want to round up my gang and go stomp those guys."

"Good thing you're a sensible adult."

"I don't know, Lauren," he said, looking into her eyes. "The last thing I'm feeling right now is sensible."

A porch light came on across the street and a woman opened her door and poked her head out. "What in blue blazes is going on out there!"

"It's okay, Teri. It's us, Lauren and Sam." She was still chuckling. "We just got egged!"

"So I see." Teri made a face. "You'd better wash that off or it'll ruin the paint." With that she shut her door and turned off the light again.

"She has a point," Sam agreed.

Lauren grinned. "Oh, I don't know. It might be an improvement." Sam scowled at her and she held up her hands to ward him off. "All right! The gas station out on the interstate should still be open. They have a coin-operated self-wash bay."

"Thanks." He reached out and took her hand. "Are you going to be okay?" he asked.

"I'm fine now. You?"

"Well, I could be a whole lot better," Sam replied, arching his eyebrows suggestively.

"One step at a time, Sam," Lauren told him, pulling away from his tempting grasp. "That's part of small-town life, too, you know. The pace is a lot slower here."

He nodded. "I know. And I agree. It's been a long time for me, too. Good night."

"Good night."

Sam got into his slime-covered car, but waited until Lauren was inside before he drove off. Lauren went to check on Jason. He'd fallen asleep with the light on and his math book on his chest. She smiled and kissed him tenderly on the forehead, then put his book away and turned off the light. A heavy sleeper, he never even budged.

"Math, huh?" she muttered as she went down the hall to her room. "I'll be darned."

It looked as if Sam was having a profound effect on them both. In a way, though, that only made Lauren worry more. Jason was quickly getting accustomed to having Sam around. So was she, for that matter. But what if something happened and they had to stop seeing each other?

Lauren didn't know what that would be, but knew it was always a possibility when it came to men and women. He might make her mad, or move too fast. She might move too slow. If they did graduate to the next step, as her body was even now telling her she should, she might not be what he expected. In short, anything could happen.

If it did, she could handle it. But what about Jason? When there was a child involved, every relationship became a triangle. Was Jason ready for that? Was Sam? Was she?

Lauren slogged through her bedtime routine and finally slipped beneath the covers, exhausted. But her mind kept going over and over things like the clues they had ferreted out that day, Missy's brush with death and especially her newfound desire for Sam. As tired as she was, her sleep was uneven, fitful and upset by disturbing dreams.

THEY WERE SMOKING cigarettes down by the hedgerow and so he smelled them long before he got close enough to hear them. The odor was much different from his own cigars.

It would be a shame, in a way. He had seen the boys around town, doing things, not nearly as good at hiding themselves as he was, but young and fast. They had such promise. But someone had to die. Their young blood would spill as easily as any adult's. Maybe more easily.

His failure shamed him. Shamed the memory. Some good had come of it, for he was back on his own land. But even that had a sour taste, because it wasn't really his anymore, not yet, and he had to hide like a mouse in the straw. There were other things to consider, too. He'd been all set up at the auditorium, and had been forced to run with next to nothing. Tonight he should have been howling in victory, instead of gagging on his own blood lust.

But that could change in an instant. He moved along the hedgerow like a wraith, making no sound. The boys were up ahead, basking in the glow of cigarettes and their own achievements. It wasn't right, what they'd done to the house.

There was a small one among them this night, one he hadn't seen before. This one wouldn't be as fast or as smart, and seemed sickened by the cigarette smoke. That pleased him. It was how it should be. Thin the sick ones from the herd.

But they were on bicycles, and it had taken him too long to track them down here from the house. As he neared the clearing, they suddenly disbanded, heading for town.

Confused, he sat down on a stump and lit a fresh cigar from one of their discarded cigarette butts. Why was this happening? How could he be given such powers and then prevented from gaining his just rewards?

Then it came to him. He had been eating too well, sleeping too warmly. He had lost sight of his goals. The boys hadn't been sent to him as prey, but as teachers.

When a guerrilla dug in, he was doomed. Only the mobile survived. Now was the time to move, to circulate, to strike quickly and disappear, then strike again. When his skills were honed razor sharp and the time was ripe, they would all gather in the killing field. They would all pay.

Chapter Ten

Lauren would have loved to shoot the alarm clock when it went off. Still, once she managed to crawl out of bed she felt fairly rested, which was amazing considering the night she'd had.

After fretting and stewing until half past one, she had finally gone to sleep, only to awaken again sometime after three in the morning thinking she'd heard a noise. She got up and prowled around the house, but found nothing. Jason had been asleep, though she also remembered his room seeming oddly cold.

Lauren checked his window, which was locked. Then she turned up the heat. That must have done the trick, because after she returned to bed she'd drifted off into a sound sleep at last.

"Have to remember to check the automatic thermostat," she muttered to herself. Then she shuffled down the hall to Jason's room to wake him for school.

It wasn't easy. "Come on, honey," she said, shaking his shoulder again. "Breakfast."

"Not hungry." He groaned.

Lauren herself could barely look at food when she first got up, but Jason always ate a big breakfast. She felt his forehead. It seemed warm, and his color wasn't good.

When he finally threw aside the covers and got up, he had all the energy of a tree sloth.

"Are you getting a cold?" she asked.

"No."

"Well, you sound stuffy to me."

"I'm fine!" he told her irritably, and pushed her hand away when she tried to feel his forehead again. "Leave me alone! I'm not a baby anymore, you know."

"Touchy!" she exclaimed, but did as he asked.

Jason just picked at his breakfast, spending most of his time staring at his plate. Lauren offered to let him stay home from school, but to her surprise he insisted on going. That made her instantly suspicious.

"You didn't sneak down here last night and play video games, did you?" she inquired.

"No, Mother. Now if the inquisition is finished, may I go to school now? Or would you like to write a note and tell them why I'm late?"

Lauren threw her hands up in surrender. "Fine! Go!"

Everyone was entitled to a bad day, she supposed. By the time she had showered and opened the first diet cola of the day, she had convinced herself it was either that or a hormone storm. There certainly seemed to be enough of those going around. Must be the moon.

Then the real cause of her own stirred-up hormones arrived unexpectedly on her doorstep. "Is there a target on my forehead?" Sam asked her.

She frowned. "No, why?"

"First the toolshed, then last night the eggs, now my kitchen windows!" he exclaimed. "I thought maybe I was a marked man."

"What happened to your windows?" Lauren asked, her frown deepening.

"Some kids broke a couple of them last night. Or early this morning, I should say, around two."

Lauren led him toward the kitchen and offered him a diet cola. He looked less than thrilled, so she went to get the instant coffee she kept for guests.

"You're sure it was kids?"

Sam nodded. "A group of boys, I think, but I can't be sure. I saw them jump on their bikes when I turned on the lights, but I couldn't identify any of them. Nice mountain bikes, though," he said. "Fast. They headed cross-country for the trees at the edge of my property and disappeared."

"Hedgerow," Lauren said absently.

"What?"

"That's what those trees are called. A hedgerow," she told him. "Just a little point of country information."

The instant coffee looked old, but it was all she had. She dumped some into a cup and filled it with hot water from the tap, lost in thought. Jason had a good, fast bike. It was one of those fancy types with fat tires and a jillion gears for zipping around or climbing steep grades. He had pleaded for one because his new friends all had them. Lauren had bought it, but it was coming out of his allowance a few dollars at a time. His old bike was still perfectly fine.

"You didn't go after them?" she asked.

"No. I think they were only toying with me. I didn't much feel like playing hide-and-seek at that hour so I just let them go," Sam replied.

Lauren handed him the cup of instant coffee. "Cream and sugar?"

"Black's fine." He took a sip and nearly gagged. "No offense, but this is awful! Guess I'll have to learn to like diet cola, huh?"

"Guess so," she replied, smiling. She got him one. "Are you going to call the sheriff?"

"With all he has to deal with already? No, I guess I'll let it slide," he said with a shrug. "I'm planning on replacing those windows anyway. But the principle of the thing *does* bother me." Sam took a gulp of soda. He seemed pleasantly surprised. "Once you get past the thought, this stuff isn't half-bad for breakfast. Especially after tasting what you pass off as coffee."

Lauren laughed, finally pushing aside her suspicions about Jason's condition this morning. "So you do have some taste, after all. I nearly abandoned hope when I found out you like beans and wienies."

"Hey! I've got loads of taste," Sam objected. "For instance, you look great today."

She had on a black cotton long-sleeved shirt that she wore unbuttoned to the waist, beneath which she was wearing a pink tank top. Her blue jeans were faded, comfortable looking and snug at the hips.

Lauren smiled. "Thanks. You're looking pretty good yourself. A little less urban."

"Thanks. I guess."

Sam had traded his usual black or gray slacks for a pair of blue jeans, and his customary white dress shirt for a New England Patriots sweatshirt. He still wore his beloved leather high-top sneakers and brown bomber jacket, though. That was okay with Lauren. She liked the mix.

"Looks like we're both dressed just right for window shopping," she said. "And I don't mean a pleasant stroll through town."

"I could just leave them boarded up for now."

She shook her head. "We have to make a start some-where, and kitchen windows are as good a place as any. You wanted the greenhouse type, didn't you?"

"Right. So I can grow herbs and maybe some flow-ers."

That had surprised Lauren when he'd first told her and still did. "Are you a gourmet cook or something?"

"No, I've just always liked the way they look in those architectural magazines," he replied. "The quintessen-tial country kitchen. But I'm a fair hand with food. A guy has to be if he wants to eat well on a budget."

"I'll keep that in mind. Shall we go?"

They took Lauren's truck and headed for the local building-supply center. It had started out as a simple feed and grain that carried some hardware and lumber, then had expanded with the growth of Beardsville and the surrounding area. Lauren had been tickled pink with the change. Now she no longer had to go to Montpelier for supplies, which also meant she no longer had to risk running into one of her ex-husband's cute-as-a-button conquests.

Of course, Demetry's couldn't afford to carry as much as that fancy franchise operation did. But with Lauren's guidance they managed to keep a good stock on hand for her and the local do-it-yourself crowd at a fair price. Of course, for that experienced guidance she also received a contractor's discount, as well.

Still, windows of the kind Sam wanted weren't cheap. He looked over the display, eyes widening at the prices.

"Isn't that awfully steep?" he asked Lauren.

She shook her head. "You get what you pay for, Sam, and that is truer with windows than almost anything else in a house, with the possible exception of plumbing fix-tures." His eyes widened even more and she laughed.

"Don't worry, we'll save that for another day, when you've had time to recover. Trust me. These windows are expensive, but they won't act like a big hole in your wall once winter comes."

Sam nodded, closed his eyes and held out his credit card. But Lauren had an account there and assured him she would bill him later. Whether she gave him the discount or not depended on how he was to work with—and who had been involved in breaking the old windows.

They made a list of lumber and other supplies they would need to do the job, paid and then pulled the truck into the yard to load up. That was when Lauren noticed the damage to one of the feed-storage sheds.

The owner's son came out to help them. "When did that happen, Frank?" she asked him.

"Early this morning. Dad was here alone, loading up for a delivery, and darn near got run over by his own truck."

Lauren gasped. "How?"

"We're not real sure. The truck checks out fine. He said he was sure he set the brake, but it must have failed somehow," the younger man told her. "Backed into him and pinned him against the shed. Broke his leg in two places."

"That's terrible! Is Antonio going to be all right?"

He nodded. "Just lucky it wasn't his head, I guess."

"Very lucky," Lauren agreed.

The incident made her wonder, though. Back at Sam's, they settled down to work, talking things over as they did. Sam had been wondering, too.

"Normally, I'd call the emergency brake failing on that truck a coincidence," he said. "But after all that's been going on around here I just can't. Does that sound paranoid?"

"Yes." Lauren paused to cut a two-by-four into proper lengths for reinforcing members. When the sound of her powerful circular saw trailed off, she continued. "But I happen to feel the same way. What do you call it when two people share the same paranoia?"

Sam finished sweeping up the mess they had made from tearing out the old windows. There were two gaping holes in his kitchen wall above the sink at the moment, a condition that made him feel a bit uneasy. But Lauren's confidence calmed him.

"I'm not sure if there is a scientific name for it," he replied. "But I guess I'd call it a hunch."

"We *know* there's something going on in Beardsville."

"'You will all pay,'" Sam intoned solemnly.

"Exactly." Lauren put one of the boards she had just cut into place in one of the openings and nailed it home. "And people are paying, all right. Missy came close to paying with her life. So did Frank's father." She nailed in another board with strong, sure swings of her hammer. It felt good to work, easing her pent-up frustration. "Unfortunately I'm of the opinion there'll be more."

"As am I."

"I'm pretty sure the sheriff would consider that a wild jump to an unprovable conclusion, however," Lauren said. "And I think I've pushed his good nature far enough as it is."

"If you hadn't, I would have. But you're right." Sam handed her the next board before she could even ask for it. "I guess it'll have to be you and me, partner."

Lauren smiled at him. "At least he's not standing in our way. I thought he would."

"He still might if we go around talking about attempted murder again," Sam pointed out. "So we'll save that as a last resort."

"When's that? When it actually *becomes* murder?"

"You know what I mean."

She sighed. "Yes, I do. Sorry." Lauren flipped the hammer around and held the handle out to him. "Care to whack a few nails? Does wonders for your attitude."

He took the hammer and hefted it. It was what she had called a framing hammer, and heavier than he'd thought it would be. Sam hoped he didn't hit his thumb.

"You trust me with this deadly weapon?"

"I think you've got the idea by now," Lauren told him, laughing. "Just frame in the other opening like I did this one. I'll go get the first window ready to install."

It took great restraint on Sam's part not to tell her the window was too heavy for her. But she hadn't asked for help and he didn't offer. That, too, made her smile.

Lauren had taken off her shirt, leaving just the pink tank top. The breeze coming in through the holes in the kitchen wall was warm and felt pleasant on her skin. So did the almost physical sensation of Sam's gaze as he watched her carry the window in and set it beneath the prepared opening. She then readied it for installation, humming softly to herself as she worked.

Sam tried to attend to his assigned task, but it wasn't easy. Lauren moved so assuredly, with strength and grace. He watched her muscles flex, loose and fluid, and realized he was becoming aroused. Jim had been right. This was quite a woman, unlike any he had known before. It was a good thing they had so much to do.

They worked steadily until noon, took a break for lunch, and then went back to work. Sam was amazed at all the tricks to Lauren's trade. This job would have taken him a couple of days to do by himself, and probably more, since she saved him from making plenty of mistakes. It was a wonder she hadn't laughed at him when they'd first met and he told her about his plans for the house.

To his astonishment, the windows were in by a little after two. There was still some finish carpentry to be done, but they looked great.

So did Lauren. Her skin was flushed from her labors and she was smiling, happy with a job well done. She turned from evaluating her work and caught Sam watching her. His gaze was appreciative. Lauren knew the feeling.

At some point he had removed his shirt, a fact that hadn't fully registered until just now. He wasn't as tanned as she was, but then, not very many people with inside jobs like his were. She was pleasantly surprised by his trim, well-muscled torso and flat stomach. Past a certain age a man had to work at that, she knew, and Sam obviously had been. She knew she was staring, so she lifted her gaze. Their eyes met.

Lauren felt a deep, pleasant ache of arousal, and suddenly turned back to the windows. "Well? What do you think, Mr. Homeowner?"

"Fantastic," Sam replied.

He had come to stand behind her so he could admire their handiwork. But he was also admiring the way her jeans hugged her hips and thighs. He slipped his arms around her and gave her what he intended to be a hug of camaraderie.

But it quickly got out of hand. The skin of his chest touched the skin of her back at the scooped neck of her tank top, and the heat seemed to sear him to his soul. He dipped his head and kissed the nape of her neck, burying his face in her feathery, cinnamon-scented hair.

Lauren moaned and leaned against him, reaching a hand back to touch his face. The movement afforded Sam a tantalizing view of one breast, the nipple turning diamond hard beneath the thin material of her tank top. He couldn't resist. His hands moved from her waist, gliding up her stomach and over her rib cage to her breasts, cherishing their weight as he softly cradled them.

"You are so beautiful," he murmured. He lowered his head again and nipped lightly at the skin of her neck.

Lauren turned within his embrace and kissed him, her hungry tongue darting out to find his. She didn't object when Sam pulled her tank top up above her breasts. She shared his need to feel them against his bare skin. Sam gasped at that first touch, and his hands glided down her back to her jeans-clad buttocks, pulling her against his hardness.

As their mouths melted together again, Lauren felt herself growing light-headed. She was on the verge of surrendering to the long-denied desire within her. Sam's readiness was in no doubt. Her hands ran up and down his bare back, stroking him, feeling his power.

Sam pulled away from her slightly, his lips brushing her cheek. "I need you, Lauren."

"Sam . . . I . . ." Lauren trailed off in a sigh, uncertain. She needed him, too, needed his touch and soft voice and the sweet knowledge of his throbbing desire for her.

But there were so many things to consider. It was important for her to remember why she had come there today. This was her work. If something like this happened every time she came out to do a job for him, it would create a conflict. In a way it would be sex in the workplace, a poor mixture no matter what the profession. Lauren was there to replace his windows, not go to bed with him. Make no mistake, she wanted to. But not now, and not like this, when she was working.

Which brought up another problem. Jason. Had he been among the boys who had broken Sam's windows in the first place? If so, it could mean there was some resentment of Sam on his part that was just now surfacing. After all, she had been spending more time with Sam of late than she had with her son, and that was bound to cause some jealousy sooner or later. She ought to know; she had been jealous of Sam herself that first day, when he and Jason had all but ignored her after they met.

Lauren pulled back from him, tugging her tank top into place as she did so. "I—I can't," she told him, though a part of her was calling her crazy.

"What's wrong?" Sam asked, confused by her withdrawal.

"A lot of things." She didn't want to tell him about Jason right now. He would probably understand, but even to her it would sound as if she was using her son as a shield. "For the most part it's this," she said, indicating the tools and trappings of her trade. "I'm at work, Sam."

He groaned and closed his eyes. "Don't do this to me."

"I'm sorry. I don't expect you to understand. I—"

"But I do," he assured her. "I'm the one who's sorry, I didn't even think about it." Sam took a step toward her, but thought better of it and stayed where he was. He didn't trust himself. "It's just that I want you so badly. I thought the feeling was mutual."

Lauren looked away. "It is. But not now. Not yet."

"I don't suppose just going upstairs would be enough, huh?" he asked hopefully.

She shook her head and looked at him. His blue eyes were full of desire for her, but she could see his intelligence and understanding now, too. This was a very special man. "It's the same. I came here to work, not play."

"I was afraid you'd say that."

As a writer, Sam knew all about self-discipline. A lot of times it was the only way he met his deadlines. He had also recently been forced to exercise a great deal of control over himself in leaving a pleasurable but self-destructive life-style. Right now, however, he wished he didn't have so much strength of will.

"I wasn't being a tease," Lauren said. "At least, not on purpose." She fanned her face with her hand and smiled, trying to inject some humor into the situation. "Believe me, I just got carried away."

Sam smiled back. "Me, too."

And no wonder. She was standing there, her tousled hair framing her face, her skin moist and glowing. He needed her so badly he wanted to just gobble her up.

Lauren was taken aback by the sudden look of lust in his eyes. "Uh, I think you'd better toss me my shirt."

"I'll say. You're driving me crazy!"

"You, too," she informed him, motioning for him to put his back on, as well. "Nice pecs, though. Maybe I will let you do all the carrying from now on."

"I know what I'd like to carry," he said. "You. Right upstairs to my bedroom."

She laughed. "The one with the falling-down wallpaper?"

"You get used to it."

"Not me. It would be the only thing I could see."

Sam raised his eyebrows. "Wanna bet?"

Lauren did her best to glare at him, failing miserably. So she made a show of starting to clean up. "I hate to pull rank on you, but give me a hand with all this, please. I think it's quitting time for today."

"I like the sound of that," he said. "It means you won't be at work anymore, right?"

"Right. But it also means I won't be *here* anymore," Lauren informed him. "Jason didn't look so hot when he left for school this morning. I need to spend some time with him." She finished putting her saw into its case and looked pointedly at Sam. "Some private time."

"Oh."

They lugged her tools outside to the truck and put them away. His hand brushed hers and she jumped. Lauren could still feel the tips of her breasts tingling from the touch of Sam's bare skin against hers.

She leaned against the truck with a sigh. "We need to cool down anyway," Lauren told him apologetically. Then she touched his arm softly. "You have eyes and ears. You know how I feel." She pointed to her head. "But up here, I'm still sorting things out."

Sam nodded. "I know that, too."

"You're a pretty smart guy."

"Wait'll you get things sorted out," he told her with a sly grin. "I'll show you a whole bunch of great qualities."

Lauren raised her eyebrows and waved goodbye, getting into her truck without a word. In her present state of turmoil, she wasn't about to touch that line. Heck, she didn't even want to think too much about the possibilities.

Sam stood at her window. "See you at the haunted house later," he said, then leaned inside the truck and kissed her quickly on the lips. "That's not really work. Maybe we can fool around in the dark."

"You're incorrigible!"

He smiled. "That's one of my greatest qualities."

Lauren just shook a warning finger at him, and then took off. She didn't let herself laugh until she was out of his driveway. No doubt about it, he was indeed a dangerous man. And she was drawn to him like a moth to flame.

Chapter Eleven

"Jason?" Lauren knocked softly on his bedroom door. "I've got dinner on the table, honey."

"I'm not hungry" came his muffled reply.

Lauren closed her eyes and sighed. To say the least, their discussion had not gone well. She hadn't exactly accused him of anything. He hadn't exactly denied anything. What it all boiled down to, at least in Jason's opinion, was trust. By asking him about the broken windows, she was as much as accusing him. So he had stalked off to his room and refused to come out.

One of the things Lauren had disliked intensely about the way her own parents had raised her was their refusal to respect her space—especially when she'd passed into the hypersensitive teens. If she had pulled something like this, they would have barged into her room, physically escorted her to the dinner table and forced her to eat.

Lauren had sworn it was something she would never do to her own children. At the moment, however, she was severely tempted. "Jason, we really need to talk this over."

"Why? You've already made up your mind, right?"

"I have not!" she shot back, a bit more forcefully than she had intended. She continued more softly. "I'm just concerned, Jason. I love you. I want to know what's going on in your life.''

It was practically a textbook thing to say, Lauren knew. After an extended period of silence, Jason countered with a response that sounded as if he were reading it *from* a psychology textbook.

''I understand and accept that. I love you, too. But I need some personal time right now.'' There was no mistaking the sarcasm in his voice.

''Jason . . .'' She trailed off with a sigh. It was no use. Both she and his father were stubborn, so he'd gotten a double dose. ''Okay. Your dinner will be in the fridge if you get hungry. Teri will be by to check on you later.''

Silence. Lauren shrugged and went back to the kitchen. She ate without much interest in her food, pondering what to do. By the time she had finished and cleaned up, she decided to wait until tomorrow and hope his attitude improved. If not, other tactics would have to be taken. But what?

The thought occurred to her that she should probably ask Sam. At the very least he could get Jason talking, she was sure. But at what cost to her own position?

Asking Sam to take a hand in this would be drawing him into a parenting role, and Lauren just wasn't sure she wanted to relinquish that much control. It might also give him ideas she wasn't quite ready to entertain, or perhaps even scare him away for the same reason.

She was, after all, just getting used to the idea of a more physical relationship herself. Both their emotions were too unsteady and their needs much too volatile for them to get involved so deeply in each other's lives just yet.

Lauren called Teri, who promised to keep a covert eye on Jason that evening. Then she headed for the haunted house. Her first duty was to repair the gas-chamber door. Another young woman, Barb Fowler, had volunteered to take over Missy's role. She didn't quite have Missy's figure, or her background, either, but made up for it with a natural flair for leering. Even the crew got spooked as she went around practicing her evil eye.

Sam arrived a bit late, having had some trouble with dinner. His stove worked fine, but as he was washing dishes his sink had backed up.

He looked at her beseechingly. "I don't suppose—"

"Nope," Lauren cut him off. "No sinks, toilets or grease traps. I'll put in new freshwater and sewer lines. I'll work on old freshwater lines. But I do not touch old sewer work. Period."

"Not even for a good friend?" he coaxed.

"I don't even do my own, Sam. But I'll give you the name and number of the guy I call when my own plumbing backs up." She finished installing the new doorknob and stood, grinning at him. "And I might as well warn you right now. He drives a nice new Mercedes."

Sam groaned. "I was afraid of that."

"Welcome to the wonderful world of home ownership."

Nancy came through on her preopening inspection tour, her sharp eyes scanning left and right as she walked. "I trust you checked for insects tonight, Lauren?"

"I did."

"Good. Door working properly?"

"Smooth as silk," Lauren returned, opening it for her.

"Fine. Sam, get into costume. I don't think anyone is going to be scared by a vampire in a sweatshirt."

"Oh, I don't know. My tailor would be shocked."

"Move it! Places, people! We've got a line!"

Nancy was determined things would move smoothly that night and they did. With the sheriff's guard on duty, there were no nasty surprises. By now, the haunted-house crew had fallen into a rhythm and the gimmicks functioned like fine machinery. So much so that Lauren was certain she could take the next night off without worry, though of course she would be on call lest anything major broke down. Otherwise Leon was a fairly capable stand-in.

After serving a near-record crowd, she and Sam were doing the nightly shutdown when the guard came looking for them. Tonight it was Tim Johnson who'd drawn the duty, a big, beefy young deputy in his mid-twenties.

"You guys better come see this," he told them. "I think I found something suspicious."

Lauren winced. "Does it . . . smell?" she wanted to know.

"No. Well, now that you mention it, there is an odd odor back there. Like barbecue or something."

"Perhaps you'd better lead on, Tim," Sam advised.

He did so, taking them through the haunted house, into the other half of the main auditorium and on toward the stage. In the orchestra pit, he pulled back the heavy velvet material draping the edge of the stage apron, and pointed to a loose piece of plywood.

"I thought I heard some strange noises down here and found this when I was looking around." He held out his flashlight. "If you yank the plywood out of the way, there's what looks like a secret passage."

Lauren was noticeably relieved, and chuckled at his dramatic choice of words. "It's a passage, all right, Tim, but hardly secret. It leads to the crawl space beneath the auditorium."

The young deputy looked relieved, too, and a little embarrassed. "I should have known you'd be acquainted with every inch of this place by now."

"Practically. Still, you said you heard noises?"

He nodded. "Have you been down there recently?"

"Not for quite a while," she replied. "A lot of the wiring is down there, or the main feeds, anyway. I haven't had to touch them this year."

"Then maybe we'd better check," Sam suggested.

Tim flipped on his flashlight. "I'll go first."

They didn't argue. With his flashlight in one hand and the other resting on his holstered revolver, Tim squeezed though the opening. It wasn't lost on Lauren and Sam that a man his size didn't have any trouble doing so.

"Gets kind of narrow back here," Tim called out.

"That's the stage foundation. Keep edging around it and it'll open up," Lauren assured him.

"Oh, yeah," he said after a moment. "Wow! It's more like a basement than a crawl space."

They were having trouble hearing Tim now. Lauren poked her head into the opening and hollered at him. "It drops off right there, too! Be careful! There should be a wooden ladder nearby you can use to get down into it."

"Got it!" he hollered back. There was another moment of silence. Finally they heard his voice again, but just barely. "All clear! But come look at what I found!"

Lauren pulled the flashlight from her tool belt and took the lead, Sam hot on her heels. They had to stoop slightly to avoid hitting their heads on the wood framing above them. On either side was a smooth concrete wall, and there was sandy dirt beneath their feet.

"Looks well traveled," Sam observed.

"Naturally. Most of Beardsville's been through it at one time or another. Sneaking down here has been the cool thing for kids to do practically since the place was built.''

"Obviously the deputy never did."

"Born with a lawman's morals, I guess."

Once past the narrow opening she mentioned, which to them wasn't really all that narrow, they made a sharp turn to the right. Lauren showed him the ladder and they descended into the dusty darkness. At the bottom, Sam found himself in a huge underground area.

The auditorium floor was about three feet overhead, forming a gridwork of pipes, wires and thick wooden joists. The dirt floor was littered here and there with construction junk and assorted trash. On all sides were the concrete foundation walls, some spray painted with amateurish graffiti, or so it seemed to Sam's jaded urban eyes.

In the distance, Tim was waving his flashlight. "Over here," he yelled. "Check it out!"

When they reached him, they understood why he was so excited. Someone had obviously taken up residence in this dark, dusty pit, and from the furnishings, it appeared to be the lair of the light-fingered thief who presently had it in for Beardsville.

"That's the kerosene lantern from my shed," Sam noted.

Lauren moved her flashlight beam around the makeshift camp set up in the auditorium basement. "And Mrs. Perkins's home-canned peaches. There's the coffee, sugar, flour and whatnot courtesy of Sandy's Place." She looked around. "I don't see any signs of a fire, though. Must have done his cooking elsewhere."

"Makes sense," Sam agreed. "Wouldn't be a good idea to cook down here. Someone would smell it."

"Another reason this is the perfect hideout. He'd have had his pick of bathrooms upstairs."

"All the comforts of home."

Tim was sniffing the air. "I still smell barbecue."

They all looked around a bit and came up with the reason, as well as the final bit of incriminating evidence.

"Here," Tim called out. "Bones."

"Looks like spareribs to me," Lauren said. "Hard to tell what happened to the rest of the meat. Could be a pig himself. Or for all we know, he's got it iced down and hidden somewhere."

Deputy Tim had seen enough. "I'm calling the sheriff."

"Good idea," Lauren agreed, more than happy to let someone else wake him up for a change.

Back aboveground, the deputy used the phone in the box office while Sam and Lauren listened in. As she'd thought, Sheriff Buckner had been asleep. Tim had to hold the phone receiver away from his ear for the first couple of seconds. After that he explained what was going on, and the sheriff was too pleased by the news to be mad.

"I'll ask them, sir," Tim said, turning to Lauren and Sam. "He wants to know if there were signs of the coat or blankets. I know I didn't see any."

"Neither did I," Lauren replied. Sam nodded agreement.

"No, sir," Tim told the sheriff. He listened for a moment, nodding his head. "Yes, sir. I will. Sorry about the interruption. Good night."

"Well?" Lauren demanded when he'd hung up.

Tim shrugged. "He's pretty sure this means it's over."

"Over!" she exclaimed. "How does he figure that?"

"Said that having a guard here must have scared the guy off," Tim replied.

Sam nodded. "I'd say that's a safe bet. But it doesn't mean this is over."

"Well, Sheriff Buckner thinks it's also possible that this guy has already accomplished whatever it was he set out to do and has abandoned Beardsville, too."

"Of all the..." Lauren took a deep breath and blew it out forcefully. "Sometimes I wonder about that man."

"He did order me to stay on guard, though," Tim offered in way of appeasement. "We'll be keeping an eye on the place all the way through Halloween."

"Good!"

Lauren stalked off to finish closing down. Sam thanked Tim and bade him good-night, then followed her. He caught up with her at the grim-reaper tableau. She reached out and flicked a switch, and the wicked-looking scythe he held in his skeletal hands ceased its relentless arc through the air.

"I wish it were that easy," Lauren said. "Just flip a switch and this guy will have left town. I really hope the sheriff is right. Somehow, though, I don't think we've heard the last of our mysterious stranger."

"Nor do I. But at least this place will be safe."

She managed a smile. "Tim's a good man."

"I understand we're hard to find," Sam said, taking her hand in his. "Anything this one can do to help erase that worried frown of yours?"

Lauren put her arm around his waist, and together they headed for the exit. "You could help me play hooky tomorrow night. I need a break before the weekend rush. Maybe I can finally make you that dinner I promised."

"Sounds great. I know I could use a rest from the rigors of terrifying people," Sam replied. "But I actually had something of a more immediate nature in mind."

She chuckled at his low, throaty tone of voice. "I'll just bet you did. But you'll have to settle for dinner. I'm pooped." Lauren could see his disappointment, and felt she owed him more of an explanation. "I'm sorry. It's just that I'm having some trouble at home. Jason's acting up."

"Anything I can help you with? I do have some insight into that abyss called the male teen years."

Lauren appreciated the offer more than she could say, but was still unsure about accepting his help regarding her son. She and Jason had become a unit over the years, closer knit than some because of his father's absence. It hurt to feel him pulling away, and although she knew his growing up was a fact she would have to deal with, she didn't see how involving Sam would help matters any.

Then again, this wasn't about growing up. Not really. She understood Jason's need to establish his independence, but must he become a hoodlum to do it?

Since they had come in separate vehicles tonight, they stood in the parking lot, reluctant to part. Lauren felt torn between loyalty to Jason and responsibility toward Sam.

"Did you ever engage in much vandalism?" she asked.

He seemed surprised at the question. "You think Jason is running with the pranksters?"

"I didn't say that!" Lauren objected. "And even if I were to say it, you never heard it from me. Clear?"

Sam laughed. "As glass," he said. Then he raised his eyebrows and pursed his lips, the light dawning. "Is that why you were so eager to help me with the windows?"

"Remember, I never said a thing! And you'll be getting a bill for services rendered in any case, believe me." She sighed. "Now answer my question."

"I broke a few windows in my day," he admitted.

"Why?"

"Some say vandalism is a cry for attention. Others believe it's a way for the powerless to express anger and take control of their environment." He shrugged. "But if you ask me, I think I just did it for the heck of it. It was fun, something to do, especially when you're with a bunch of other guys. In this particular instance I'd consider that the key."

"Peer pressure?" she asked. "If it was him, I mean."

"Something like that. I haven't caught the slightest hint of resentment from him, if that's where this is leading," Sam told her. "Do you want me to talk to him?"

She shook her head. "No. Or not yet, anyway. Like I said, I'm not even sure that's what this is all about. If it is, I'd prefer he came out and told me himself."

"That would be best," Sam agreed. He breathed on his hands to warm them. "Chilly tonight! Care to step into my cab and get warm?"

"Tempting," Lauren replied with a smile at his roguish expression. "But I think it's best if I get home now. See you tomorrow?"

"You couldn't keep me away even if you met me in your yard with that hammer of yours," Sam assured her. He pulled her into his arms and kissed her soundly on the lips, then let her go before she knew what hit her. "Good night. And don't worry so much."

"I—I'll try," she said, a bit breathless from the unexpected ardor of his kiss. "Good night."

They got into their respective vehicles. Sam was the first to drive away, waving as he did so. Lauren waved back. It was indeed a chilly night, and her truck needed a moment more before it wanted to move.

But Lauren felt plenty warm. "If he keeps doing things like that," she muttered to herself, "he's the one who's going to need protection!"

When she got home, the first thing she did was to check on Jason. He was quite soundly asleep, not faking this time. She watched him for a moment, enjoying the sound of his breathing and his angelic expression.

She sincerely hoped he wasn't dreaming of breaking more windows. What had really started worrying her, though, was the incident with the scarecrows.

Had Jason been with the other pranksters when they'd manipulated the straw figures into those positions? If so, had he known what he was doing? Worse, being the creative individual he was, could he have even come up with a couple of those positions himself?

That was a thought too full of unsettling implications for a mother to handle while looking at her sleeping thirteen-year-old son. Lauren sighed and left his room, shutting the door behind her. Too bad locking him in was out of the question. Not for long. Just until he was eighteen or so.

Instead, she simply got ready for bed and climbed under the covers, hoping for the best. She couldn't guess what the next disaster would be.

Chapter Twelve

Jason was only slightly more communicative the next morning. Lauren felt obliged to press a bit harder, but that went over like a lead balloon and he left for school in a huff. For her part, Lauren indulged in a rare bout of self-pity and a good cry, more out of frustration than anything else.

Afterward, she went to take a nice, hot bubble bath. This was her usual panacea, and Lauren lolled there reading until her fingers and toes wrinkled.

She emerged feeling like a new woman and decided to look the part, donning her most feminine bra and panties and a soft brown skirt that showed a lot of leg, topped by an oversize cardigan of burnt orange with gold patch pockets.

It was then time to go grocery shopping, which she found a much more enjoyable task when it was for a special dinner. Her menu was a fairly ambitious one, consisting of four-cheese vegetable lasagna, fresh-baked homemade sourdough bread and a complex salad with as many fresh greens as the local store had on hand.

When she returned home with her purchases, she found Sam waiting for her. Since she was starting to wonder whether she'd bitten off more than she could chew, food-preparation-wise, Lauren was happy to see him for more than just the pleasure of his company.

His eyes widened when she climbed from the truck. This was the first time he'd seen her in anything other than jeans. Evidently he liked the change.

"Wow!"

"What? You didn't think I had legs?" she responded.

"Oh, I knew you had them. I even figured they'd be nice. But I wasn't prepared for great!" Sam exclaimed.

Lauren fought a blush. "Thank you."

Sam grabbed the sack of groceries she thrust at him, still taking in this new revelation. "I mean really! If we were in the city I'd have you pegged as a dancer."

"Well, now you know that carpenters can look pretty good, too. It's all the ladder climbing, I guess. And to think, some women have to buy exercise machines."

In the kitchen, Sam put down his burden and relieved Lauren of hers. "I came over to talk about the story, but it looks like I'd better start by helping with dinner."

"Thanks. I think I'll need it. And we can do both," Lauren told him. "As long as you can chop and talk at the same time."

"I believe I can handle that."

In fact, he proved to be more than a fair hand in the kitchen. While he grated cheese and chopped vegetables, Lauren attended to the other tasks, such as getting her bread ready. She wore an apron to protect her clothes, but Sam waved away the frilly one she offered him.

"I've got a shop apron in the garage," she said.

"What? Do I look like a messy person?"

"Suit yourself." As they worked they discussed their leads. "I've come to a rather unnerving conclusion," Lauren began. "Whoever this guy is that's stalking Beardsville, he must have a lot of local knowledge."

"How do you figure?"

"His targets. Take Sandy's Place, for instance," she said. "The window he used to gain access hasn't had a lock on it in over twenty years."

"Thin," Sam remarked doubtfully. "But go on."

"Not only did he seem to know that Mrs. Perkins is an avid and excellent home canner, he also knew where she kept her stock. He even targeted her peaches specifically."

Sam nodded. "Better. But he might just like peaches."

Lauren measured out her flour, added the water and sourdough starter and then dug in with both hands. "Okay, how about Henry Joseph? He isn't the only farmer in the area with hogs. And his farm isn't the farthest from town or least secure, either. But he sure as heck is the oldest. No way could he catch a thief, or even hit the broadside of his own barn with a shotgun. Probably slept through the whole thing anyway."

"Now that's a valid point," Sam agreed. He was grating cheese by hand, being careful not to grate himself in the process. "And I think I see what you mean. That opening to the auditorium crawl space isn't something a transient would just stumble on, is it?"

"Not likely. But there are a lot of residents who know about it, especially the adults who played in there as kids."

Sam glanced at her recipe, found he had enough provolone grated and went on to the mozzarella. "Can we establish a link to the victims somehow?" Sam asked. "Something they have in common, maybe?"

"Besides the fact they live in Beardsville, you mean." Lauren thought a moment. Kneading the bread dough helped. "Sandy is a member of the BPS. So is Antonio

Demetry, the lumberyard owner," she told him. Then she frowned. "But Mrs. Perkins certainly isn't."

"All three of them are long-time residents, though, aren't they?" Sam asked.

"Yes, but you're not, and neither is Missy Jenkins."

"True."

"Still, I think we're on to something," Lauren said. "Somehow the town as a whole must be the key to all this."

With enough mozzarella, Sam started grating the fresh Parmesan. "How about my theory that somebody is out to settle a grudge?"

"It's the only thing that really makes sense, isn't it?" Lauren agreed. Her bread kneaded, she covered it and set it aside to double. There was a dusting of flour on the countertop, and she wrote in it with the tip of her finger. You Will All Pay. "And a nasty grudge at that. Do you suppose it's against the whole town? Does he want everybody here to pay for something?"

"Seems that way. But for what?"

"I don't know! You're the true-crime expert!" There was water boiling on the stove, and Lauren started cooking the lasagna noodles. "What would cause someone so much grief that he would take it out on any resident he could get close to, no matter who they are or how long they've been here?" she asked. "It's as if this guy considers the town itself his enemy."

Sam thought for a moment, measuring out the last of the cheeses, a nonfat ricotta, which thankfully didn't have to be grated. "There's an old saying. Follow the money."

"As a motive?"

He nodded. "That and problems concerning love or sex are the most common reasons for holding a grudge or seeking revenge. And I'm still betting on a businessperson."

"Then maybe we'd better make the rounds again," Lauren suggested. "See if we can find a nice, juicy grudge."

"Sounds like fun."

"Let's get the lasagna assembled first, though. Then all we'll have to do is pop everything in the oven when we come back."

While Lauren fiddled with her sauce and kept an eye on the pasta, Sam put the cheeses aside and started chopping vegetables. The recipe called for spinach, zucchini, bell pepper, carrot and onion, but he was good with a knife and was done before Lauren. They then put the dish together, covered it with foil and slipped it into the refrigerator.

"All this cooking has made me hungry," Sam announced. "How about we go have a bite of lunch at Sandy's place before we start the inquisition?"

"Okay, but something light," she told him. "I don't want you spoiling your dinner."

"Don't worry. I've worked up quite an appetite." He eyed her legs again as she preceded him out of the house. "For a lot of things."

They had just sat down at one of the tables near the front café window and placed their orders when Sheriff Buckner walked through the door. He came over and joined them, taking a seat beside Lauren.

"You look tired, Sheriff," Sam observed.

"I am," he said. "Been chasing my tail all morning. Something real strange going on over on the west side."

Lauren raised her eyebrows in sudden interest. "Oh?"

"Some darn fool's been leaving these all over," he said, handing her a piece of paper.

She put it on the table so Sam could see it, too. It was ordinary notepaper, upon which someone had pasted what looked like letters that had been cut out of magazines.

"'I'm watching you,'" Lauren read. She looked at the sheriff. "Do they all say that?"

Oswald shook his head. "No. I've got a couple more here somewhere." He fished them out of his jacket pocket and handed them to her. "There. And don't give me a hard time about not treating evidence properly. I'm not in the mood. Besides, by the time I got them they'd been passed around the whole neighborhood anyway."

Lauren read these two notes aloud, as well. "'Don't even think about it.'" She frowned and looked at the next one. "'If he does it again, I'll come after *you*.'" The "you" had been underlined in crayon.

"You're right," Sam told him. "That's pretty strange."

Sandy delivered their food, a club sandwich that they had decided to share. She gave her husband a cup of coffee.

"No doughnut?" he asked plaintively.

"No, Oswald. Remember your diet."

She shot him a look that made him wince. "Yes, dear," he said, and morosely dumped a packet of artificial sweetener into his coffee. He eyed their club sandwich with an expression akin to lust.

"Would you like half of my half?" Lauren whispered.

His eyes went wide and he nodded eagerly. But as he reached out to take it, Sandy bellowed from the kitchen.

"I see that, Oswald!"

The sheriff slumped in his chair. "Yes, dear."

"Oh, well," Lauren said, then tried to take his mind off food. "Did you find out anything?" He looked at her blankly. "About these notes?"

"Oh. Sorry. Isn't the inability to concentrate a sign of starvation?" Sheriff Buckner wanted to know.

Both Sam and Lauren laughed. "Maybe so," she replied. "But I think you're a long way from that stage. Now about the notes?"

"No, I didn't come up with anything. You know those westsiders. Close-knit bunch."

Lauren nodded her understanding. Even in a small town, cliques formed, usually around political lines, but in this the common denominator was geographical. The west side was closest to the hills, and the residents there considered their neighborhood to be the only true Beardsville. Of course, the north, east and south parts of town all felt the same about their own neighborhoods. It was, for the most part, a good-natured disagreement. Obviously, though, there was unrest on someone's part, for reasons unknown.

Lauren opened her mouth to speak, but Sam was way ahead of her. "Would you mind if we took a stab at it?" he asked. "Sometimes people clam up around the law, even if they know it by name."

Oswald sipped at his coffee and waved a hand. "Knock yourselves out. I've got more important things to do anyway," he said, his voice full of sarcasm. "Sandy overheard the call last night and is demanding the return of all the stuff stolen from her kitchen. So now I'm going to be crawling around in the dirt all afternoon, I suppose."

Sam had finished his sandwich quickly so as to take temptation out of the sheriff's way. Lauren had followed suit. Now, however, she was feeling sorry for him.

She leaned close and whispered, "There's half a jar of Mrs. Perkins's peaches left down there."

Oswald stood immediately, nearly spilling his coffee in the process. "Well, guess I'd better get over to the auditorium. You two have fun with those notes. 'Bye!"

With a parting wink at Lauren, he was gone.

"You shouldn't have done that," Sam told her.

"A couple of peaches won't make much difference. But look at him go! At least he's getting some exercise."

They paid their bill and left the café, heading for the west side of town. There, it didn't take long before they were feeling as dispirited as Sheriff Buckner. Nobody knew anything, and if they did, they weren't talking.

Many of Beardsville's largest homes were on the west side, as many of the town professionals lived there. So finally they decided to go have a talk with Howard Conner's wife, Alma. She received them graciously enough. At first.

"Tea? Some cookies, perhaps?" she asked when they were seated in her antique-filled colonial parlor.

"No, thank you, Alma," Lauren replied. Evidently this was one stop the sheriff hadn't made, or he wouldn't have been in such dire straits. "We're here about the notes."

The older woman's face hardened. "Yes, I thought this would reach Jim Ferguson's ears eventually. He sent you here snooping, did he?"

"Actually, we heard about it from Sheriff Buckner," Sam replied smoothly before Lauren could open her mouth. He'd caught her look of irritation. Evidently Alma Conner was not her favorite person in town. "As you may know, we're doing a story on the wave of pranks and—"

"Story?" Alma interrupted. "Is that what they call mudslinging where you come from, Mr. Burdett?"

Sam was quickly learning to share Lauren's opinion of this woman. "Had I the intention of slinging any mud, Mrs. Conner, I assure you I'm perfectly capable of doing so without hiding behind a euphemism," he replied coolly. "What we're after right now is facts."

"And have you any?" she asked sarcastically.

"A few," Lauren interjected. It was her turn to keep Sam from exploding, sort of like a tag-team wrestling match. "The pranks are a fact. They have happened. So have several thefts. In a town this size, that is considered news, and we are in the process of reporting it. Do you wish to contribute, or be cited as unavailable for comment?"

Alma sniffed contemptuously. "Neither, I think, given the publication in question."

"For heaven's sakes, Alma!" Lauren exclaimed. "You were quick enough to demand coverage for that garden club award you won. What's your problem?"

"Howard said this could damage the upcoming Halloween pageant," she replied tersely.

"The next edition of the *Razor* doesn't even come out till the Monday after Halloween! What are you afraid of?"

"Nothing!"

To Lauren, the older woman seemed terribly on edge. And while being snotty was simply a part of her character, such direct use of it was not. Lauren studied her face and came to the conclusion that she really was afraid.

"Alma," she began quietly, "we believe the person or persons who are behind all this have a grudge to bear of some kind. The notes being spread around this neighborhood also seem to be the work of someone who holds a grudge. There could be a connection. What do you think?"

She nodded, a stricken look on her face. "I think it's him," she whispered.

Sam frowned. "Him who?"

"Shh! The man you're looking for, of course!"

Alma took a piece of paper out of the pocket of her housedress and handed it to him. It was a pasteup note like the others. Lauren was sitting by his side on the antique settee, so she could read it over his shoulder. The message was indeed more ominous than the others.

"'If you talk about me behind my back one more time, you'll pay dearly,'" Sam read, speaking quietly so Alma wouldn't have a nervous breakdown.

"He could do it, too," Alma told them, nodding her head. "He's so crass and—" She suddenly stopped and looked around, eyes wide, as if the walls had ears.

"You think you know who made this note?" Lauren asked.

Alma nodded. "It's that horrible Mr. Judd," she managed to squeak, quite obviously expecting a lightning bolt or some other form of immediate retribution. "All the things Howard told me. It all fits. He's big. A hunter. And he hates us all!"

"The west side or Beardsville?" Lauren asked.

She made an expansive gesture. "Everyone! But you mustn't tell Howard I told you! And you mustn't tell . . . him!"

They promised they wouldn't, calmed her the best they could and then took their leave. Back in Sam's car, Lauren explained the situation.

"Allen Judd does have something of a reputation around here," she said. "I should have thought of him before, in fact. But I'd always heard his feud was only with the westsiders.'' She pointed. "Go up two blocks and hang a left."

Sam did as she directed. "What's the feud about?"

"Class prejudice, if you ask me. Judd is that bane of high society, the poor man who got lucky. He was a back-country guide in Florida before his paternal grand-mother died and left him her house here and a pile of money to go with it," Lauren explained.

"Let me see if I can guess," Sam said. "You can take the man out of the swamp, but not the swamp out of the man.''

"That about covers it," she agreed. "He's...rough. If they didn't have protective covenants around here, he might actually try to turn his front lawn into a swamp. As it is he does just the bare minimum maintenance and goes out of his way to irritate his neighbors."

"Well, it seems as if they may have done something to irritate him back, if the notes are any indication."

Lauren nodded. "Takes two sides to make a feud."

"Do you really think he could be behind the other note and all the rest, though?" Sam asked.

"Who knows?" She shrugged. "Let's ask."

"Maybe we should call the sheriff first."

"I don't think so. With the mood he's in, Oswald might just shoot the poor guy to relieve his frustra-tions."

Sam didn't have to ask which house was Judd's. He could see it all the way down the block. It stood out like a sore, ill-bandaged thumb among the big, fine homes lining the tree-covered hills. Out front sat a battered, hulking old four-wheel-drive truck that made Lauren's look showroom fresh. Hitched to it was a shiny brand-new speedboat that probably cost more than Sam had paid for the Addison place. The contradiction was striking, and clearly calculated.

Another such contradiction was the yard itself. There wasn't any trash lying around; undoubtedly Beardsville had an ordinance about such things. But everything looked dead and dingy. No legislating that. In Beverly Hills, maybe, but not this part of Vermont.

"Conspicuous consumption in reverse," Sam observed. Lauren started to get out of the car, but he put a hand on her arm to stop her. "You're sure we won't get shot?"

She chuckled. "Where's your sense of adventure?"

"Must have left it home today."

"I brought enough for both of us. Seriously, by now the whole neighborhood knows we're here. Even if he is our mysterious stranger, I don't think he'll attack us in broad daylight."

"No, he'll just track us down and butcher us while we sleep," Sam muttered.

Lauren got out of the car. Sam joined her in the driveway. Together they went up and knocked on Allen Judd's door. It was doubtful the doorbell worked, since it was dangling by its wires.

The door swung open on creaky hinges and a large, gruff-looking man with a day's growth of beard greeted them in a voice made gravelly with beer and cigarettes. One dangled from his lips as he spoke.

"I didn't call for no cab."

Since they hadn't discussed any strategy, Sam decided honesty was the best policy. "Hello, Mr. Judd. We're with the Beardsville *Weekly Razor* and—"

Lauren cut him off. "Did you do this?" she asked the man, holding up one of the pasteup notes.

Sam glowered at her. She didn't notice. Her attention was focused on Judd, who looked at the note with bleary red eyes and nodded once, curtly.

"You bet. Wrote 'em all." His eyes shifted to her now. "What's it to you?"

No doubt about it, he was a very intimidating man. But Lauren was no ordinary individual herself. "They're rather threatening, don't you think?" she asked.

He belched, adding to the general aroma of stale beer that surrounded him. Peering more closely at the pair standing on his front porch, he frowned and belched again.

"Lovely," Sam muttered under his breath.

"You I don't know," Judd said. "But I've seen you before. Kent, right? Lauren Kent?"

She nodded. "Last December. You spliced two hundred strings of Christmas lights together and wired them to your security timer. Blew out the whole system."

"Oh, yeah! Little Miss Fix-it! Only time I ever wanted to see somebody's tool-belt cleavage." He sighed. "Wish I could've made those lights work. They were all purple."

"I noticed. Most of southern Vermont would have noticed, too, if you'd gotten them lit."

"That was the whole idea."

"Why did you make these notes?" Sam asked.

He stared at Sam. "You I don't know," he said again.

"Sam Burdett. Bought the old Addison place," Lauren explained. "Answer the question, Mr. Judd."

"I don't see no badge on that pretty chest," he said.

Sam was getting close to losing his temper. "You're going to be seeing stars! Answer the lady's question!"

"Tough guy, huh?" Judd asked, puffing out his chest.

"As a matter of fact, I am. But you're half in the bag, Judd. My ninety-year-old grandmother could take you."

The man considered that for a moment, then nodded sagely. "Yeah. I wrote 'em because they teed me off, see? Always watching me. So now I watch them! And that old bat, Alamo or whatever, talking behind my back. She has somethin' to say, she should come out and say it to my face!"

"Or else she'll pay dearly, right?" Lauren asked. "That's what you wrote, Allen. Just what are you planning on doing to her?"

"Talk about her the same way, that's what!" he replied. He leaned closer and continued in a conspiratorial way. "I seen her going through people's trash when they ain't home. Nosy old bat. Tell the neighbors, see how *she* likes it."

Lauren held up another note. "How about this one? 'Don't even think about it.' Think about what?"

"Jerk parked his car in my driveway. Does it again, I'll let the air out of his tires."

Sam rubbed his chin and gazed balefully at the other man. "I'm beginning to detect a pattern here."

Judd stared at him. "You I don't—"

"Don't know," Sam finished for him. "I think there's a lot you don't know. What about the note that says, 'If he does it again, I'll come after *you*'? What's that about?"

"Lady thought she'd get cute, started sending her dog over every day to do his business on the front lawn. I mean, I like to keep it brown, make 'em mad. They deserve it, the snooty sons-a-ducks. But that's disgusting. He does his thing again, I will go after her!"

Sam was shaking his head. Lauren gave it another try. "Okay, Allen. You're a hunter, right? Do you skin and butcher your own game?"

"Can," he replied. "Have. Don't anymore. I plug 'em and let my nephew do the rest. Little dip'll inherit all this when I'm gone, might as well work for it."

"All this," Sam said, looking around. "My, my."

"What are you two digging around for, anyway?" Judd asked. "Is it about that stuff that happened in Sandy's Place? 'Cause if it is, I hope you find the guy. She's nice. So's old Henry Joseph. Wish my house were on the other side of town. Wouldn't have nearly the grief in my life. Money can be a curse, you know?"

Lauren gave up. "That about answers all our questions, Mr. Judd. Now if you'll excuse us—"

"Hang on a sec!"

He had spied one of his neighbors on the sidewalk that ran across the front of his property. With a gleeful grin, he spun around and bent to turn a valve on the wall beside his porch. There was a hiss, and the sprinkler system came to life, spraying the poor soul who had chosen the wrong moment to take his constitutional. He yelled and shook his fist at Allen Judd.

"Hey, sorry about that!" Judd yelled back. "Have to water the lawn now and then in the fall or it'll winter kill, you know!" He turned back to Sam and Lauren. "Yep. Wouldn't have nearly the grief if I didn't live on this side of town. But I wouldn't have near the fun, either!"

They made their way back to the car, carefully avoiding the puddles of brackish water that had formed in the driveway. Sam started the engine and sped away.

"Dead end," he said.

"Plenty juvenile, though. Maybe we should have asked him about the scarecrows."

Sam laughed. "He probably does it *with* scarecrows!"

"You may have a point there." She settled back in her seat. "I'd be depressed if it weren't for the dinner we have waiting for us. Home, driver. And step on it!"

As they turned the corner at the end of the street, an old red Chevy that had been parked across from Allen Judd's house started up. The driver tossed the stub of a cigar out the window, then pulled away from the curb and followed at a discreet distance.

Chapter Thirteen

Their foray had taken them longer than planned, and Jason was already home when Sam and Lauren arrived. He came out of his room to greet them, which Lauren considered an improvement. But he was still distant, and had trouble looking Sam in the eye.

Sending them off to play video games, Lauren put the lasagna in the oven to bake and then formed loaves from her bread dough, ready to pop into the oven at the right time. Meanwhile, she made the salad.

A while later she called Jason to set the table, which he did without complaint for a change, perhaps because Sam helped him. The spontaneous banter that had marked their relationship thus far was conspicuously absent, however.

This situation continued into dinner. Everything had turned out marvelously, though, so it wasn't too difficult for Sam and Lauren to enjoy themselves.

However, Jason's monosyllabic responses to their attempts at conversation eventually got on both their nerves. While in the kitchen helping her get dessert, a store-bought angel food cake with lemon icing, Sam finally spoke up.

"If I'm out of line, tell me to butt out, okay?"

She shook her head. "I know what you're going to say, and it's not out of line. He's driving me crazy, too!"

"It can't be all that great for him, either," Sam noted. "I mean, maybe I'm wrong, but the poor kid seems like a guilty wreck to me."

"No, that's what it looks like to me, too. What should I do? I was really hoping that seeing you would bring out the truth."

"Gee, and here I thought you wanted to show off your cooking skills," he said. Sam dodged her playful slap and slipped to one side, kissing her on the cheek. "Seriously, I think your plan is working. He just needs a little nudge, that's all. Follow my lead."

They went back in with dessert. Lauren sliced three pieces and gave them each one, then took a bite of her own, waiting for Sam to make his move.

He did so just as Jason took a bite of cake. "Those new windows work great, Lauren," he said. "Almost makes me glad somebody broke them."

As planned, Jason choked on his cake. He started coughing, and Sam reached over and patted him on the back. Lauren did her best to keep a straight face.

"Whoa!" Sam exclaimed. "Something go down the wrong way, Jason?"

He nodded, gulping milk to clear his throat.

Lauren kept up the pressure. "Anyway, I'm glad you like them. I know they cost more than you wanted to pay, but you'll appreciate it in the long run. Too bad you can't take the expense out of those boys' hides."

Jason was glancing from one adult to the other, but they carefully avoided looking back.

"Too bad," Sam agreed. "But if Sheriff Buckner is right, they're the same ones doing all the other damage around town, and he'll catch them eventually. I wouldn't want to be in their shoes when he does."

Lauren shook her head. "Neither would I."

"Where is the nearest juvenile detention facility?"

"I'm not sure," she replied. "Quite a ways from here, though, I think. It'll be tough on their families."

At last, Jason cracked. "Stop it! I know what you're doing, okay? So stop the act!"

"Is there something you'd like to tell us, Jason?" his mother asked patiently.

He let out a big sigh and slumped in his chair. After a quick, guilt-filled look at Sam, he stared at the remnants of his cake. "I was there. When they broke the windows."

Lauren closed her eyes. Until just then she had really hoped she was wrong. "You sneaked out of the house," she said. "At two in the morning, when I was asleep." She opened her eyes and glared at him. He nodded. "Jason, why?"

"I—I don't know why I did it. The guys were out, playing around, and they wanted me to come with them." He looked at Sam. "I didn't throw any rocks. I didn't even know what they were going to do, and when I figured it out I tried to stop them." He looked away. "But they just laughed and did it anyway."

"Were you involved in the other things?" Sam asked.

Jason shrugged. "Some, during the day. The mailboxes and pumpkins." He looked up quickly. "But I didn't really do anything. A pumpkin or two. Mostly I just watched."

"That's just as bad, Jason," Lauren informed him. She took a breath and blew it out slowly. There was something she just had to ask. "Were you with them when they moved the scarecrows?"

He seemed puzzled. "What scarecrows?"

Lauren sighed again, this time with relief. But her anger quickly returned. "It's not the things you did that have me so upset. It's that you were out running around in the dead of night! Something could have happened to you!"

"Oh, Mother!"

"Don't you 'Oh, Mother' me! Jason, how could you! What on earth were you thinking?"

"They're my friends!" he exclaimed, defiance creeping into his voice now. "They were going to have some fun, that's all. And they asked me to go! I wasn't thinking anything!"

"Obviously," she returned.

"You don't understand."

Lauren was fuming. "You've got that right! I want you to give me the name of every boy who was involved. And then we're going to talk with Sheriff Buckner."

Sam shot her a warning glance. "Lauren..."

"This is my problem, Sam, and I'll deal with it." She turned back to her son. "You're going to tell the sheriff who they are and what they've done."

"No!" Jason cried. "I won't, and you can't make me!"

"We'll see about that! You're grounded for life! It'll be just school and your room from now on for you! And no video games ever again!"

Jason pushed away from the table and stood facing her, his complexion reddening. "You can't do that!"

"No? I've been worrying about you for a long time, buster. Moping around, running with the wrong crowd. What do you say we start looking into military schools?"

"Fine!" Jason thumped the table with his fist. "If it'll get me out of this house, I'm all for it!" With that he turned and stalked off to his room.

"I'm not finished with you yet!" Lauren called out.

Her answer was the slamming of his bedroom door. She put her elbows on the table and her face in her hands, so mad she couldn't see straight.

But it wasn't just anger. She was scared, too. He was her only child, and the thought of him tearing around town at all hours, playing with firecrackers and doing who knew what else, was enough to make her tremble.

Sam came to stand behind her chair and put his hands on her shoulders. "I think grounding him for life might have been a bit much," he said quietly. "And military school?" He chuckled. "Come on now. You couldn't stand to be away from him that much."

"No," she muttered. "I couldn't. But he *will* go with me to talk to the sheriff."

Sam gnawed at his lower lip. "Uh, bad idea, Lauren."

She lifted her head and glared at him. "What would you know? You don't have any kids!"

"I can't argue that," Sam replied evenly, trying to keep his own temper in check. "But this is a guy thing, Lauren."

Lauren pulled away from him and stood. "Oh, bull!" she exclaimed sarcastically. "A guy thing, my rear end! What kind of sorry excuse is that?"

"Fine!" Sam threw his hands up in a gesture of surrender. "Do it your way! Alienate the kid!"

"He's my son!"

"That makes you an expert on male behavior?"

"And you are?" Lauren shot back.

Sam clenched his jaw. "At least I have the apparatus."

"Why, you...I don't envy...ooh!" She was so mad she thumped the table just as Jason had done. "Go ahead, then! Explain this asinine masculine reasoning of yours!"

"First of all, I'm not condoning his actions. What he did was wrong and he'll have to be punished for it," Sam told her, his voice returning to normal. "But you're asking him to rat on his buddies. Worse, these are older boys."

"So?"

"It's pretty clear to me that Jason is running with them simply because they asked him to."

"What kind of stupid reason is that?" Lauren demanded.

"He feels flattered by it," Sam continued calmly. "To him it represents a form of masculine acceptance he isn't getting anywhere else."

Lauren was calming down now, too. Sam had a way with words that always seemed to soothe her temper. And he had touched her own guilty conscience. "What do you suggest?"

"I think he regrets what he's done. Guilt is nature's punishment, at least for a sensitive individual like Jason, so he's suffering already," Sam told her. "But he has to understand why you're so angry. It's the scare he gave you by running wild like that, right?"

She nodded. "Especially now. What if he'd run into this mysterious stranger?" Lauren shuddered. "What you're saying makes sense, Sam. But what about his friends?"

"I admit it's a tough call. But I say back off. They have parents of their own," he replied. "Concentrate on making sure Jason gets the right message from you— you're concerned for *his* welfare. If those other boys have parents who don't care, that's another problem entirely and one you can't solve. You can't choose Jason's friends, but you can set the rules about when he can see them.''

"Darn right! And after midnight isn't on the list!" she frowned. "Now all I have to do is get him to listen."

"Again, if I'm in the way here, just tell me. But would you like me to break the ice?" Sam offered.

She smiled at him. "You're not in the way. I'm glad you're here. And I'd really appreciate it if you would go beard the lion cub in his den for me."

While Sam went to have a word with Jason, Lauren cleared the dinner dishes. If she didn't know better, she would suspect this of being a plot the pair of them had contrived to get her to do all the work.

As she cleaned up, she tried not to eavesdrop, but couldn't help hearing an occasional tidbit. Once, they both laughed. Maybe it *was* a plot. Finally the pair emerged.

Jason stood at the kitchen door for a moment, looking sheepish. "I'm sorry," he said at last. "I didn't mean to worry you. I just wanted to be...cool, you know?"

"Believe it or not, Jason, I do. And as surprising as it may seem, I don't have anything against a prank or two at Halloween, either. But vandalism is against the law."

"I know." He looked at Sam, who gave him a nudge of encouragement. "If they do stuff like that again, I'll just leave. Okay?"

Lauren would have much preferred to hear him say he'd never see the boys again, but knew Sam was right. She couldn't pick his friends.

"Okay. But there are other laws, too, Jason," she told him seriously. "My laws. You know curfew is ten on school nights and only when you've done your homework and I know where you are. You broke that law."

"I know. And I'm sorry." He glanced at Sam again. "I'm sorry about your windows, too, Sam. I didn't want for it to happen. I told them we were friends."

"We still are. Apology accepted."

"Okay," Lauren continued. "I know there's a bunch of stuff going on this week, and I can hardly take Halloween away from you." She chuckled. "In this town, there's probably a law against *that!* So I'll just ground you for the month of November. Only school functions, and no video games except on the weekends. Maybe this will help you get your math grades up, as well."

Clearly that wasn't what Jason had expected. He looked up at Sam. "Hey! You said she'd go easy!"

Sam cleared his throat. "Evidently your mother's idea of easy and mine are different. But like she said, her word is law. Sorry."

By the hurt look on the boy's face, Sam could tell that it was a shock to see the adults put up a united front like this. He had started to consider Sam a friend.

"It's not fair!" he exclaimed.

"Jason..." Lauren warned, her temper rising again.

"Maybe you'd better hit the books, kid," Sam suggested.

"I don't have to do what you say! Either of you! You just like pushing me around, that's all. Maybe next time I'll stay gone!"

Again he stalked off to his room and slammed the door. Sam and Lauren breathed a collective sigh of exasperation and looked at each other.

"Well, that sure went well," Sam said. "However did you manage without me around to straighten things out?"

Lauren shook her head. "It wasn't your fault."

"I did lead him to believe his punishment would be substantially reduced," he noted. "Sorry."

"From forever to a month is pretty substantial."

"I was thinking more along the lines of a week."

She shrugged. "That's usually all I can stand anyway, and Jason knows it. I think we're butting heads on general principle, really, trying to establish who's in control of his life. He's at the age where he thinks it should be him. He just forgot I have a harder head than he does, that's all."

"It probably confused him, me taking your side like that. Confused me, too, actually. I felt like a traitor. Guess it'll take some time for both Jason and I to accept me as an authority figure."

Lauren cocked her head curiously. "I wasn't aware you were auditioning for that role."

"You know what I mean."

She turned back to the sink and the task of putting dishes into the dishwasher. "Do I?"

Sam joined her at the counter. He put his arms around her from behind and kissed her softly on the back of the neck. "I'm long past sowing wild oats, Lauren. I thought you understood what I had in mind."

The touch of his lips on the sensitive skin of her neck made her shiver with delight. But his words troubled her.

The little scene between the three of them tonight was a graphic example of how much things would change if she allowed Sam into their lives. The trouble was, she wasn't sure she really had any choice. He was already involved, and showed no signs of backing down.

"I suppose I did know you were serious," Lauren said, turning in his embrace to look him in the eyes. For a moment she was caught in their piercing blue depths. "I didn't want to think about it, that's all. And I'm not sure I'm ready to start just yet."

He nodded his understanding. "Fair enough. But I'm not going away."

"You'd better not." Sam pulled her closer to kiss her, but she edged out of his grasp and toward the kitchen door. "Let's go into the living room, shall we?" she asked with a pointed look in the direction of Jason's bedroom.

"Oh. Right." He followed her, muttering under his breath. "Yet another thing that will take some getting used to. Please, dear, not in front of the children."

"What are you mumbling about back there?" Lauren asked.

"Oh, nothing. Would you like me to build a fire?"

"That would be cozy. But you don't have to build it," she said. "It's natural gas. Better for the environment, you know."

Sam sighed. "They're taking all the masculine arts away these days."

But it was still very cozy. They cuddled up on the sofa in front of the fire, watching the flames cavort beyond the marble hearth. All along, from the first time they'd met, Sam had caused Lauren to feel things she hadn't felt in years.

Now, however, curled up beside him like this, Lauren wasn't so sure she had ever felt this close to a man, not even her ex-husband. Maybe it was the way Sam cared so much about her feelings, or the way he cared for her son. All she knew was that she was finding him more irresistibly sexy with each passing day. And to think, that first day she wanted to ride him out of town on a rail!

She turned from the flames to look at him, finding his eyes already upon her. "My goodness," she murmured. "That look is hotter than the fire."

"So is this."

Sam pulled her even more tightly against him and kissed her, plunging his tongue into her mouth. Lauren didn't resist; she opened her mouth wider and demanded her own measure, as well. His hand went to her thigh, gliding along her hose beneath her skirt and up to her hip, then around to grasp her firm buttocks.

At this Lauren gasped, but her surprise quickly turned to ardor, and she pressed herself against him, feeling his incredible arousal.

"If Jason weren't here..." she murmured against his lips.

Sam nibbled on her ear. "You wouldn't have made it through dinner."

He kissed her throat, then buried his face in the lush cleavage exposed at the neck of her cardigan, groaning with need and frustration.

"You would have taken me on the table?" Lauren asked.

"In the kitchen," Sam informed her. "Right in the middle of the lasagna."

"You're crazy!"

"Never said I wasn't." He lifted his head and kissed her again. "That's life in the big city. What do the country folk do?"

"The same," Lauren breathed. "But we move the food first. We're always hungry afterward."

"I'm hungry now."

Sam kissed her throat, then the tops of her breasts, and then started to unbutton her cardigan and explore new ground. He marveled at the smooth radiance of her skin, his tongue blazing a path along her stomach.

Lauren knew where he was heading and the thought made her quiver, but she put her hands on his cheeks and demanded he return to safer territory.

"We can't, Sam. Not with—"

"Jason in the house. I know. And you want to ground him for a month?" He moaned and nibbled on her fingers. "I'll explode!"

"So would I! It's not that he's in the house. It's that he's awake and just a few feet away," Lauren informed him softly. She traced a line down his chest with her fingertip, feeling him shudder. "Maybe a bit later, when he's asleep—"

Suddenly a pounding on the front door interrupted her. Eyes wide, Lauren fumbled with her buttons, once again feeling like a teenager caught in the act. Sam helped her up and she stood there a moment, unsteady on her feet.

"All my blood must be elsewhere."

"Tell me about it," Sam grumbled.

She smiled at him, but the pounding on her front door started again, this time more strident, and the overzealous visitor called out to her.

It was Sheriff Buckner. "Lauren! Open up! Oh, God, Lauren, please be home! There's been an accident!"

Her heart thumping in her chest, she ran to the door and flung it open, Sam right behind her. "What's going on, Sheriff? Who's been in an accident?"

He looked at her, his eyes wide and sad. "I—I'm afraid it's Jason, dear. He's been hurt."

Lauren started to laugh. "That can't be, Sheriff. My Jason is in his room—"

"It's Jason," the sheriff insisted, grabbing her arm. "He's been hit by a car. They're taking him to the emergency room right now. You've got to hurry!"

Chapter Fourteen

First blood! Exhilaration raced through his veins like wildfire. Now they would know there was something out there in the dark, waiting for them, counting the moments until it was their turn to feel the terror of approaching death.

The boy had known that feeling. He had been there in the street, tagging along last, the weak member of his herd. Suddenly he saw the car, speeding toward him out of the still night. His eyes had gone wide, as wide as saucers.

It was simple as pie, hitting a target that size. The lessons had been learned long ago, on the dirt ovals and fairground tracks. An expert could put any part of a car within six inches of a target that size, even at a hundred miles an hour. The old red Chevy wasn't going anywhere near that fast. But it was fast enough.

In an instant the boy was airborne, flying into the bushes at the side of the road. The impact had been brief. But he had known what hit him. Oh, yes. He had known *who* hit him. Not that it would do him any good.

That was all right. The time was coming now when they would all know, and all would pay. Now he had the scent.

"HE LAUGHED WHEN he hit me. I remember hearing it above the roar of the engine. He was laughing real hard."

Lauren was wringing her hands, wanting to hug Jason to pieces, but worrying that it would cause him pain. He had a cast on his left arm from wrist to elbow. It made everything about him look so thin and frail.

But the doctor had said it was his youth and resilient bones that had saved him from more serious and permanent injury. Instead of breaking under the impact and subsequent diving fall, his body had flexed, like a sapling bending in the wind. He had some bruises and a fairly deep cut on one ankle, and a simple fracture of the ulna. That was all.

From his and the other boys' descriptions of what had happened, he was lucky there was anything left of him but a spot on the pavement. None of them called it an accident.

They were out fooling around. One second it was quiet, the next headlights flashed and an engine roared. Someone had been waiting for them at the dark end of the street and tried to run them down. Jason, the youngest, was also a step or two slower. He had seen the driver clearly for an instant before the car hit him. It was a big man wearing a navy blue pea coat and smoking a cigar.

"How about the car?"

"It was red. An old Chevy."

"I don't suppose you caught the license plate, did you, Jason?" Sheriff Buckner asked.

"Sheriff!" Lauren exclaimed. "You can't expect—"

Jason rattled off the number. "And it was a New York plate," he added, with a sly smile at his mother.

"Well, I guess his head is okay," Sam observed, laughing. "Do you want a soda, Jason?"

"Yes, please."

"But no caffeine," Lauren ordered. "He's going home and straight to bed." She gave in and put her arm gingerly around her son, hugging him gently.

He didn't mind. The doctor had said the shot he'd given him would numb the pain for several hours. And he didn't mind being hugged in any other way, either. He wasn't even pretending not to need one.

The incident had rattled all the boys, to the point where they had confessed to being the pranksters. Sheriff Buckner hadn't charged them with anything yet. That might change, however, depending on the property owners involved.

But Jason was even more contrite than the rest, and with good reason. The others had seen him get hit, which had obviously been terrifying enough. Jason, however, had been the one confronted with his own mortality. The sullen, defiant teen of earlier that evening was a very different boy from the one who sat in the emergency room waiting area now. Somehow Lauren didn't think he would be sneaking out to run wild in the streets again.

"I guess that's all," Sheriff Buckner told them. "I'll get this out over the radio, see if we can track this guy down. If we come up with anything, I'll give you a ring."

"Thanks, Sheriff."

He left. Although he wasn't quite buying into Lauren's theory that there was a brutal, vindictive individual on the rampage in his town, he was weakening. She just hoped no one had to die to convince him.

Sam returned with Jason's soda. He took it gratefully and drank it as if it was the best thing he'd ever tasted. Then looked at his mother. The time had come.

"I'm sorry, Mom. I just..." He trailed off, his voice cracking. There were tears in his eyes. "I'm a stupid jerk. Go ahead and ground me forever. I deserve it."

Lauren sighed and looked at him, her expression as stern as she could make it. She was too happy he was still alive to be very angry.

"I suspect you learned a lesson tonight that you'll carry with you for a long time. I'm sure it's had a greater impact on you that any loss of privileges ever could," she said. "And I think you realize now that I wasn't pushing you around or punishing you arbitrarily. I'll bet you know why I didn't want you running around at all hours now, right?"

He nodded, eyes downcast. "You said it."

"I'll bet you wish you'd listened to me now, too, don't you?" Lauren asked.

"Yes."

"Good. We'll leave it at that, then," she told him, dabbing at his eyes with the wadded-up tissue she had in her hand. "Now let's go home, shall we?"

Jason stood. "Mom?"

"Yes?"

"I love you."

He put his good arm around her and hugged her fiercely. She hadn't realized how tall he was getting, or how strong. It brought fresh tears to her eyes. She reached out to Sam and included him in the hug, as did Jason. Sam was too big a man to cry, so he just sniffled a little.

On the ride home Jason drifted off to sleep, leaning on his mother's shoulder. He woke up enough to walk inside the house by himself and get ready for bed, but once his head hit the pillow he went out like a light.

"He's zonked," Lauren told Sam when she emerged from the bedroom. "But he insists on going to school tomorrow."

"Well, of course he does. How else can he show off his cast?" Sam pointed out. "I imagine there'll be a few highly impressionable young girls who'll want to sign it, too."

She groaned. "Oh, no. Not another guy thing."

"Bragging rights are very important to us males." He grinned slyly. "Would you like to see my scar?"

"That depends," Lauren returned. "Does it involve taking off your pants?"

"How did you guess?"

"Just as I thought." She started pushing him toward the door. "I think you'd better go home and give your guy thing a rest. You'll need your strength for tomorrow."

Sam's eyes lit up. "As in meet you here the moment Jason leaves for school?"

"No, as in meet me at the *Razor* tomorrow morning at nine-thirty so we can start going over old records," Lauren informed him. "There's a ton of them, so don't be late."

"My idea sounds much more exciting."

It sounded pretty enticing to her, as well, but at the moment she was a woman with a mission. "Be that as it may, the first thing on my agenda is to get the man who tried to make a pancake out of my son tonight."

They had arrived at the front door. Sam turned to face her, his expression serious. "Mine, too, Lauren. I didn't mean to make it sound otherwise."

She put her arms around him and kissed him lightly on the lips. "I know. And you never can tell what a new day will bring," she told him softly. "But records first."

"What do you hope to find?"

"I'm not sure. But I am sure we're on the right track," Lauren replied. "The man we're after knows this town, and he's obviously got a very large bone to pick with us. All I can think of is to try and figure out why."

Sam nodded thoughtfully. "I get it. You think that whatever made him this mad might have been in the papers. Good thinking," he said appreciatively. "Pretty tall order, though. I take it Jim has a morgue on the *Razor*?"

"And other sources, as well. Most of it's on microfilm. But you're right," she agreed. "It'll take some doing. Which is why I'm escorting you out the door."

They kissed again, more deeply, and Lauren melted in his arms, reveling in the feel of them wrapped around her. She began to have second thoughts, but decided that Jason would have enough to deal with in the morning without discovering that Sam had stayed the night, too.

Then again, that was probably a cop-out. She had the feeling Jason would adapt to that situation more quickly than she would herself.

At last they pulled apart. Sam gazed into her eyes, his brow furrowed with concern. "Are you going to be okay?"

Lauren nodded. "I've got a shotgun and I know how to use it. But I don't think Jason was targeted specifically. If that was the case, this would be much easier to figure out."

"At least we'd have a starting point," Sam agreed. "As it is, we're trying to put a pattern to random acts of violence. Somehow, though, we'll do it."

"Yes, we will. We have to."

They kissed good-night, and Sam departed, waiting on the porch until he heard the sound of Lauren turning her dead-bolt lock into place. Lauren watched him pull away.

It had been quite a revealing evening for all concerned, Jason included. As for her and Sam, their relationship was turning very serious, ready or not.

But so was the trouble confronting their town.

FRIDAY MORNING FOUND Jason stiff and sore but still adamant about going to school. If Sam hadn't clued her in as to his probable motivation, Lauren might very well have insisted he stay home. As it was, she simply hoped that the girls who did line up to sign his cast were his own age and not *too* impressionable.

She did insist on taking him to school herself, though, both to make sure he got there safely and to have a talk with his principal and teachers.

But the school had already been informed of what had happened. Lauren also discovered how much things had changed since she'd been in school. It seemed all the boys involved in the vandalism were to be scheduled for counseling, starting with a group session after school that afternoon. Lauren gave her approval and went on her way.

As she left the school grounds, she noticed that Jason had developed a sudden interest in his old friends again. And Sam was right—he was the center of attention and loving every second of it. Lauren felt as if a great load had been lifted from her shoulders.

But there was still something weighing her down. She headed for the *Razor*. Sam's unmistakable vehicle was already parked out front when she arrived.

"'Morning, all," Lauren said as she breezed into the office. Her first stop was the refrigerator for a diet cola, her second the desk where Sam was sitting. In front of him, she noticed, was a cola can and not a coffee cup. She smiled. "Created another addict, have I?"

He shrugged. "Maybe. I discovered that Jim's coffee is even worse than yours."

"That's because he uses the same grounds for a month."

"Hey! I'm not that cheap!" Jim objected. "A couple of days maybe. A week tops."

Thus assured she had Jim's full attention, Lauren leaned over and kissed Sam full on the lips. It surprised Sam, but Jim practically fell out of his chair.

"Say it isn't so!" he cried. "I was hoping to get a whole winter's worth of fighting out of you two before you got mushy on me!"

Lauren chuckled. "Don't give up your ringside seat just yet. We haven't hung wallpaper together. There could still be some serious bloodshed."

"Promise to invite me?" Jim asked.

"Promise," Sam replied.

That seemed to satisfy him. "Sam was telling me about your theory. I like it. Make good reading, too. Sorry Jason had to get in the way of this guy, though," Jim said with a worried frown. "He okay?"

"He'll be fine," Lauren told him. "His biggest worry right now is running out of room on his cast," she added with an appreciative wink at Sam. "Mine is stopping this guy. I want the story, but mostly I want him behind bars."

"My morgue is your morgue," Jim assured her.

"Then let's dig into it, shall we? Before somebody around here ends up in a real one."

They proceeded to sort through the vast array of filed and microfilmed clippings. Lauren felt certain the person they were looking for was a former resident of Beardsville with an ax to grind. Unfortunately it soon became clear that small towns like hers were prone to a goodly number of internal feuds.

They worked until eleven-thirty, then ate Sandy's take-out special of the day at their desks. Or rather, Sam and Lauren did. The special was tuna salad sandwiches, and Jim had his with ketchup. They made him eat in the back room.

Since his old microfilm reader was harder on the eyes than the loose clippings, they took turns on it. By noon, however, it was obvious they were going nowhere fast. Lauren turned off the reader and rubbed her eyes.

"I think it's time we put our heads together on this," she said. "And since your head is older than ours, Jim, I'm expecting great things from you."

He rolled his chair over to hers. "Shoot."

"There have been lots of spats, arguments and even a few free-for-alls in Beardsville over the years," she began. "I've read about water and land disputes, heated debates over divorce settlements and even a few custody battles concerning cattle. And while I'm sure all of them were serious to the people involved at the time, I have trouble believing that any of them would lead someone to do what this guy has done."

"Unless he's just plain crazy," Sam pointed out.

Lauren sighed and nodded her head. "That's always a possibility, of course. But if it's true, we really are in trouble, because crazy people don't always have motives for what they do. I prefer to think there's some method to his madness."

"Isn't that what we've been looking for?" Jim asked.

"It is, but everything we've found has been so petty. What we need is the real nasty stuff. A bitter fight that involved the whole town. I can't remember any, but then again I didn't really start getting involved in town politics until after my divorce. I was hoping you could shortcut some of this rooting around.''

Jim leaned back in his chair, thoughtfully sipping a diet cola. ''Well, the worst I can recall was the big tax battle. That was about fifteen years ago.''

''Tax battle?'' Lauren asked, frowning. ''Sounds familiar.''

''The town voted to increase property taxes to create a general fund for civic projects,'' he explained. ''That was about the time the BPS was formed, as well. A lot of people were angry, especially the antigrowth contingent.''

''I was only seventeen at the time, and hardly the most civic-oriented young woman.''

Jim chuckled. ''True. As I recall, you were more of a boy-oriented young woman.''

''And two years later I had a baby boy of my own,'' she noted with a wry grin. A light was dawning in Lauren's mind. ''But since my political awakening, so to speak, I have spoken with plenty of antigrowth people. And now that you mention it, most of them do talk about 'the vote,' as if it was some big, significant event in the downfall of Beardsville.''

''Depends on your point of view, of course,'' Jim said. ''But it was a pretty big turning point. The community woke up. The vote opened the floodgates to more development, set the stage for progress.''

''Or put you on the road to ruin,'' Sam interjected. Both Jim and Lauren looked at him strangely. ''Hey, just playing devil's advocate.''

''You have a point, though,'' Lauren agreed. ''That's just the way some of them look at it. Which is why I was so worried when I read that article of yours. I thought they'd found an eloquent spokesman. But you're not quite that rabid an antigrowther, are you?''

"Let's just say I would rather have a modern supermarket on the corner than a dusty old general store and leave it at that, shall we?''

She laughed. "Close enough for me.''

"Oh, please!" Jim complained, holding his stomach. "I had such hopes for your relationship. Screaming matches on Main Street, maybe even a food fight at the café. But, no. You have to dash my hopes by making peace! I think I'm going to be physically ill.''

"It's that disgusting sandwich you ate, you mean old curmudgeon,'' Lauren told him.

"I am not that old!" He cleared his throat. "Anyway, that's the biggest fight I can remember. And you're right, Lauren—some people still have their noses out of joint because of that vote.''

"But mad enough to seek deadly revenge?'' Sam asked.

He shrugged. "Money does strange things to people.''

"Follow the money,'' Lauren said thoughtfully. "That's what you told me, Sam. I think it's time we went and had a word with what used to be my opposition.''

Jim's eyes widened. "You don't mean the Macklins?''

"They're the most adamant antigrowth family in the area. Who better to ask where the bodies might be buried?''

"Maybe so,'' Jim agreed reluctantly. "Just make certain two of those bodies don't end up being your own.''

Although Jim was being rather melodramatic, it was true that Lauren was much less welcome on Tom and Sherry Macklin's property than anywhere else in town. And they were even less fond of strangers.

With that in mind, Sam and Lauren decided on two things. The first was to go in her truck so as not to alarm them. The second was to take a copy of Sam's article as an introduction.

Both worked. Tom Macklin called off his pit bulls when he realized it was Lauren coming down his driveway. They seemed a bit unnerved to hear Sam had bought the old Addison place, but his article was well received, as was the news that Lauren had recently decided to step down from the progrowth soapbox. Of course, it didn't hurt that *True Behavior* was one of the Macklins' favorite television shows, either.

"You want to see a real crime, you just take a look at that," Tom Macklin told them.

They had settled down in the Adirondack chairs on the Macklins' front porch. Tom was pointing west, toward an adjacent house. It blocked the view of the nearby mountains and would undoubtedly spoil any sunset watching, as well.

"I take it you were here first?" Sam asked.

"Four generations of Vermonters have lived on this property, Mr. Burdett," Tom informed him. "You bet we were here first. And I can't say some of the blame isn't ours for not buying that little slip of land a long time ago. But to tell you the truth, I didn't think anybody would want to build a house on that small a piece of property. City people." He used the words as an epithet.

"They wanted to make a bed-and-breakfast out of it," Sherry Macklin said as she joined them with glasses of fresh lemonade. "Can you imagine? Luckily we fought the zoning on that and won. They're talking about leaving, but the damage is done. We can't afford to buy the land now that they went and put the fancy house on it. It's a shame."

"It's a crime," Tom maintained. "I'm not saying I'd start anything, mind you, but if that place happened to catch on fire, I wouldn't even go spit on it."

"Tom!"

"Well, it's true," he said, sullen. He looked at Lauren. "But I suppose you didn't come out here to listen to me complain. This is about the trouble in town, right?"

Lauren nodded. "Yes. And in a way, Tom, we did come to hear about your problems, and those of the other people opposed to growth. We think the terrible things that have been happening might have to do with a grudge somebody has against Beardsville. In particular, we were wondering if you knew anybody who really got hurt by that property-tax vote fifteen years ago."

Tom's eyes had narrowed. "A lot of people got hurt." He jerked his head at the interlopers' house again. "We got hurt. That vote started the ball rolling, and it hasn't stopped since. But all we want is a voice in our affairs and some justice. So if you've come here to accuse—"

"It's not like that at all, Tom," Lauren interjected in a soothing tone. "We're not talking about people like you, or your friends. The man we're looking for is after far more than justice—he wants revenge. And he's taking it out on innocent people. My own son was nearly killed last night."

"Oh, my!" Sherry exclaimed. "Is he okay?"

"His arm is broken, but he'll be all right. But you heard about Missy Jenkins. She came within a few moments of dying. And Antonio Demetry could easily have been crushed by that truck. We're talking about a madman here. Is there anything you can think of that can help us find him?"

Tom looked concerned now, as well. "What have you got to go on?" he asked.

"Not much, I'm afraid," Sam admitted. "From the things he's done and the way he's managed to move around, we're pretty sure he either lives in Beardsville or knows the place like a native. That's why we're approaching it from the angle of a grudge or vendetta."

"And we have a vague description," Lauren added. "Based mainly on supposition, though Jason did get a glimpse of him last night. He's a big, husky man. Since he also did a pretty good job on Henry Joseph's hog, we think he either is or has been a butcher or farmer. Oh, and he smokes a special kind of sweet cigar."

Sherry Macklin dropped her glass of lemonade and it hit the wooden porch with a crash. She gasped and put a hand over her mouth. "Oh, dear God! That's Hank Addison! He really is alive!"

Chapter Fifteen

Sam and Lauren were staring at Sherry Macklin. Lauren was the first to recover. "What do you mean, Hank really is alive? The whole town knows he's dead!"

"That's what we thought," Tom said. "Dead and buried several years ago in an unmarked grave in some New York cemetery for the indigent. Or so the story goes. But then last week we got a letter from him."

Lauren's eyes opened wide. "That's impossible!"

Sherry had regained her composure and went to get the letter in question. While Lauren and Sam read it, she cleaned up her broken lemonade glass. She was seated again by the time they finished.

There was nothing particularly ominous about the letter, other than the signature at the bottom that indicated it was from a man who was supposedly dead. It was chatty in a gruff sort of way, a how-are-you, my-life-stinks type of thing, with a hint that conditions would soon be looking up.

"Were you good friends of Hank's?" Sam asked them.

Tom shrugged his shoulders. "As good as any Hank ever had, I suppose, which isn't saying much. We felt sorry for him more than anything. Fed him when he was hungry, things like that. But he never wrote to us before now."

"It seems he knows a lot about you."

Sherry was nodding. "That's the part that convinced me the letter was genuine. He mentions our boys by name, and how much he loved my fried chicken."

"But it's strange at the same time," Tom noted. "As if he's still living in the past or something. For instance, you see there where he talks about Buster?"

Sam looked at the passage, nodding. "One of your dogs?"

"Yes, but twelve years ago. And Buster was old even then. You'd think a person would ask if he was still alive, not how he was doing. But then I guess Hank's brain never did work all that well," Tom admitted. "Did you know him, Lauren?"

"Only by reputation. I don't think he and I ran in the same social circles, if you know what I mean. The Blue Moon Bar was strictly off-limits."

Tom chuckled sadly. "And that place was Hank's second home, all right. Heck, the way he treated his house, I guess the bar was actually more important to him."

"I can testify to that," Sam said.

"Now *there* was someone who got hurt by the tax vote," Tom continued thoughtfully. "I mean, he was a lousy farmer and a drunk to boot, so he was just barely hanging on to that land by the skin of his teeth. But the new property tax was the straw that broke the camel's back. A year later he was in arrears on the taxes and every debt he had, as well. I remember when he lost the place I had to go pull him out of the Blue Moon before Sheriff Buckner threw him in jail."

That caught Sam's interest. "Did he make threats?"

"Sure, he hurled some words around. But I never remember him saying we'd all pay, if that's what you mean," Tom replied. "And nothing ever came of it. In fact, he left town just a few weeks later."

"Was he a violent man?" Sam asked.

Tom shrugged, but his wife was quick to answer. "Yes, he was a violent man," Sherry told them. "He had a hot temper and it was worse when he'd been drinking. Mind you, I wouldn't be saying such things about him if he were still dead." She paled slightly at the thought. "I mean if he was ever dead. Oh, I don't know what I mean!"

Lauren sympathized. She wasn't sure how much stock to put in all this. On the other hand, she wanted to believe that the letter was genuine and that Hank Addison was alive, because then they would have a perfect match for her theoretical mysterious stranger. But Hank was dead, and everyone knew it. Or, as Tom had said, so the story went.

Was that the explanation? Was it just a story? In truth, it did have the suspicious ring of a parable. Strong drink will lead to ruin and an early death in a pauper's grave.

"May I keep this for a while?" Lauren asked, holding up the letter. "I want to check on a few things."

"Of course," Sherry told them. "I hope it helps."

Tom remained doubtful. "Something's fishy about this, if you ask me," he said. "Hank was a severely depressed alcoholic when he left Beardsville, and already having physical problems. I'm still inclined to believe he crawled into an alley and drank himself to death, letter or no letter. But I'll tell you this. If it is him, and he has somehow managed to get himself back in shape again, you watch yourselves. Hank Addison was one cruel human being."

Thus encouraged, Sam and Lauren got into her truck and headed back to the *Razor*. The first thing Lauren did was ask Jim what he knew about Hank Addison's death, and got the same story, word for word.

"How do you know that?" she asked.

Jim blinked owlishly. "Well, I just heard it, that's all. I never saw an obituary, or printed one, either, if that's what you mean."

"It's not like you to accept something on face value."

"That's true, but in this case I didn't have much choice," Jim pointed out. "It's sad, but when a man like Hank Addison dies that way it doesn't make the newspapers anywhere, especially not in New York City, which is where he supposedly went after leaving here."

"I suppose you're right."

"Hank was a drunk, Lauren, and a pretty lousy excuse for a human being in any case, if you'll pardon my being so frank. There were other people who got hit by the tax, but they didn't fold. You can't help someone who won't help themselves. I believed Hank died the way everybody said he did, because it fit the way he lived."

They checked the clip files again but didn't come up with much on Hank Addison except for his sad, seemingly inevitable descent into ruin, as chronicled by reports of an increasing number of arrests for drunken disturbances and notices of his past-due taxes.

"Drat," Lauren muttered. "If only we had something with his signature on it, maybe we could at least verify this letter as being his."

"Sheriff Buckner would probably have something over at city hall," Jim suggested.

Lauren didn't look too thrilled by the thought. "I don't think I'm quite ready to mention this to the sheriff just yet," she said. "I finally have him on my side, sort of, and that's where I want him to stay until we can prove Hank is still alive and after revenge.''

"Or prove he's dead," Jim told her. "I have to admit it'd make a great story, but keep an open mind, okay?"

She nodded. "Don't worry. I have Sam to help me keep my feet on the ground. Right, Sam?"

"Sure."

But Sam wasn't really listening. If Hank Addison was the one stalking Beardsville, it wouldn't be just a great story. It would be a fantastic story. A highly marketable story. Right down *True Behavior*'s twisted alley. And he was on the spot, hot on the trail.

"Hey!" he exclaimed. "I remember seeing some old papers in the attic when I was checking the insulation. Maybe Hank's signature is on some of them!"

It was the first time Sam had showed some genuine excitement over this story, and Lauren found his mood to be catching. "Then what are we sitting here for?" she asked, jumping to her feet. "Let's go!"

This time Sam drove, much to Lauren's dismay. She had been driving these roads more or less every day since her sixteenth birthday, while as a big-city dweller Sam wasn't nearly as practiced at driving, period. At normal speeds this wasn't a problem, but he was in a hurry. He quickly discovered that gravel could be as slippery as ice, and nearly put them in the ditch.

"Heaven help us all when the snow comes!" Lauren cried, hanging on for dear life. "It's a good thing this beast is so noticeable. We can see you coming and get out of the way!"

"Maybe I should get a big truck like yours."

"No! Please, have mercy!"

They arrived at Sam's place in a cloud of dust, but in one piece. He retrieved the papers from his attic and they sat on the front porch going through them, but found nothing with Hank Addison's signature. For the most part it was still more evidence of his looming downfall, in the form of unpaid bills and overdue credit notices.

Sam refused to give up. "Maybe in the back of a closet somewhere, or in the root cellar."

"Good idea," Lauren agreed. "You look here, I'll go check the barn. It's been a long time, but there has to be something around here with his scrawl on it."

In addition to the barn, there were also the remains of an old chicken coop and the storage shed. Lauren checked the smaller outbuildings first, but found nothing of interest. She then headed for the barn. As she approached it, she thought she heard a noise.

"Sam?" she called, thinking he'd beat her there.

But there was no answer except the cooing of some pigeons in the hayloft. Carefully she stepped inside the dilapidated old structure.

It was dark inside, and smelled not unpleasantly of straw, dust and age. What light there was came from the open door and cracks between the barn's rough-hewn siding. But it was enough to see by, and from what Lauren could tell, it didn't look promising. She stepped over to the ladder leading to the loft and started to climb.

When she reached the top, she peeked around, but saw nothing interesting there, either. Then she spotted some old wooden boxes stacked in one corner of the loft. She hoisted herself the rest of the way up and made her way over to them, checking with each footstep to make sure the creaky wooden floor would hold her weight.

The boxes contained old, rusted farming implements, twisted lengths of baling wire and a great deal of what looked like rodent droppings. But down in the bottom of one box, Lauren thought she saw a scrap of paper in the dim light of the loft. Gingerly, lest a mouse leap out at her, she reached her hand into the box.

That's when she heard it. A scraping noise from down below. She spun around just in time to see the ladder disappear from view. Seconds later it landed with a crash on the barn floor below.

"Very funny, Sam," she called out. "Now how am I going to get down from here?"

Indeed, the person below must have thought it was very funny. He laughed loudly, a harsh, terrifying sound in the still, dusty air of the barn. The hair on the back of Lauren's neck stood up.

"Is that you, Hank?"

There was more laughter. "It's time to pay, trespasser. See you in hell!"

Stuffing the paper she'd found in her pocket, she crept over to the edge of the loft. But all she saw was a glimpse of a man's back. It was broad, the back of a big man, and he was going out the barn doors. Those doors then slid closed, and Lauren heard what sounded like a chain being wrapped around the metal pull handles.

Suddenly she smelled smoke. At first she thought it was his cigar, but then she heard the sharp crackle of fire consuming ancient straw below her. A moment later she felt the heat. This old barn was tinder dry, she knew, and would go up in just a few minutes. Already the air was filled with a thick, choking haze. What little light there was left was rapidly being blocked out by the smoke.

But, of course, in just a few moments she would have plenty of light. The first tongues of flame licked at the edge of the loft, igniting the loose straw. And there she was, trapped.

It was at least thirty feet to the barn floor, and none of the remaining hay piles were big enough to land in safely.

But even if she could jump down without breaking a leg, all that waited for her was a rapidly expanding fire and a door some madman had chained shut.

The hay door! She ran over to it and gave it a kick. Sweet, blessed sunlight flooded in. But so did a fresh source of oxygen. Behind her, the fire responded like a living thing, surging higher with a snarling roar.

She now had a way out. But it was still a long way to the ground. From this height a broken leg was almost a certainty, and a broken neck a definite possibility.

From her vantage point she could see the house, and Sam had just stepped out onto the porch. She put two fingers in her mouth and let out a shrill whistle to get his attention.

"Help me, Sam! Fire!"

Sam might not have been much of a driver, but he was one heck of a runner. He was there in seconds flat, standing below her and looking at the barn doors.

"What the...? They're chained and locked!"

"Do you have a ladder?"

He shook his head. "Just a small one in the house. Is there a rope up there?"

Lauren checked the swing-out hoist that was used for lifting hay bales into the loft. But what rope was left had long since rotted to shreds.

"No good," she called back. "How about the toolshed?"

"No, I don't remember seeing any."

Sam thought furiously, painfully aware of the flames that had started streaming up the walls of the barn. He could kick in the old wood siding, or even drive the car through, but getting himself inside on the ground floor wouldn't do any good. It was almost entirely in flames

now anyway. What he needed was to get Lauren out.
Now.

"The lumber!" he suddenly exclaimed.

While at the lumberyard, they had purchased some
extra two-by-fours, which Lauren had told him always
came in handy around any restoration project. They were
going to come in very handy right now.

He took off running. Lauren shouted after him.
"You'll need six! And a hammer and nails!" She glanced
behind her and saw that the fire was now firmly in control of the loft and coming her way. "And hurry!"

Sam raced to the house, grabbed the materials she had
requested without giving it much thought and then raced
back to the barn. Each board was eight feet long, so it
was a tricky load to carry, but he managed by balancing
the lumber on his shoulder and holding it with one hand.
In his other hand he had a hammer and a plastic bag full
of nails.

Lauren had eased herself out to the very edge of the
loft and was sitting there with her legs dangling down.
Smoke billowed around her, making her cough. In about
two more minutes she would have to jump and take her
chances.

Sam dropped the boards. "What now?"

"Start nailing them together, overlapping them a
foot."

He went to work, talking to her as he did so, as much
to calm himself as Lauren. "How am I doing, Profes-
sor?"

"Good. But use three nails, and nail both sides."

"Picky, picky!" he muttered, but did as she said.

When he started to nail the sixth board to the rest, she
yelled at him again. "Stop!"

"But—"

"Just start sliding it into place," she interrupted.

Again Sam did as she said, but wasn't sure why. Then he realized the angle was too steep. He couldn't get the makeshift ladder more than three quarters of the way up the side of the barn because of the way it flexed.

"Now use the last board to shove it up to me!" Lauren cried. "Hurry! I'm starting to feel like a marshmallow!"

From about halfway along the length of the ladder, Sam used the sixth board to lift it up to her waiting grasp. It totally amazed him how coolly she'd estimated the materials they would need. And it was a good thing, too, because there was no time left. Flames spilled out the top of the hay door, flirting with the roof.

Lauren went out. The nailed-together boards bowed under her weight as she came down them hand over hand, but they didn't break, and the nails held. When she got within his grasp, Sam grabbed her and helped her down.

He hugged her fiercely. "I was scared to death!"

"So was I." She looked around. "I saw him, Sam. He laughed as he locked me in there to die, just like he laughed when he tried to kill Jason."

"He must have taken off before I came out." Sam looked around now, too. "Damn you, Hank Addison! Or whoever you are! You're the one who'll pay!"

Lauren was hot from the fire and her strenuous climb, but she still shivered. "Come on," she told him. "We'd better call the fire department, though I don't think there's much they can do."

There wasn't. By the time Beardsville's aging pumper truck arrived, the barn was a total loss. The volunteer firemen sprayed down what was left to avoid any flare-ups. Sam assured them he'd report in to Sheriff Buckner, who had gone to Montpelier to check on something. They packed up their gear and went back to town.

A couple of neighbors stopped by to see what was going on and offered sympathy and their future help in rebuilding. But they soon left, as well. It was as if there was a pall hanging over the old Addison place.

"Word must be getting around about the letter," Sam said.

Lauren's eyes went wide and she reached into her pocket, coming up with the paper she'd found in the barn. She unfolded it, then showed it to Sam.

"It's an old order for hay," she said. "He signed it!"

"The letter's in the car. Let's see if they match."

Neither of them was a handwriting expert, but the two signatures were close enough to make them both look around uneasily again. Then they gazed at the burned-out barn.

"I'm worried, Sam," Lauren said. "He called me a trespasser. I think maybe Hank is trying to tell us something."

"Like get lost," Sam agreed. "To tell you the truth, I'm not wild about the idea of staying here, either."

Lauren hugged him. "Then pack a bag and come stay with me. I have a guest room."

"I'm not going to let him run me off my own land!"

"Then do it for me," she said softly, meeting his angry gaze. "I need you with me." Lauren hugged him again. "That guest room is right next to mine," she added.

His expression softened. "You don't have to bribe me. If you don't want me to risk staying here, I won't."

"That wasn't a bribe," Lauren informed him. "That was a hint." She glanced at her watch. It was half past three. "If you're interested, Jason has a counseling session after school today. He won't be home for another hour and a half.''

Sam grinned, then turned and ran for the house. Lauren helped him pack. They emerged scant minutes later, Sam with his blue gym bag in hand.

"I'll drive," he said.

"The heck you will. I don't want to spend what little time we have getting towed out of a ditch."

The old cab was hardly a race car, but it handled at least as well as Lauren's truck. Sam, she observed, wasn't at all bothered by her speed.

"You're taking this well," she said.

He shrugged. "This? If we had a few hundred more cars around us and about a million impatient pedestrians at every intersection, I might be a bit edgy," he told her. "But only if you were going twice as fast, and yelling obscenities in four different languages at the same time."

When they arrived, they raced inside and up to Lauren's room, where they fell on the bed, entwined in each other's arms. It amazed her what a brush with death had done for her libido. Sam was equally passionate. They kissed deeply, tongues dueling. Then suddenly they both pulled back at the same time and looked at each other.

"You smell like smoke," Lauren observed.

Sam nodded. "You, too, times ten."

"I have a suggestion, if you promise not to think me a wanton, sex-starved divorcée," she said. "Which, of course, I am. But I don't want you to think of me that way."

"Never," Sam agreed. Lauren whispered in his ear. His eyes went wide. "Oh, my! Can we *do* that?" he said in feigned shock.

The hot water of the shower felt heavenly as it cascaded over her body, loosening every muscle. But even better was the slick feel of Sam's skin against hers. They took turns washing each other, discovering one another with awestruck wonder.

Sam cherished every full curve, holding her breasts in his hands like the treasures they were as he kissed each nipple in turn. They hardened at the touch of his lips, and he gently stroked them with his teeth before suckling them softly. His hands then smoothed down over her hips to cup her firm buttocks, pressing her against him.

Lauren moaned with anticipation as his hardness slipped between her willing thighs. She lifted her head and kissed him, her tongue darting between his lips, while her hand explored every inch of his well-muscled form. Impatient, she teased him with a wriggle of her hips, smiling at the way he groaned and stiffened.

She gasped as he ever so slowly filled her, then cried out in joy as he set a rhythm to match the need burning within them both. For Lauren, who had been without such pleasure for so long, the climax came swiftly and with a force that had Sam holding her tightly against him so she wouldn't slip away. And then, knees weak, she clung to him and watched his eyes as he achieved the same shuddering peak.

They remained wrapped in each other's arms for a while beneath the hot, stinging spray, savoring their afterglow. Slowly they again became aware of the passing of time.

Barely sated, their passion still smoldering, they stepped out of the shower and toweled each other off. Lauren could see the need in Sam's eyes, and could feel that need pulsing within herself. But time had run out.

They held each other for a moment, feeling the beating of their hearts. "Jason will be home any minute," Lauren reminded him softly. "Explaining why you'll be staying here will be easy. It'll even be easy to explain the showers in the middle of the day. But if we both come out of my room at the same time soaking wet, he's going to know something's up."

"Something *is* up," Sam told her.

She moaned and rubbed against him. "Mmm. I know. And may I take this opportunity to tell you how magnificent you are? But Jason—"

"Jason in a smart boy," Sam interjected. "He'll figure out something's up no matter what we do. What I meant was, I have feelings for you that I couldn't hide even if I wanted to." He smiled. "But thanks for the compliment."

"Oh." She smiled back. "I...I have those feelings, too. And I suppose you're right. He'll know."

"But you have a point, too," Sam agreed. "No sense in flaunting it just yet. Let's observe some decorum."

"Exactly."

"See? I'm becoming less urban all the time."

They kissed again. Before she knew it they were moving toward the bed, as if it were a magnet and their bodies made of steel. Just as they tumbled atop it, however, they heard the sound of a door slamming downstairs.

"Mom! I'm home!" Jason called.

Lauren bounced off the bed and dashed frantically around her bedroom in a dither, flinging on her robe and trying to straighten her damp, tangled hair.

"You go meet him," Sam ordered softly, gently grabbing her arm and calming her down. "I'll pretend I'm just taking my shower now." He grinned. "Heck, maybe I had better take a cold one anyway."

Lauren found Jason downstairs in the kitchen, getting a glass of milk from the refrigerator. He gave her an odd look when he saw her, but she managed to maintain her cool.

"Hi, honey! How was school?"

He shrugged. "It was okay. Lots of people signed my cast, see?" He held it up. "How come your hair's wet?"

She explained all that had happened. Jason listened, eyes wide, then came and gave her a one-armed hug. Much to her surprise, he even responded possessively.

"But Sam doesn't have to stay here. I can take care of you," he assured her.

"I know that, Jason, and so does Sam. He wanted to stay out there. But I'm worried about him."

Jason smiled slyly. "I know. I like him, too. It'll be cool having him here."

Lauren imagined the temperature would probably be at the opposite end of the scale, especially between Sam and her. But she nodded. Jason turned and headed for his room, saying he had homework to do. That surprised her. Obviously he was turning over a new leaf.

If his back hadn't been to her, she would have seen a knowing grin on his face that would have surprised her even more. He went into his room, chuckling quietly and shaking his head. Adults were so transparent.

When Sam came down, all dressed and bright eyed, he told Lauren he would do the honors of calling the sheriff while she got dressed in turn. He watched the gentle motion of her rear end beneath her robe as she walked down the hall, and felt himself stir. But there was business to attend to.

Sheriff Buckner was naturally concerned about the fire, but was still reserving judgment on the Hank Addison theory.

"I'd appreciate it if you'd give those signatures to Tim this evening at the haunted house, and we'll have an expert look them over," Oswald said. "By the way, the old red Chevy this guy used was reported stolen from a parking lot in upstate New York last week. I've got an inquiry working on that to see if I can come up with any details. And I've already put out a bulletin to see if I can find out what really happened to poor old Hank."

"Good. But Hank or no Hank, someone is bent on doing damage around here, Sheriff."

"No doubt about that. I've arranged to put an extra man at the haunted house for the duration. Whoever this is, we're not going to let him spoil Halloween!"

Lauren returned as he was hanging up. It amazed him how fabulous she could look in just jeans and a sweater. When he told her what the sheriff had said, spots of color appeared on her cheeks and she reached for the phone.

"Am I the only one in town who takes this seriously?" she muttered, dialing Howard's number. When he answered, she didn't give him time to go into his sympathy spiel. "Can it, Howard. You heard about Jason last night, didn't you? And the fire today?"

"Yes, but—"

"I assume you've also heard the rumors that Hank Addison might still be alive, and bent on revenge?"

"I have," Howard replied. "It's a load of rubbish, if you ask me—"

"As a matter of fact, I didn't," Lauren interrupted again. "All I want from you is the order to cancel the haunted house."

Predictably Howard exploded. "That's insane! Our business is up thirty percent over last year, Lauren!"

"A fat lot of good that'll do if somebody dies there!" she shot back. "We have no idea where Hank or whoever this is will strike next. That means—"

"Precisely!" It was Howard's turn to interrupt, and he did so forcefully. "Maybe he'll hit the art fair! Or the parade! Or maybe he won't hit anywhere at all where a lot of people are gathered. He hasn't yet, you know."

"Oh, really? How about Missy Jenkins?"

"That was different," Howard pointed out. "He left a trap, and she triggered it. *If* that was his work at all."

Lauren hated the smug tone in his voice. "So what prevents him from laying some more traps at the auditorium?"

"Two of Oswald's best men, an alert crew and you, their fearless leader."

"Flattery will get you nowhere, Howard."

"Face it, Lauren. Closing down the haunted house won't do anything except hurt our fund-raising efforts," he told her. "Why, it might work to our advantage if he should try something there. With all the security, he's bound to get caught."

This was a waste of breath, Lauren realized. And as much as she hated to admit it, the greedy old goat had made a pretty good point. Closing the haunted house could make Hank concentrate on other, less easily controlled targets.

"All right," she said with a deep sigh. "I suppose the show must go on."

"That's the spirit!" Howard exclaimed. "And according to the reports I'm getting from area innkeepers, you'll be playing to a packed house the whole weekend. Relax!"

He hung up. So did Lauren. "I won't relax until the first of November," she muttered.

"He didn't set a deadline on his threat," Sam noted.

"Perhaps not, but he'll come after us this weekend, all right. Maybe even Fright Night itself."

"What makes you so sure?"

"I'm sure because it fits. Economically this is one of the most important weekends of the year for this town, and I'm betting he wants to hit us where we hit him, below the money belt," Lauren replied. "I don't know what he has planned, but it's bound to be nasty. Nasty enough to put an end to Beardsville's Halloween pageants for a long time to come. Because that way, even if he only hurts a few people physically, we'll all pay in the end."

"You sound as if you're positive it's Hank Addison."

"Aren't you?" she asked.

He sighed and shrugged his broad shoulders. "I don't know, Lauren. Part of me hopes it is, because of the sensational story it'll make. But another part remembers what Tom Macklin said this afternoon. Hank doesn't sound like the sort of guy you'd want to meet in a dark alley."

"Or a haunted house," Lauren agreed. "But like I told Howard, the show must go on."

"Can we get something to eat first? I'm so hungry I couldn't frighten a flea."

She laughed. "I'll bet you could throw a pretty good scare into a hamburger and fries, though, couldn't you?"

"Lead me to it!"

Lauren still hadn't decided whether she was going to punish Jason or not, a fact he was responding to by being very, very good. Nevertheless, it didn't seem to be a wise idea to reward him right now, either, so she decided to cook at home. Afterward it was back to the books for Jason and off to the haunted house for her and Sam.

Howard hadn't been kidding about the crowds. It was a Friday night, and the spooks did a land-office business. He might have been right about the crowds keeping Hank at bay, too, since there wasn't even a hint of trouble. But people kept coming, and the place didn't shut down until two in the morning.

Elated by the money pouring into the town coffers but exhausted with the hours they put in, Sam and Lauren went home and fell into separate beds. They were proud of themselves for showing such decorum, but in truth were asleep almost as soon as they turned out the lights.

Chapter Sixteen

The next morning was Saturday, and Lauren had forgotten about the day-before-Halloween party at Jason's school. She graciously allowed him to go. As he strolled down the street, she closed the front door and looked at Sam. They exchanged mischievous smiles.

Yesterday afternoon they had been pressed for time. Now, with the party not scheduled to end until noon, they had hours at their disposal. They were determined to make the best of each and every minute.

"At last, we've got the house to ourselves."

Sam moved toward Lauren but she slipped around him in a twirling circle, her hand grabbing hold of his as she headed for the stairs. "Come with me."

"I'd love to."

They ran up the stairs and fell on her bed like eager, giddy teenagers, kissing each other passionately, unable to get enough.

"Hours," Lauren mumbled against Sam's tanned throat, her fingers busily unbuttoning his shirt. "We have hours together." They kissed greedily.

His smooth fingers were caressing the soft skin of her back when Lauren suddenly sat up and unzipped his pants.

Sam chuckled. "Still in a hurry?"

"You'd better believe it." All through breakfast there had been only one thing on her mind. Sam and her, together again, exchanging pleasure.

There was no stopping Lauren as she took control, the desire deep inside her belly driving both of them into a passionate frenzy that exploded quickly, taking both of them by surprise.

"Next time," Sam murmured as Lauren snuggled against him, her sweatshirt rubbing his bare chest, "we'll do it without our clothes."

She laughed wickedly. "I wasn't that picky."

"I noticed." Sam breathed a deep sigh of contentment. "And I'm not complaining, but this time it's my turn. Sit up."

Puzzled, Lauren did as he asked, and a moment later her sweatshirt went flying across the room, her lacy white bra and the rest of their clothing following it in short order.

"That's better."

He leaned back against a stack of pillows, admiration filling his eyes as he looked at Lauren sitting beside him, her legs curled gracefully to one side. Her glowing beauty stunned him, leaving him speechless.

Unable to find the words to express his feelings, he instead worshiped her with his touch. The satiny skin of her shoulders gave way to even softer curves.

His palms cupped her plump breasts, savoring their weight as his thumbs teased the dusky nipples into smooth pebbles. Leaning forward, he buried his face in their softness. Her scent was earthy, feminine and irresistible.

When his mouth covered one breast, Lauren moaned softly, her fingers clutching his shoulders as he began a gentle sucking. He took his time, his lips kissing every inch of each milky white orb, his hands sliding down to her waist and around to cup her buttocks.

With his hands Sam eventually eased her up on her knees, his tongue and lips trailing leisurely down her midriff and across the smoothness of her belly. As he slid lower Lauren tried to back away, but he held her firmly in his grasp, his fingers kneading her buttocks as he continued to caress and tease her with his tongue.

Her erratic breathing was punctuated by gasps and sexy moans, the sweet sounds driving him crazy. His teeth nipped at the inner softness of her thighs as he eased her back on the bed. They came together like lightning, unable to stop the thundering tides that whipped them up in a furious storm, hurling them beyond where they'd ever been before.

A while later Lauren stretched like a sleek cat and sat up, a mischievous grin on her face. Sam eyed her balefully.

"What?"

Eager to explore every inch of him, Lauren skimmed a teasing finger across his chest. "My turn."

"You think so?"

He moaned when Lauren's touch became intimate. "Mmm, I'm going to enjoy this."

"So am I," Sam mumbled, groaning softly as she continued to tease him.

Hours later they slowly drifted back to reality, still wrapped in each other's arms. "I could stay here forever," Lauren said. "But duty calls."

Sam hugged her close. "In a minute."

"All we have is a minute. Jason will be home any time now," Lauren reminded him, snuggling closer.

Sam jumped out of bed when he heard the front door slam. "Rats! He caught us again!"

"If I look as happy as I feel," Lauren said, sliding lazily off the bed and groping for her clothes, "I don't think I'll be able to put anything over on him this time."

Indeed, Jason couldn't help but notice his mother's elated spirits. Again he hid his knowing smile, and tried to take advantage of the situation by asking to go to a friend's house.

"No dice," Lauren told him. "You'll have all day tomorrow to mess around, and trick-or-treating tomorrow night, as well. Then I suppose you'll stay up half the night watching trashy horror movies. So today I want you to stick around and study."

"I finished my homework last night."

"Then read a book. But no garbage."

Jason accepted her wishes without further complaint, since she'd actually given him more leeway than he'd expected. The volume of collected horror tales Sam had brought from home and now slipped him behind his mother's back also appeased him. He went happily to his room.

"I'm going to go check on my house," Sam announced.

Lauren scowled. "I don't think that's such a good idea. What if he's still hiding out there and tries another stunt like yesterday?"

"I'll be careful."

"That sounds as if you plan to go alone," Lauren said.

"I do. No sense in both of us taking the risk."

"If you're going to insist on doing this, I insist on coming along," she informed him.

Sam knew that look in her eyes by now. It meant there wasn't any use in arguing with her. "Then let's go."

"Just a sec. I'm not ready." The weather was pleasant but a bit breezy, so she grabbed her windbreaker. She then grabbed her shotgun and a pocketful of shells. "Okay," she said, joining Sam at the back door. "Now I'm ready."

"For what? Bears?"

Lauren nodded. "Of the human variety."

They made the trip out to Sam's place at a leisurely pace. As they rolled up his driveway, all looked quiet and normal, except for the charred remnants of his barn, of course. They got out of the car at the same time, Lauren with her shotgun in hand. She loaded it.

"You did say you know how to use that thing, right?"

"Beardsville women's skeet-shooting champ two years running," she told him proudly. "Of course, there were only two of us competing. But the other woman was Nancy."

Sam raised his eyebrows. "Oh." If the way Nancy could shoot from the hip verbally was any indication, he figured he was now in expert company. "In that case, you lead."

Lauren did so. The house was locked up tight, and when they went inside to check, nothing had been disturbed. They split up and prowled around outside for a while, but didn't find anything unusual there, either. Lauren went to check the toolshed; the lock was still in place.

As she came around the corner of the shed, she saw that Sam was heading for the old chicken coop. It was certainly big enough for a man to hide in, so she hurried to catch up.

That's when she noticed the smell. She stopped in her tracks and called urgently to Sam. "Sam! Stop!"

But Sam had already ducked his head inside the chicken coop. Suddenly he pulled his head back out, spun around and started running toward her. There was a second of preternatural silence.

And then the chicken coop exploded, disintegrating in a ball of hot, white flame and a deafening explosion. As Lauren watched, helpless, Sam was knocked flat on his face by the powerful blast. Then the shock wave hit her, rocking her back on her heels. Splinters of wood, clods of dirt and a fine dust rained down on her head.

"Sam!" Lauren cried. She dropped the shotgun and ran to him, kneeling beside him. "Sam! Are you all right?"

He rolled to his side and looked up at her. "Oh, man! Somebody answer the phone!"

There was a gash over his eye. Lauren pulled a tissue from her pocket. "You're bleeding!"

"I can see your lips moving, but all I hear are bells!"

"Come on. Let's get you to the house," Lauren said, helping him to his feet. His first couple of steps were unsteady, but then he regained his balance. Still, she made him sit down on the front porch steps. "Do you have a first-aid kit?" she asked.

Sam frowned. "Third-base hit? You must be kidding! That was a home run!"

"First-aid kit!" Lauren repeated, enunciating clearly.

"Oh! Yeah. Downstairs bathroom. Bottom drawer of the vanity. Am I bleeding?" He touched his forehead, then looked at his bloody hand. "Guess so, huh?"

"Men," Lauren muttered under her breath as she went to find the kit. "It's a good thing they're cute, otherwise they'd be too much of a pain to tolerate!"

She returned and tended his wound, which looked much worse than it was. By the time she was finished,

Sam was hearing clearly. Together they went to spray down the smoldering remnants of the demolished coop with a garden hose.

"That's two," Sam observed, looking around his property with a forlorn expression. "Only two more buildings to go. I guess I should be glad he started with the ones that were already falling down." He noticed Lauren stepping gingerly amid the muck and poking around with a stick. "What are you looking for?"

"I'm not sure. What were *you* looking for?"

"I smelled something strange coming from the coop and went to investigate," Sam replied.

"Propane," she informed him. "It doesn't quite smell the same as natural gas. And it's tricky because it pools on the ground instead of floating in the air. Must have been leaking for quite a while."

"Well, the house is on natural gas now, so I've never encountered the stuff before. But believe me, I'll remember all that next time," he said ruefully.

"Then what made you run?"

"When I poked my head in, I heard a clicking noise," Sam replied. "That I *have* encountered before, on my new stove—once I plugged it in, naturally."

Lauren bent to retrieve something from the muddy ashes at her feet. "So you ran."

"Right."

"Good thing you're fleet of foot." Lauren pointed to a misshapen lump across the yard. "There's what's left of the tank." She then came over to him and showed him a twisted hunk of plastic and metal. "And this is about all that's left of the little heater that was used to keep the chickens warm in the winter."

"Defective?" Sam asked, but already knew the answer.

Lauren shook her head. "No. I've fiddled with lots of these, and even though this one is mangled I can tell it's been tampered with." She looked at him. "Someone deliberately blew up the coop, Sam, undoubtedly hoping you or I would be inside when it went. And you know who that someone is."

"Hank," Sam agreed. "Because we're trespassing on what he still considers his property. He's obviously taking a personal interest in us, Lauren, and that could be deadly."

She went and got her shotgun, then headed for the car. Sam was right beside her. "You'd better drive," he told her. "I'm still feeling a little loopy. Besides, I want to get away from here fast."

"You said it."

Back in town, their first stop was Sheriff Buckner's office. What they told and showed him only added weight to a conclusion he'd already come to on his own.

"The signatures are a match," he told them. "I even sent an old one I had on file here from an arrest report I had on Hank for disturbing the peace."

"Did you get anything back on the bulletin you sent out on him?" Lauren wanted to know.

Sheriff Buckner shook his head. "Not yet. But I don't have to know where he's been or what he's been doing to figure out what he's up to now," Oswald said. "Hank Addison is back in Beardsville, and he plans to make us pay for what he thinks we did to him."

Lauren wasn't the sort to say I told you so. But she settled for the next best thing. "Sam and I came to that conclusion ourselves. Yesterday. What's our next move?"

If the sheriff noticed the dig, he didn't mind. "I've got the whole town on alert. Heck, before this weekend is over, I'll probably have to deputize half of the able-bodied citizens!'' he exclaimed. ''But the way I figure it, canceling the pageant is just what Hank wants. With all these people primed and ready, it'd put a blot on our reputation that would last for years.'' Oswald scowled. ''I'm not going to give that worthless sot the satisfaction.''

''We agree,'' Sam told him, looking at Lauren for confirmation. She was nodding. ''So far he's been able to move around the area like the ghost everyone thought he was. But now maybe we can catch him in the act.''

''I have Tim out distributing copies of Hank's picture,'' Sheriff Buckner informed them. ''It's an old one, but it might help. With all these strangers in town, though, our best bet is just to be on the lookout for anything suspicious. We won't go down without a fight, by golly!''

As Lauren and Sam headed home, they noticed that the rest of the town shared that sentiment. No one was letting this threat dampen their Halloween spirit. Wherever they looked, people were getting ready for the big parade and other festivities tomorrow.

''Wow!'' Sam exclaimed. ''This is really something!''

''It's the one time of the year when a tourist can say Beardsville looks ghastly and mean it as a compliment,'' Lauren said, enjoying the way her town was pulling together.

Lauren again thought it best to stay in for dinner that evening, not for Jason's benefit, but because every restaurant around was likely to be packed. This time, Sam insisted on cooking. He made what he called his famous enchiladas. Lauren and Jason called them very tasty, although they were spicy enough to burn holes in their plates. The triple-fudge ice cream they had for dessert cooled them off nicely.

Jason pleaded to come with them to the haunted house, and Lauren relented. She decided it was probably the safest place in town, especially with Nancy to keep an eye on him. What with two watchful guards on duty, as well, they all felt pretty safe.

As it turned out, they needed Jason's help, for the place was overflowing. Still, Lauren sent him home early with Teri, and a good thing, too. They had a line around the block that lasted until midnight. And once again, she and Sam dragged home, too exhausted to do much more than kiss each other good-night in the hall and head for their rooms. Tomorrow was Halloween, a holiday in Beardsville that started early and ran late.

Providing Hank Addison let it take place at all. Only time would tell what he had planned for them. Unless he was caught, this year Fright Night could bring with it a very real terror.

Chapter Seventeen

For many Beardsville residents, Halloween morning was a lot like Christmas morning. Rather than jumping out of bed to open presents, however, this day started with a fantastic parade that wound around the streets, paying homage to all the hard work of those taking part in the decoration competition. Though every house in town had at least a jack-o'-lantern, some people went to the opposite extreme and expense. These were the true contestants, and their friendly but intense rivalry was the essence of the pageant.

Since she was involved in the haunted house, Lauren didn't really have the time to participate in the yearly competition. At her place, a couple of pumpkins and some mock spiderwebs on the porch had to suffice. But she and the rest of the haunted-house crew always marched in the parade in full costume, as did nearly the whole populace. This was Beardsville on display for the tourists, and they ate it up.

Of course, this year there was a darker side. The sheriff had deputized an extra force to keep an eye on the crowd. They paid particular attention to any large adult male in a costume that completely concealed his identity. Several gorillas were asked to remove their heads, and only the children got by with a full face mask.

Jason was among these, and justifiably proud of the mask Lauren had procured for him from one of the specialty suppliers she dealt with. It was the visage of a particularly hideous wolflike monster with large fangs and huge bulging eyes. At the touch of a hidden button, those fangs dripped blood, its eyes narrowed to thin, glowing slits and a chilling growl came from an audio chip in its mouth.

Naturally Jason put these gruesome features to their best use. As he, Sam and Lauren walked along with the rest of the bizarre parade, he scared as many girls as he could.

"Did you see that one?" he asked them. "I thought she was going to spew!"

Lauren looked at Sam.

"At least they're verbally creative," Sam observed.

"Right. Steinbeck would be proud."

The parade continued on, now passing Mr. Anderson's house. Evidently the pranksters had given him an idea. Rather than returning them to their original positions, storming his porch, he had arranged the scarecrows to look as if they were climbing all over his house, peeking in windows. The crowd laughed as they filed by. That made Mr. Anderson happy, since their response was taken into account in the judging. But his competition was formidable.

Down the block, someone had staged a mock hanging, complete with working gallows. The homeowner himself played the part of the condemned prisoner. While the crowd watched, a hooded executioner, played gleefully by his wife, pulled a lever and he dropped through the trapdoor, dangling at the end of his rope. The crowd gasped as one, a reaction the judges duly noted.

Farther along the parade route, one front lawn had been turned into an eerie graveyard scene, with mist-shrouded tombstones and moaning ghosts. Another had jack-o'-lanterns of every shape and size, a regular pumpkin gallery, amid which stood still more ghosties, ghoulies and a human skeleton or two. Yet another was a monster zone, from legend and movies both, all played by family members who chased after people in the crowd as the parade passed by. Audience participation was a big hit with the judges, too.

But by far the most impressive house in Beardsville that Halloween was Lee Patterson's. A past winner and current holder of last year's second-place award, Lee had spared no effort or expense in going for the gold this time around.

At first, everything about the three-story colonial home appeared normal, as if no decorating had been done at all. But then there came a slow transformation. A hazy mist started forming around the house, hissing from hidden jets near the eaves. Some sort of little furry creatures with gleaming eyes popped out of unseen holes in the yard, first ten, then twenty or more, all looking at the crowd and squeaking strangely.

These were used to draw attention away from the house itself, so that when the crowd heard a noise and looked back at it, they saw that an odd pair of spectral forms draped in black had appeared on the front porch, dancing a waltz to the eerie music of a clavichord.

There was another noise, this time from the huge oak trees overhanging the street. The crowd looked up, and much to their uneasy amazement discovered hundreds of lifelike bats hanging from the branches, gazing back at them with blazing red eyes. Again this was to trick the eye, for when their attention returned to the house, the figures on the porch were gone.

But that's when they noticed something happening within the house itself. Strange forms appeared at one of the windows of the first floor, then slowly took shape. It was a man and woman, dressed in colonial-era clothing. The man had a knife. He raised it as if to stab the woman, who turned and disappeared from view, only to reappear in the next window, and then the next. As the chase continued, the crowd surged forward, caught up in the drama unfolding before them.

After a moment, the couple appeared in a window on the second floor. The man had caught her. As the crowd gasped, he slit her throat, spattering the window with blood. But as he moved to the next window, the man seemed wracked with guilt and remorse. Then he disappeared from view again...

Only to reappear on the third-floor balcony. After a moment, he raised a flintlock pistol to his head and fired, shocking the crowd yet again. As they waited to see what would happen next, the clavichord began to play. All eyes were drawn to the porch, where sure enough, the eerie specters danced. But then the hidden steam jets hissed, concealing them. When the mist cleared, they were gone. And to the amazed eyes of the people watching, the house and yard had once again returned to normal.

The applause lasted for a full minute, during which Lee and his wife, Bev, came out to take a bow. There was little doubt as to who would win the first-place award.

After all the other prizes had been parceled out to the rest of the contestants, it was time to head for the center of town and the annual art fair and mass picnic. Still, Sheriff Buckner and his enlarged force of deputies kept a watchful eye on the proceedings, lest it turn into a mass murder.

Jason went with his friends to find some more girls to frighten. Lauren counted herself lucky that it seemed the only emotion he was interested in evoking within them at the moment. Meanwhile, she and Sam went looking for the sheriff to get an update. They caught up with him at the hot-dog stand.

"I doubt that's on your diet, Oswald," Lauren told him as he hungrily poked the last bite into his mouth. "What would Sandy say if she saw you?"

Oswald swallowed, a look of sheer ecstasy on his face. "She wouldn't say anything. She'd just kill me on the spot," he replied. "But she's busy serving up sandwiches right now, so I'm safe." He looked Sam. "You ought to try one of these. They're great!"

Sam looked vaguely ill, no doubt remembering his last encounter with pork. "Uh, no thanks. I've got my eye on those pretzels over there. With plenty of mustard."

"Anything on your bulletin?" Lauren asked.

"I got in some old arrest reports this morning that prove Hank did leave here for New York," Oswald replied. "They list his place of employment, and evidently he found work, at least at first, in a couple of different slaughterhouses there. But he was still drinking and causing trouble. The last report was for vagrancy about seven years ago, so I guess he couldn't hold a job anymore. After that, it's as though he dropped off the face of the earth."

"Or into a homeless shelter somewhere," Lauren said.

Sam made a face. "Same difference sometimes."

"Anyway, I'll keep checking," Oswald assured them. "Normally I wouldn't bother on a Sunday, but since this is Halloween, everybody has extra help on. Speaking of which, the haunted house opens at noon today, right?"

Lauren nodded. "We're headed over there as soon as we grab a bite to eat. What looks good?" she asked. "Other than the hot dogs and pretzels, I mean."

"I'm the wrong person to ask," Oswald replied, gazing around wistfully. "So much food, so little time."

He headed for the cotton candy. Sam and Lauren went the other way, across the town square, where vendors were selling everything from homemade cinnamon rolls to imported olives. The sun was warm and there were people all over the place, looking and buying, seeing and being seen. Many were in costume. All were having fun.

It was quite a scene, with jugglers, roving musicians and even one dreaded mime competing for attention, as well as whatever money wasn't flowing in the direction of the street vendors and artisans. Beardsville's best were on display. Particular favorites were the handmade jewelry, stained glass, carved wooden statuary and watercolor landscapes of the surrounding hills in full autumn color.

After they strolled around for a while, Sam and Lauren settled on pretzels as an appetizer, pizza for the main course and caramel apples for dessert. Feeling full, happy and a bit decadent, they then headed for the haunted house.

Today the crew worked in shifts, spelling one another when it was time to eat or take a break. There were more children than usual, so everyone turned the fright level down a notch. They would make up for it later when they closed down for the special all-adult tour that preceded the Weirdsville Bash.

As evening approached, Sam and Lauren took their break, both for dinner and to take Jason trick-or-treating. Normally Lauren would have let him go alone, but in light of what had nearly happened to him the other night, she insisted on escorting him this year.

He didn't mind. In fact, he had some ideas of his own. Both adults were still in costume. Sam was directed to insert his fangs and play his vampire role to the hilt. Then Jason studied Lauren in her brown hooded robe.

"With a little help, she'd make a great Pekoe, the demented monk," he said, looking at Sam for confirmation. "Like in the video game. Don't you think?"

Sam grinned. "I do, indeed. She keeps her makeup in the upstairs bathroom, doesn't she?"

"Uh-huh."

"Hey!" Lauren exclaimed. "Wait a minute!"

"No time, Mom," Jason told her. "I hear tons of candy calling to me out there." Sam was already heading upstairs. Jason joined him. "You get the makeup, I'll get my water pistol. Should make a great plasma blaster."

"Good thinking. And instead of water, let's try a little recipe for disappearing ink I read about."

"Can we make it green?"

"I think so," Sam replied.

"Cool!"

Lauren simply stood in the living room and shook her head. "I think I may be in trouble here," she muttered. "But I guess I did want to be part of the fun."

Once she got past the painted black circles around her eyes and bright purple nose, Lauren conceded that she really did look like the video game character.

Armed with a squirt gun full of Sam's green disappearing ink, which they tested first, they headed out to terrorize the neighborhood. All three were a big hit and had a great time. To Lauren it felt as if they were becoming a family. But she cautioned herself not to jump to conclusions. Sam was serious about her and she about him. That did not mean marriage was in their future, nor had either said anything about love. Lauren knew how she felt; saying it aloud was another matter entirely. She'd said it only once before, to a man who had taken her heart and crushed it.

Leaving Jason with his mountain of candy and an admonition not to eat it all or watch too many horror movies, Lauren and Sam went back to the haunted house to help with the changeover. For the most part that meant spiffing up the tableaux and making sure the atmosphere was still good and creepy. The caterers would take care of setting up the food and refreshments.

Even with all the security, there was still some concern. Though there hadn't been any problems so far, they all felt Hank Addison was out there somewhere, perhaps waiting for the cover of darkness. But no one could get into the haunted house now except those who had bought a ticket for the party, and every one of them would be totally scrutinized as they came through the door. Since all of them were in costume, that could take a while, but Deputy Tim had plenty of patience.

Nancy was in an unaccustomed dither, looking out at the people waiting in line. This wasn't just the average group of thrill seekers. These were the high-paying, party-going ticket holders to the Weirdsville Bash. They would expect nothing less than the best performance the haunted-house crew could give.

"Okay, people!" she called out. "This is the moment you've practiced for. Make me proud!"

She opened the door. Fright Night had arrived.

Chapter Eighteen

For this crowd, the spooks put a little extra zip into their performances. And with each group that went through the haunted house, the scene got a little more bizarre. At last, there were only five more people left, and Sam was elected to take them through. By now the crew were playing their roles with abandon, experimenting with new techniques and ad-libs. After all, next year they would have to top themselves yet again.

Lauren had gotten the idea of piping cold outside air into the opening gag with the truck, thus adding one more aspect of realism. It left the last guests with a suitably worried look about them as they were led to the next step along the horror trail. There, in the mad scientist's laboratory, Leon had decided he was hungry and sat down to dine—upon the dissected corpse that lay atop his operating table. The grossed-out guests forged onward, leaving him chewing delicately on a rib.

The final group got one thing they hadn't bargained on, that being the attention of the entire crew. As they went through each tableau, the players would abandon their posts and follow behind, zombielike. At the guillotine, with its hideous twitching corpse and shifty-eyed disembodied head, the five people noticed their creepy escort numbered ten. Passing the grim reaper, that number had grown to fifteen.

Finally they reached the gas chamber, and Barb Fowler went into her act. But this time, as she appeared behind the startled guests and started advancing toward them, she was accompanied by the entire crew of twenty.

Leading the crew was Sam, having now made his full transformation into a vampire. "This concludes our tour, ladies and gentlemen," Sam told the last, lucky five.

He bared his fangs. Lauren stepped up beside him and lowered the hood of her robe. She, too, grinned to expose sharp, white fangs. "And now you'll learn the true secret of Beardsville," she said. "You see, the reason we hold this party every year isn't to raise funds."

Nancy was also among the group advancing upon the five remaining guests, who now found they had their backs against the partition wall. "We don't need money," Nancy agreed, showing her own fangs. "Do we, people?"

"No!" the crew agreed, speaking at once. They now had completely surrounded the wide-eyed guests. "We don't need money! We need blood!"

As the rest of the haunted-house crew surged forward, snarling and displaying their vampire fangs, Sam opened the exit door, and the last group to go through this year's haunted house ran out screaming and laughing, much to the amusement of the crowd assembled for the Weirdsville Bash.

One by one the crew exited, as well, taking their bows as the crowd applauded. It was time for Nancy, Sam, Lauren and all the others to let down their hair and join everybody else at the party, their admittance a free perk for all their hard work.

Most headed for the bar. Sam caught Lauren as she turned to go back into the haunted house. "Haven't you spent enough time in there for one year?" he asked.

She grinned at him. "Plenty. I'm just going to get something I left at the box office. I'll be right back."

As promised, she returned quickly, carrying a paper sack she'd brought with her from home. Sam had noticed it earlier, and his curiosity was killing him.

"What's in there, anyway?" he demanded. "Some new trick you cooked up?"

"Nope." Smiling mischievously, she pulled a pair of black high heels out of the bag. "It's a treat. You wait here and I'll show you."

Lauren headed off toward the backstage wardrobe room, leaving Sam to mingle and wonder. The party was in full swing. Toward the middle of the room, people were dancing to the music of a live band playing pop favorites. Still more people had hit the buffet line and were seated at the tables that lined the perimeter of the auditorium, eating, drinking and having a ball.

The crowd was an unusual mix, with townsfolk outnumbered by about two to one. But even some of the Beardsville people were hard to spot, being in costume.

Sam located Sheriff Buckner quickly enough, standing near the food with a frustrated expression on his face. He had come dressed as a sheriff of the old west, naturally. Sandy looked to be the dance hall madam, and was keeping a close eye on her hungry cowboy.

Henry Joseph was there, much to Sam's surprise. It was hard to tell whether the suit he wore was supposed to be a costume. Given his age, it was probably just his usual Sunday best. Whatever, he looked quite the ladies' man, with slicked-back hair and a twinkle in his eyes. Those eyes were tracking Marge Tandy. As Sam watched, laughing, Henry cornered her and swept her out on the dance floor. She protested vehemently, but there was a twinkle in her eyes, as well.

Even Jim Ferguson was there, dressed like the nifty, fresh-faced cub reporter he had once been. Though the big camera he hoisted from time to time was an old flash model from his youth, Sam had every reason to believe it worked, and that Jim was prepared to snap a picture of anyone who engaged in newsworthy behavior that night.

A party on Halloween night was a good bet for any reporter. That was when the true spirit of the season emerged. When in costume, no one was quite what they seemed, and people did things they normally wouldn't. Everyone had on some kind of mask, even those who weren't wearing one.

Like Mr. Judd. Dressed to the nines, he was smiling and having a great time, with a group of the westsiders, no less, the Conners among them. But Judd's smile concealed a secret. A late arrival, he had gone around the parking lot letting the air out of the tires on every one of their vehicles.

Sam caught Jim's eye and waved. Jim smiled. Then his eyes went wide and he raised his camera, taking a picture of someone across the room near the stage. Sam turned in that direction, wondering who had caused such a stir.

It was Lauren. And she was causing a stir, all right. Every red-blooded male in the room was soon gazing at her.

Tired of looking like a refugee from a monastery, especially when standing next to Sam in his Victorian era finery, Lauren had decided to pick another costume for this evening. She had chosen well.

The black sheath-style evening gown was made of satin, and it shimmered beneath the spotlights at the edge of the stage. Its low-cut neckline displayed an amount of creamy cleavage that made Sam's pulse race, and when she started to walk toward him, he could see that the gown was also slit high on the side. With every step, he was treated to a brief, tantalizing flash of her long, perfect legs.

"Hello, handsome," Lauren drawled as she joined him at the edge of the dance floor. "See something you like?"

Sam blinked, watching as she took a deep breath and the twin mounds of her breasts swelled at the gown's neckline. Then she turned slightly, showing him a bit of nylon-encased thigh. He stepped closer to her, drinking in her beauty.

"Something? I see a whole candy store," he replied hoarsely. "Would you like to dance?"

Lauren leaned near, giving him an even better view of her barely concealed breasts, and kissed him on the cheek. "I'd love to," she replied, her breath soft upon his skin.

It was a slow song, and they stepped out on the dance floor, amid the envious glances of both males and females. Sam cut quite a figure himself in the rich evening attire of a former age. Together they made a striking couple as they slowly swayed to the music.

"You're really something, Lauren," he whispered softly in her ear. "Good with a saw and a saucepan. Tough as the nails you can drive with one swing and yet as soft as a feather." Sam kissed her gently. "And now a bombshell. Any man who would willingly risk losing you didn't deserve you in the first place."

Lauren held him close. "Thank you. I've always thought so, too. But it's nice to hear out loud."

"Well, it's true. If it weren't for Jason, I'd say the whole thing was a mistake," Sam told her. "As it is, all I can say is that I must be the luckiest guy alive."

"Lucky?" she asked, feeling her heart skip a beat.

Sam whirled her around in a slow circle, gazing deep into her eyes. "Lucky to have found you," he replied. "Lucky that you would even speak to me, after being hurt so badly." He pulled her close again, kissed her and then sighed. "But most of all, I'm lucky to have enough of a heart left myself to fall in love with you. I do love you, Lauren. I want to be with you forever."

Lauren's eyes widened. "I—I love you, too, Sam. With all the heart I have left, as well. And I accept." Her eyes widened a bit more and she added quickly, "That is, if you meant to say—"

Sam interrupted her by kissing her quickly on the lips, then chuckled softly at her expression. "Spoken just like the woman you are. Strong and sure. It's part of what made me fall so hard for you," he said. "And, yes, that's exactly what I meant to say. I want you to marry me. If you and Jason will have me, that is."

"I'll have you," Lauren told him, wrapping her arms around him and hugging him hard. "If Jason doesn't like it, I'll send him to his room until he's old enough to get married himself!"

The next song was up-tempo, and they whirled across the dance floor, giddy, well aware of the stares of townsfolk and strangers alike. Most of the Beardsville residents knew what this sudden happiness on Lauren's part meant, however, and heartily slapped Sam on the back as the couple danced by. And it was all so appropriate. To become engaged on Halloween!

Finally Sam and Lauren had to take a breather. They sat at the edge of the activity, sharing a glass of champagne and watching the lively crowd.

Then something caught Sam's attention and he frowned, pointing toward the doors at the other side of the room. Lauren looked in that direction. Deputy Tim was at the auditorium exit doors, waving frantically at the sheriff. She frowned, too, wondering what was up.

They found out soon enough. Sheriff Buckner noticed his deputy at last and went to have a word with him. He made a motion with his hand that seemed to indicate for Tim to look around, then turned back toward the crowd. Spotting Sam and Lauren, he headed in their direction.

"You're not going to believe this," Oswald told them as he took a seat at their table. Though the noise level was fairly high, he still leaned close so as not to be overheard by the other nearby party goers. "I just got word. Hank Addison is dead."

"What do you mean?" Lauren asked, confused. "Did one of your guards shoot him or something?"

The sheriff was shaking his head. "No, I mean dead and buried. The story we all heard was true. You see, I got to thinking about that stolen car, and made some inquiries to the local police up that way. I was just wondering if maybe there was any place around there that Hank might have ended up. You know," Oswald said. "Like one of those homeless shelters you mentioned or something."

"And?" Sam demanded impatiently.

"There is a place. Not a shelter, though. A mental institution. Had a file on poor old Hank and everything. Seems he wandered around the streets of New York City for a while after he lost that last job, just panhandling and drinking. By that time he had cirrhosis of the liver pretty bad, and I guess some priest took pity on him and got him placed in this facility. That's where he died. Not a red cent to his name. They buried him in the potter's field there. Evidently a lot of their patients end up that way.''

Lauren was stunned. ''When?''

''Five years ago.''

''Then who's stalking Beardsville?'' Sam wondered.

''And why?'' Lauren added.

Sheriff Buckner stood. For the first time, they noticed that the gun in the Western holster on his hip was very real. ''I don't know. Right now, the thing worrying me is that we've been looking for a dead man. That means the real stalker could be anywhere.'' Oswald slowly scanned the crowd. ''Even right here in this room with us.''

Lauren shook her head. ''No,'' she said firmly. ''I looked at every man who came through the haunted house tonight, and there wasn't one with size-thirteen feet.''

''Well, no one got past my guards back here, either,'' the sheriff assured them. ''There's only three doors to this place, and no windows. That's why we needed a new civic center—this design was so outmoded.'' He sighed. ''Maybe we're safe in here, after all.''

At that moment, Deputy Tim stuck his head back inside the auditorium. He didn't bother using hand signals this time, because everyone could hear the ruckus outside.

''Sheriff!'' he bellowed. ''You'd better come quick! There's some guy out here playing demolition derby with the cars in the parking lot!''

Sheriff Buckner raced for the door, moving surprisingly fast considering his girth. As he went he tried to calm the crowd. "Now take it easy, folks! Everything's under control. No reason to be alarmed."

But the sound of screeching tires and grinding metal outside convinced them otherwise. There wasn't a panic, but most everyone was hot on Sheriff Buckner's heels.

The sight that greeted the hundred or so people attending the Weirdsville Bash as they filed out the double doors was sheer vehicular mayhem. An old but powerful-sounding red Chevy sedan was selectively plowing into the parked cars. The pattern wasn't random by any means. Whoever was at the wheel had a marked preference for expensive models.

"My Beemer!" someone cried.

"I just made the last payment on that Jag!"

Sheriff Buckner pulled his gun and fired several shots into the air. "Stop in the name of the law!"

The driver did pause for a moment. He was at the far end of the lot, so they couldn't see his face, but there was the sudden flare of a match in the darkness as he lit a cigar. Smoke billowed from the driver's-side window. Then he showed the sheriff how he felt about the order to stop, and put on a driving demonstration, as well.

He hit the gas, backed into a Mercedes, then shifted gears and stomped on the gas again, turning a neat loop as he crossed the lot so that the battered rear of the Chevy again connected with a parked car, this one a Cadillac. Again the engine roared, the Chevy surged forward, and he spun in a complete circle in the middle of the parking lot.

There he stopped again. Now facing the crowd, he revved the engine, a powerful, frightening sound in the chill night air. Then the Chevy came right at them in a cloud of burning rubber and flying dust.

This was a bit too much like the first tableau in the haunted house for anyone's taste. They scattered left and right, diving for whatever cover they could find. But the sheriff stood his ground, and leveled his pistol at the approaching car.

"Oswald, you fool!" his wife, Sandy, cried. "Run!"

Since the man in the battered red Chevy could be heard laughing above the roar of his engine, and showed no sign of slowing down, Oswald decided that perhaps discretion really was the better part of valor. He ran.

But the driver was good, and had never intended to run into the auditorium. In one fluid motion, he yanked hard on the wheel to send the car into a spin, shifted gears as the nose came around, and stomped on the gas. Gravel sprayed the auditorium wall like machine-gun fire. When the crowd dared look again, the Chevy was going in the opposite direction, back to the far end of the lot.

"Damn it!" Sheriff Buckner exclaimed. "I don't know who that is, but it sure as heck ain't Hank Addison's ghost! Let's get him!"

He and his deputies took off running, with Tim in the lead. A few others followed, bent on avenging the destruction of their precious vehicles. Sam took a step forward, as well, but Lauren caught his sleeve.

"He's playing with them," she said. "And the sheriff is right. That's not Hank. Whoever he is, he's a pro with that car."

"Stock-car driver or something," Sam agreed.

Jim came out from behind the patrol car and joined them. They were all watching as the driver of the red car played cat and mouse.

"Ace driver," Jim said. "Butcher. Knows Beardsville and the people who live here, and moved among us like a master thief. Or a guerrilla. Must be an excellent forger, too, judging by the signature on that letter." He looked at them. "Are we any closer to figuring out who this guy is?"

Lauren shook her head. "Beats me. But I'll tell you one thing. I found something else I'm afraid of. That guy."

"Look out!" Jim cried. "Here he comes again!"

Having successfully separated the people with guns from the other, more helpless individuals, the driver was now headed back toward the auditorium at top speed. This time, it didn't look as if he was going to stop.

Jim dived back behind the patrol car. Sam, Lauren and an older couple decided the safest place was back inside. They had just barely gotten through the door when they heard the sound of squealing rubber and a heavy thud that shook the building. They turned to look, thinking the driver had misjudged this time and crashed.

Then, to their dawning horror, they saw that in fact he had hit exactly on the mark. The car had slid broadside against the auditorium wall so that the passenger-side door was square in the middle of the entranceway.

That door now opened, and out stepped a big, burly man dressed in rubber-soled hunting boots, dark camouflage pants and a navy blue pea coat. Quick as a wink, he turned and closed the auditorium double doors and slung a length of chain through the handles. He secured the chain with a heavy padlock. He then turned around and looked at his captives, touching a match to the stub of a cigar and taking a leisurely puff. They could smell its sickly sweet aroma.

The older couple started backing away, but the big man didn't even glance their way. He was looking directly at Sam and Lauren. A broad grin spread across his haggard, unshaven face.

"Well, well," the man said, his voice as cold as the wind out of a graveyard at midnight. "Look what we have here. A couple of trespassers. And don't you know, old Hank knows just what to do with trespassers."

Pulling a large, gleaming butcher knife out of the inside pocket of his coat, he tested its edge with one huge thumb, then started toward them, laughing with every step.

He stood about six-three and weighed approximately two hundred seventy-five pounds, very little of which looked to be fat. His feet were every bit of thirteen triple E, and he had hands to match. He had virtually no neck, legs like telephone poles and the arms of a gorilla, long and thick.

Sam mentally added weight lifter to the guy's résumé. Unfortunately, though, he wasn't muscle-bound. When Sam feinted a move to the left, the big man simply countered and laughed louder, as light on his feet as a cat. One thing seemed certain—not even the both of them put together could outmuscle this freak. They would have to outthink him. Sam was thinking as fast as he could.

So was Lauren, and along the same lines. But there was one other thing of which she was certain, and she saw no reason not to say it aloud.

"You're not Hank Addison."

The man stopped laughing. But his scowl told her that was not necessarily a good sign. Then the scowl cleared, and his cold green eyes focused on her breasts.

"Old Hank sure would like a taste of you," the man said. He laughed again, a curt chuckle. "Before he cuts you up into steak to feed the dogs, that is! And tonight, what Hank wants, Hank gets!"

He lunged at Lauren. She backpedaled, no easy feat in high heels, and nearly tripped. Sam stepped between them and the big man slashed deep into the fabric of his suit coat with the butcher knife, but failed to draw blood. Still, Sam now knew to keep his distance. Those big hands were incredibly fast.

Outside, they could hear the sound of the sheriff and his deputies pounding on the doors. But they were made of thick, solid wood, and the chains holding them shut were strong. Since there wasn't help coming from the other two possible directions, Lauren had to assume this maniac had somehow blocked those entrances, as well. The windowless design of the old place was working in his favor, doubtless his plan all along. For the moment, they were trapped.

Lauren kicked her shoes off. "But you're not Hank Addison," she repeated.

"Uh, that seems to be ticking him off, Lauren, dear," Sam observed quietly. "Perhaps we'd best move on to another subject."

The man calling himself Hank had been so intent on the pair that he hadn't noticed the other couple. Neither had Lauren. But now she looked over at them, and saw that it was Bev and Lee Patterson, owners of this year's winning house in the decoration competition. They were older, and certainly no match for this lunatic. But Lee was a retired electrical engineer. She had consulted him on some work she'd done for the haunted house one year.

"Lee," Lauren said simply, then looked up at the lights.

He got the message and both he and his wife immediately moved toward the backstage area where the circuit breaker panel was. Hank didn't like the activity, but when he turned and went after them, Sam and Lauren took the opportunity to put some distance and a few tables between themselves and him. This didn't go over at all well.

The man roared in anger. "The hunter who chases two rabbits loses both!" he exclaimed. He forgot about the Pattersons and focused red-rimmed eyes on Lauren and Sam.

They looked at each other and nodded. They were in the hands of a homicidal maniac. One who had made a decision on who he wanted most, and was about to pounce.

Help would come soon, for even now they could hear the sound of an ax chopping into the heavy wooden doors. But the man could hear that sound, too, and was shoving tables aside like toys as he stalked them across the room. What she and Sam had to do was make sure they kept out of this madman's way until help arrived.

The lights went out. That was step one. "Now hide!" Lauren yelled out to the Pattersons.

She then grabbed Sam's hand and pulled him toward the partition wall. There was some light, from the moon that shone through the skylights overhead. But Lauren didn't need it to find the back door to the haunted house. They stepped inside and she grabbed one of the flashlights that the crew had left there.

"Are you sure this is a good idea?" Sam asked uneasily.

"You got a better one?"

"I wish I did."

"Then come on!"

All the ghastly paraphernalia took on a new, gruesome look beneath the sweeping beam of the flashlight, reminding Sam of an awful childhood nightmare. He shuddered, but stayed right with Lauren. As she had hoped, the strange setting confused the maniac on their tail. They heard him bump into things, and once he cried out in what sounded like fright.

But still he came.

"Where are we heading?" Sam whispered.

"I don't know! I thought the sheriff would be coming to our rescue by now!" Lauren thought furiously. "The lab! Leon has some real surgical instruments there."

"Are you nuts! We can't face that monster with a pair of forceps and a scalpel!"

"You would prefer a stick of gum? That's all I have on me at the moment. I left my tools in the wardrobe room."

Sam searched his own pockets. All he had were his keys, wallet and a pair of fangs. He supposed biting the guy wouldn't do much good. "The lab it is. Lead on!"

They didn't make it.

He caught up with them just as they entered the grim-reaper tableau. "Now you'll pay!" he cried, his knife at the ready as he advanced toward them. "I'll show you how Hank deals with trespassers!"

The knife arced through the air with a wicked sound. Lauren jumped clear, but Sam tripped on the pile of dirt beside the open grave. As he fell he instinctively held up a hand to ward off the attack, and the blade sliced into his arm, bright red blood splattering onto his white shirtfront.

"Sam!"

"Run, Lauren!" he cried.

The man was laughing again, that horrid, terrifying laugh of the hopelessly twisted mind. He raised the knife high over his head, ready to plunge it into Sam's chest.

Suddenly someone turned the power back on. Just in time for Lauren to see clearly as the madman who tried to kill her son now killed the man she loved.

"Hank Addison is dead! And you're no ghost!"

Lauren was a strong woman, who also knew this place like the back of her hand. She knew that other things came on with the power besides the lights. Lunging forward, she shoved the big man as hard as she could. It was like trying to topple a tree. Still, he teetered, and took a single step back. But a single step was all that was needed.

It put him directly in the path of the grim reaper's mechanical arm. The scythe pierced his chest, and added the most horrible tableau ever to the Beardsville haunted house.

"Sam!" Lauren knelt beside him. "Are you all right?"

He nodded, holding his arm tightly to stop the flow of blood. "I—I think so. I've never been too fond of the sight of my own blood."

She hugged him fiercely. "Don't you dare leave me!"

"Don't worry." He kissed her tenderly. "I won't leave you, my love. Not ever."

Epilogue

"His name was Claude Hill. And he was just what you thought, Lauren—a homicidal maniac."

It was the morning after Halloween, and welcome sunshine streamed through the windows of the sheriff's office, where Oswald was finally sorting out all the details concerning the mysterious stranger who had perished in the haunted house last night.

Sam and Jason sat on either side of Lauren. They looked like bookends, Jason with his cast, Sam with his bandaged forearm. Jim was there, as well. Today's edition of the *Weekly Razor* couldn't go to press without this story, but Lauren and Sam couldn't write it until they had all the facts. He was pacing irritably.

Sheriff Buckner was seated at his desk, upon which he had propped his feet. He had a strange tale to tell, and was enjoying every word. "Or at least, Claude Hill was his given name," he continued. "The guy had used many others throughout his lifetime, assumed many different identities."

"You mean he took over other people's lives?" Sam asked.

"Not really. According to the doctor I spoke with earlier this morning, what Hill did was study other people, learn everything about them that he could and then re-make himself in their image," Oswald explained. "Evidently his own life became unbearable to him at some point. They never found out what set him off, and aren't sure they would have even if he'd lived. The doctor said it was an extremely deep psychosis, totally consuming."

Lauren had a little tape recorder going, and was scribbling notes, as well. "In other words, Claude Hill really believed he was Hank Addison?"

"Completely," the sheriff replied. "Although the doctor also said Hill always retained certain elements of former personalities, as well."

Jim stopped pacing for a moment. "Let me guess. Among the identities this guy had assumed before, was there by any chance a stock-car driver?"

"He drove sprint cars, actually, and as a matter of fact, that was his real identity coming through. But the rest he learned from studying his target's abilities. They don't know what all he had taught himself to do, but we saw a pretty good sample. Forgery. Outdoor survival. Even some of the skills of a guerrilla soldier, though—thank heaven—that seemed limited to an ability to sneak around undetected."

"Amen to that!" Jim exclaimed. "If he'd shown a penchant for guns instead of knives—"

"I'd rather not think about it," Lauren interrupted, with a quick, possessive glance at Sam and Jason. "Where did Hill meet Hank Addison, anyway?"

"The same place he met the other people he cloned, so to speak," Oswald told her. "Hill spent a great deal of time in mental institutions."

"Why didn't they hold him in any of them?"

The sheriff shrugged. "He wasn't considered a danger to anyone until the past few years. In a way, maybe that's the part we can blame on Hank," he said. "When he was sent to the institution where Hank was, the two of them became fast friends. The doctors didn't see much in Hank for Hill to emulate, so they actually encouraged their contact. But, of course, all the while Hill was learning everything he could, including the way Hank felt about Beardsville, the town he felt was responsible for his downfall."

Sam was nodding. Everything was coming into focus for him now. "Then Hank died, and Hill snapped."

"Not right away," Oswald said. "After Hank died, Hill dropped deeper into his insanity, grew more violent and had to be transferred to another facility. There, unbeknownst to his former doctor, he sank deeper into his new target identity, until in his mind he had actually become Hank Addison. Driven by the need to avenge what he now saw as his own death, he escaped. There was a bulletin out on him, but it got lost in channels. The rest, as they say, is history."

Jim was pacing again. "It's a corker of a story, that's what it is!" he exclaimed. "It'll be picked up by the wire services before the ink is dry. Imagine! A story that first appeared in the *Razor* going national!"

"Maybe wider than that," Sam informed him. "The crew from *True Behavior* will be here tomorrow, and I hear the show is quite popular in Europe."

Jim hooted, then glared at Sam and Lauren. "But first you have to write it. So get writing!"

Lauren just grinned at his bluster. But she stood, as did Sam and Jason. It was time to go anyway. She had wanted Jason in on this, since he had nearly lost his life at the hands of Claude Hill.

"Thanks, Sheriff," she said. "As you can see, duty calls. And I have to get this young man back to class."

"No, thank *you*," Oswald returned. "All of you. I couldn't have solved this case without you. Especially Jason, who had the presence of mind and sharp eyes to catch that license-plate number." He got to his feet and came to shake the boy's hand. "Have you ever considered a career in law enforcement, son?"

"He has not!" Lauren quickly hustled him out the door. "I'd rather he figure out how to design video games for a living, thank you very much! And he'll learn the math if I have to tutor him every day till he graduates college!"

"All right!" Jason cried. "Mom's back!"

He and Sam exchanged a high five with their good hands. Lauren shook her head and led the way to the car. "Am I getting a husband, or just another son?"

"A bit of both," Sam told her. Then he leaned close and added, "With a little luck and some time in bed, maybe we really can make it both. Or how about another boy and a girl? Doesn't that sound nice?"

"Hah! That'd make it three against two!"

"If a daughter turned out anything like you," Sam informed her, "I'd say that would just about make it even."

Jason got in the car. Before Lauren could slip in beside him, Sam caught her hand and pulled her into an embrace, kissing her passionately, not caring that they were right in the middle of town.

"Sam! What will people think?"

"They'll think we're madly in love," he replied.

Lauren kissed him again. "And they'll be right."

. . . . And here's more of the best in romantic suspense!

Turn the page for a bonus look at what's in store for you next month, in Harlequin Intrigue #253 WHAT CHILD IS THIS?—a special Christmas edition in Rebecca York's 43 Light Street series.

In the hallowed halls of this charming building, danger has been averted and romance has blossomed. Now Christmas comes to 43 Light Street—and in its stocking is all the action, suspense and romance that your heart can hold.

Chapter One

Guilty until proven innocent.

Erin Morgan squinted into the fog that turned the buildings on either side of Light Street into a canyon of dimly realized apparitions.

"Guilty until proven innocent," she repeated aloud.

It wasn't supposed to work that way. Yet that was how Erin had felt since the Graveyard Murders had rocked Baltimore. Ever since the killer had tricked her into framing her friend Sabrina Barkley.

Sabrina had forgiven her. But Erin hadn't forgiven herself, and she was never going to let something like that happen again.

She glanced at the purse beside her on the passenger seat and felt her stomach knot. It was stuffed with five thousand dollars in contributions for Santa's Toy and Clothing Fund. Most were checks, but she was carrying more than eight hundred dollars in cash. And she wasn't going to keep it in her possession a moment longer than necessary.

Erin pressed her foot down on the accelerator and then eased up again as a dense patch of white swallowed up the car. She couldn't even see the Christmas decorations she knew were festooned from many of the downtown office windows.

"'Tis the season to be jolly...'" She sang a few lines of the carol to cheer herself up, but her voice trailed off in the gloom.

Forty-three Light Street glided into view through the mist like a huge underwater rock formation.

Erin drove around to the back of the building, where she could get in and out as quickly as possible. Pulling the collar of her coat closed against the icy wind, she hurried toward the back door—the key ready in her hand.

It felt good to get out of the cold. But there was nothing welcoming about the dank, dimly lit back entrance—so different from the fading grandeur of the marble foyer. Here there were no pretensions of gentility, only institutional gray walls and a bare concrete floor.

Clutching her purse more tightly, she strained her ears and peered into the darkness. She heard nothing but the familiar sound of the steam pipes rattling. And she saw nothing moving in the shadows. Still, the fine hairs on the back of her neck stirred as she bolted into the service elevator and pressed the button.

Upstairs the paint was brighter, and the tile floors were polished. But at this time of night, only a few dim lights held back the shadows, and the clicking of her high heels echoed back at her like water dripping in an underground cavern.

Feeling strangely exposed in the darkness, Erin kept her eyes focused on the glass panel of her office door. She was almost running by the time she reached it.

Her hand closed around the knob. It was solid and reassuring against her moist palm, and she felt some of the knots in her stomach untie themselves. With a sigh of relief, she kicked the door closed behind her, shutting out the unseen phantoms of the hall.

Reaching over one of the mismatched couches donated by a local rental company, she flipped the light switch. Nothing happened. Darn. The bulb must be out.

In the darkness, she took a few steps toward the file room and stopped.

Something else was wrong. Maybe it was the smell. Not the clean pine scent of the little Christmas tree she'd set up by the window, but the dank odor of sweat.

She was backing quietly toward the door when fingers as hard and lean as a handcuff shot out and closed around her wrist.

A scream of terror rose in her throat. The sound was choked off by a rubber glove against her lips.

Someone was in her office. In the dark.

Her mind registered no more than that. But her body was already struggling—trying to twist away.

"No. Please." Even as she pleaded, she knew she was wasting her breath.

He was strong. And ruthless.

Her free hand came up to pummel his shoulder and neck. He grunted and shook her so hard that her vision blurred.

She tried to work her teeth against the rubbery palm that covered her mouth.

His grip adroitly shifted to her throat. He began to squeeze, and she felt the breath turn to stone in her lungs.

He bent her backward over his arm, and she stared up into a face covered by a ski mask, the features a strange parody of something human.

The dark circles around the eyes, the red circle around the mouth, the two dots of color on his cheeks—all wa-

vered in her vision like coins at the bottom of a fountain.

The pressure increased. Her lungs were going to explode.

*No. Please. Let me go home. I have a little boy. He
needs me.*

The words were choked off like her life breath.

Like the rapidly fading light. She was dying. And the
scenes of her life flashed before her eyes. Climbing into
bed with her parents on Sunday morning. First grade.
High school graduation. Her marriage to Bruce. Ken-
ny's birth. Her husband's death. Betraying Sabrina.
Finishing college. Her new job with Silver Miracle Char-
ities. The holiday fund-raiser tonight.

The events of her life trickled through her mind like the
last grains of sand rolling down the sloping sides of an
hourglass. Then there was only blackness.

Don't miss this next 43 Light Street tale—#253
WHAT CHILD IS THIS?—*coming December
1993—only from Rebecca York and Harlequin
Intrigue!*

**Relive the romance...
Harlequin and Silhouette
are proud to present**

by Request ™

A program of collections of three complete novels by the most-requested authors with the most-requested themes. Be sure to look for one volume each month with three complete novels by top-name authors.

In September: **BAD BOYS**

Dixie Browning
Ann Major
Ginna Gray

No heart is safe when these hot-blooded hunks are in town!

In October: **DREAMSCAPE**

Jayne Ann Krentz
Anne Stuart
Bobby Hutchinson

Something's happening! But is it love or magic?

In December: **SOLUTION: MARRIAGE**

Debbie Macomber
Annette Broadrick
Heather Graham Pozzessere

Marriages in name only have a way of leading to love....

Available at your favorite retail outlet.

REQ-G2

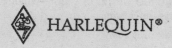
HARLEQUIN®

Silhouette

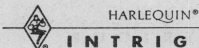

CHRISTMAS STALKINGS

All wrapped up in
spine-tingling packages,
here are two books
sure to keep you on
edge this holiday season!

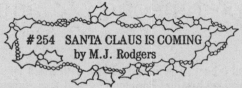

#254 SANTA CLAUS IS COMING
by M.J. Rodgers

On the first day of Christmas, newscaster Belle Breeze was
sung a bad rendition of "The Twelve Days of Christmas."
Then, one by one, the gifts started to arrive, and Belle knew
the twelfth gift would play havoc with her very life....

#255 SCARLET SEASON
by Laura Gordon

The night was *too* silent when, on a snowy Denver street,
Cassie Craig found herself the lone witness to a crime that no
one believed happened. Her search for the truth would make
this Christmas season chilling....

**DON'T MISS THESE SPECIAL HOLIDAY INTRIGUES
IN DECEMBER 1993!**

HIX

Familiar is back! The fantastic feline with a flair for solving crimes makes his third Harlequin Intrigue appearance in:

#256 THRICE FAMILIAR
by Caroline Burnes
December 1993

When a valuable racehorse is stolen from a horse farm in Scotland, it's Familiar's first chance to gain international acclaim. And it's the perfect opportunity for him to practice his pussyfooting panache, as he tries to matchmake the horse's owner and trainer, Catherine Shaw and Patrick Nelson—two people as opposite as cats and dogs!

Don't miss #256 THRICE FAMILIAR—for *cat*-astrophic intrigue and *purr*-fect romance!

FEAR-F

1993 Keepsake

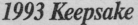

Stories

Capture the spirit and romance of Christmas with KEEPSAKE CHRISTMAS STORIES, a collection of three stories by favorite historical authors. The perfect Christmas gift!

Don't miss these heartwarming stories, available in November wherever Harlequin books are sold:

ONCE UPON A CHRISTMAS by Curtiss Ann Matlock
A FAIRYTALE SEASON by Marianne Willman
TIDINGS OF JOY by Victoria Pade

ADD A TOUCH OF ROMANCE TO YOUR HOLIDAY SEASON WITH KEEPSAKE CHRISTMAS STORIES!

HX93